This much is
TRUE

TIA LOUISE

This Much is True
Copyright © TLM Productions LLC, 2020
Printed in the United States of America.

Cover design by Lori Jackson Design.
Paperback wrap by Shanoff Formats.
Photography by Wander Aguiar.

Dedicated to my amazing readers.
It's been a tough year.

I hope you're hanging in there. I hope your loved ones are well. I hope this story helps you laugh, swoon and forget about your worries for a little while.

Sending you so much love,
Thank you always for your support,
Tia

"Love lights more fires than hate extinguishes."
—*Ella Wheeler Wilcox*

In the waves of change we find our true direction.

Prologue

JR

WITH MY BACK TO THE SAN FRANCISCO TRAFFIC, I HOLD THE railing of the iconic, vermillion bridge and watch the sun set over the Pacific Ocean.

Two hundred and forty-five feet below me, the frigid water of the bay swirls past, and behind me is the building where I spent the last eighteen months of my life, paying for a crime I didn't commit.

My hair is long to my collar. My body is lean and ripped with muscle to intimidate anyone who thought he'd get the best of me.

I've lived with the funk of brown Lysol, body odor, and urine so long, I forgot fresh air could smell so sweet.

At five p.m., a guard came to my cell, rattled the bars like some old cheesy black and white movie, and told me to get my shit together.

Time to go.

I was halfway through a four-year prison sentence, and last night, they said it was over, early release.

Confused is an understatement for how I felt, but I wasn't about to argue. I started making plans.

"You can thank the tree huggers for this miscarriage of justice." The woman behind the desk scowled as she spoke, like the words tasted bad. "Wouldn't want you getting sick. It might violate your civil rights."

Rage smoldered in my chest, and I didn't make eye contact with her. This whole eighteen months has been a violation of my civil rights, but why should she care?

Since the start of this nightmare, nobody cared. I said it once, twice, three thousand times. *I. Didn't. Do. It.*

Nobody gave a shit.

Not even my court-appointed lawyer believed me. I was caught with illegal human growth hormone, and that's all they saw. No one looked at the receipt for perfectly legal adaptogen supplements, which is what I thought I was picking up. I was a redneck from South Carolina with a trunk full of HGH. Case closed.

I entered San Quentin and kept my head down. I made allies with the biggest, meanest guys, and the quiet ones who stayed to themselves. I learned to be ready to fight always.

I started my prison sentence resolved the next time I saw my father, I wouldn't let up until he was begging for mercy.

Now I'm a free man.

Sort of.

I'm out, and I'm headed back to look him in the eye. He sent me here, and I want to know why.

Staring out across the dark waters, I make a vow. I'm getting back everything I've lost. I don't know how the man who put me here will make it happen, but we'll sort that out when I get home.

Snatching my navy canvas bag off the ground, I start walking.

CHAPTER
One

Hope

I SHOULDN'T HAVE DRUNK THAT WHOLE BOTTLE OF WINE.

The sea breeze pushes my blonde hair off my face and twists my skirt between my legs. I pull my fluffy beige coat tighter around my chest, and when I wet my lips, salt touches my tongue.

It's rough out tonight, the wind whips hard and the waves crash, but it suits my mood. My insides are twisted and stormy, everything is crashing around me…

The beach path along the shore of San Francisco bay is deserted—just like everything these days—and I cut a wobbly path in my progress towards the bridge.

Two iconic, vermillion towers rise in the distance, a string of lights tracing the edges, and I think of a ship passing in the night.

Blurring my eyes, I imagine I'm in an Alfred Hitchcock movie… or Mike Myers… *So I married an axe murderer…*

A dip in the soft sand makes me stumble, and the empty

bottle slips from my fingers. It hits the ground with a dull thump, but I keep walking. I should go back and get it, be a responsible citizen, carry it to a recycling bin, but I don't.

I push on.

Large boulders separate me from the path up to the bridge. They feel metaphoric. I gaze up at the network of iron and cables and try to sing my favorite ABBA song. *"I have a dream…"*

My voice wavers and breaks on a sharp inhale, but I push back. I square my shoulders and summon my daily affirmations…

I am doing better than I think I am.

My future is bright, and my best days are still ahead of me.

I am strong enough to face what's in front of me.

My life isn't over, and I never give up without a fight…

But I'm so tired. I'm not sure I believe them anymore.

Pulling out my phone, I text my best friend Yarnell. **How long would it take for me to walk to Half Moon Bay?**

At this point, I think I could walk all night.

Her reply buzzes the phone in my loose grip. **Why would you walk all the way to my apartment?**

Staring at the words, I sway slightly as I tap the phone icon. I need to hear a voice.

"If you're at my door, I'm not letting you in without a temperature check." My bestie is such a drama queen.

"I'm having an existential crisis."

"You're such a drama queen."

My jaw drops. "You are!"

"Why are you threatening to walk all the way to my apartment? Just drive."

Inhaling slowly, I clear the thickness in my throat, looking up at the fading twilight so I don't cry. "I sold Metallicar."

"What?" A loud gasp then, "Nooo…"

"Yep. They're picking it up tomorrow. I am officially destitute."

And miserable.

Years ago, we nicknamed Dad's cherished black 1967 Chevy Impala "Metallicar" after our favorite TV show *Supernatural*.

He gave it to me before he went into the nursing home after his bilateral knee replacement. It was supposed to be for short-term rehab... Neither of us expected it would turn into long-term rehab, and I can't even visit him. He's stuck there for the duration, and I'm flat broke.

"I'm so sorry, Hope." At least the sarcasm is gone from her tone. "Where are you?"

"I'm at the bridge."

"Hope Eternal Hill! What are you thinking?"

Placing my fingers against my forehead, I scrub against the turmoil mounting in my brain. "I'm thinking about my name. Is it *Hope Eternal*? Or is it *Eternal Hill*? Because this hill feels like it's growing taller and taller..."

"What can I do? What do you need?"

"I need a job, dammit! I've been doing my best to wait for things to go back to normal, but I don't think I can wait any longer."

Ever since the shutdown killed Pancake Paradise, my dream restaurant business that I sank every dime into opening, it's been harder and harder to make ends meet.

"Work at one of those Amazon distribution centers. Everybody's doing that now."

"And as a result, they're not hiring."

"That's impossible! They're sending people into space so they can have Amazon distribution centers on the moon."

"Well, the earth-bound ones don't need me."

I gaze up at the giant metal bridge again, wondering... There's a sign up there—I can see it in my mind.

Dad used to take me for a walk across the bridge when I was little. If we were feeling energetic, we'd try to jog all the way. Or we'd stand and look out at the Pacific Ocean, and I'd strain my ears, listening for the sound of the angels…

Squinting my eyes, I try to hear them, but it's all silence. It's the hush of nonstop wind and the groan of barges.

I used to hear them…

Something moves along the edge, and I think I see a figure standing there, far away. A silhouette of a man.

"Are you listening to me?" My bestie's voice cuts through my thoughts.

"Sorry, what?" My head is swimming, and I know I'm not thinking straight. Too much wine.

"When we were kids, who said we could save our lemonade stand after Mrs. Blackburn ran over all our lemons with her car?"

My brow furrows, and I shake my head. "Mrs. Blackburn was the worst driver. She almost hit me when I was riding my bike in the neighborhood. Twice!"

"You said we could save it!" She pushes onward. "You didn't let us give up!"

"We were going to squeeze the lemons anyway…"

"When we were in middle school, who said, 'Our football team's mascot might be a dove, but we can still have a kick-ass fight song!'"

"We were twelve, Yars. I don't think I said *kick-ass*."

Our parents were peace-loving super-hippies, but they still wouldn't let us swear.

"'Peck 'em up, Doves' was a fight song for the ages!" Her voice rises like she's giving the pep rally speech in one of those *Friday Night Lights* episodes.

"More like a fight song for doofuses."

I can still see the large, white dove appliquéd to the front of our knee-length, royal blue cheer jumpers. *Shivers.*

Our home-school collective played flag football because our parents said tackle football led to cognitive deficiencies and mood and behavior disorders.

They tried to make us feel like all the other kids, but we knew we were weirdos.

"Maybe I've always been a loser, and I just didn't know it."

"You are not a loser! You're the strongest person I know. You have always found a way through tough situations. And you always will!" I imagine the music swelling in the background, lights rising behind my bestie, and the roar of the crowd bursting through the stands. "Now say it! I am *not* jumping off that bridge!"

My chin jerks back, like a record scratch. "I'm not jumping off the bridge, Yars."

"That's the spirit!"

"No, seriously, I wasn't—"

"You're going to get through this tough time. We all are, and we're going to come back stronger for it."

"No, seriously. I was listening for the voices."

A beat.

Silence on the line.

I hold my phone out before putting it to my face again. "Did I lose you?"

"The voices?" Her tone is cautious.

"When I was a kid and we'd stand on the bridge facing the ocean, I believed I could hear angel voices singing above the water."

"Did you actually *hear* angel voices singing?"

"In my imagination I heard them."

"Phew!" She exhales dramatically. "For a minute I thought we had a bigger problem."

"Bigger than me jumping off the bridge?" I'm teasing, but I'm still sad. "I don't hear them anymore, Yars. They've stopped singing. I think that means something."

"It means you're an adult living in the real world now."

Dropping my chin, I start back the way I came. The wind

pushes my hair roughly, and I feel a tear on my cheek. "If only I could talk to Dad. I need a hug."

My dad could always help me regain my perspective. He would put his arm around me and tell me a story, something from when he was growing up or how he solved a problem.

"I know you're worried about him." My friend's voice softens. "But Shady Rest is taking great care of those guys. Heck, with your dad's age and athleticism, he's probably enjoying himself."

My eyes narrow. "He's stuck in a nursing home, Yars."

"Your dad could always make the best of a bad situation. It's where you get it from."

I'm approaching my family's old beach house, noticing the graying boards and chipped paint. "He'd probably tell me to paint."

"You know…" Her voice grows quiet. "That old place is probably worth a million at least."

"I can't sell the house. It's been in our family since forever." I don't mention how it's not even in my name. It would be admitting I'd considered it.

"So you want to come here? You can crash on my couch."

"Maybe." The small gate is stuck, so I walk around to the driveway. When I see the shiny black Impala parked out front, heaviness presses on my chest. I can't imagine it being gone. "I'll figure it out and see you in a few days."

"Hang in there, friend."

We disconnect, and I go to the car that holds so many memories, sliding my fingers along the fender to the door. Dad loved this car. He held onto it from when he was a teenager, maintaining it and updating it as needed.

It was his pet project, and he always made sure it ran like a charm. All the belts were oiled, all the nuts and bolts replaced. How could anyone love it as much as he did?

My heart is broken. I feel like I'm selling a cherished pet.

"Oh, Dad." I lift up on the driver's side door handle and climb into the backseat, pressing my body against the leather and hugging my knees to my chest beneath my teddy coat. "I wish there was some way I didn't have to do this."

Closing my eyes, I slide down to my side as the memories flood my mind. I remember being a little girl, seatbelt across my lap, holding the open window as we took her out for a spin.

Dad would put on his favorite station, Sirius XM's 60s on 6, and crank it.

He was born in the 1960s, but for whatever reason, he loved that silly old beach music. "Dawn" by Frankie Valli and the Four Seasons was his favorite.

Moving my lips, I speak the words in a broken whisper, *Go away, I'm no good for you...*

I remember my gleaming eyes, my hair in pigtails. I remember smiling so hard my cheeks ached. The sun shone as we drove along the coastal highway singing along to the eternally cheerful surfer tunes.

Hope Eternal...

Like a spark from a match, the smallest flicker of light smolders in my chest. The tiniest hint of faith standing up to the fog of despair trying to wrap me in its suffocating darkness.

This is not where our story ends. I'm not going down without a fight. I will turn this sinking ship around. I will get back what we've lost.

I just need to take a little nap so I can think about it more clearly. I'll find a solution...

CHAPTER
Two

JR

THE SUN IS JUST WARMING THE EDGE OF THE HORIZON WHEN I REACH the ancient beach house on an unfashionable stretch of the coastal highway.

The place barely has a driveway, and I double-check the address. I don't really need to—the car I bought is waiting for me, unmistakable. Thanks to contact-less delivery, the keys should be waiting a combination box under the fender. I should be able to get in and take off right away.

Walking here was a strange experience. I only passed one person hitchhiking, and hardly any cars on the freeway. But I don't have time to worry about it. I've got a lot to do and a short amount of time to do it.

Feeling around, I find the keys. I'm not happy the driver's side door is unlocked, but when I turn the ignition, the engine roars to life, sounding as good as Car Heaven promised.

I'm kind of amazed at how trusting these online car services are. I didn't even have to make a downpayment. Still, I suppose they can track me down and reclaim it if I don't... and send me back to prison.

In my bag are the few personal belongings I had on me when I entered San Quentin—an old iPhone, my wallet with a few credit cards, and my driver's license.

A plain white envelope containing two hundred dollars in cash is new. Apparently, that's the amount you get when you're released from jail, like it's fucking Monopoly or something.

My jaw flexes, and I briefly feel the fiery anger of how much I've lost and where I am now. I used to have it all.

I was the biggest guy in town, the homegrown hero. It still stings, and I double-down on my mission. I've got seven days to get it done.

Three hours down the road, my phone is charged enough to make a call. I'm only a little surprised it still works—I handled all the bills, and we had a family plan. I'm sure they didn't even think to take me off it.

Family, I exhale a bitter laugh. I've learned a lot about family through this experience, specifically who I can trust.

"Scout here." My younger brother's voice is scruffy like he's just waking up.

I imagine he's been sawing logs as usual, and my tension eases a notch. "You sleeping?"

He clears his throat, and I hear a rustle in the background. "JR? Is that you? What the hell?"

"It's eight o'clock in the morning. Don't you work anymore?"

"No!" He says it like it's the most obvious thing in the world. "I'm about to lose my apartment. What's new with you?"

"They let me out early."

"No shit!"

"Yeah. One of the inmates had a good lawyer, said it was a civil rights thing."

"You're shitting me."

"Nope. I'm out."

"Not sure how I feel about that." He laughs, and it sounds like he's walking. "Who else is running around loose?"

"You won't catch me judging." It's safe to say I have a whole new perspective on the penal system.

My hand tightens on the steering wheel, and I squint away from the rising sun.

"So… are you okay?" Hesitation is in his voice. I'm sure he's thinking of all the exaggerated bullshit he's seen in movies.

"I'm okay. But I need your help."

"Oh, sure. Need a place to crash? Everything's closed, so finding work is tough, but I could see—"

"Can you get away for a week? I'm making a road trip, and I need you to help me drive."

"A week?" It sounds like he's rubbing his face. "I don't know. I mean, the studios are closed, but they could reopen at any time—"

"I'm an hour outside the city. Text me your address, and I'll pick you up. I'll have you back in seven days."

"You sound awful sure about that."

"I'm sure." My jaw tightens.

I'm not totally free, which only fuels my anger. I'm furious I have a record. Otherwise, I could do this myself, instead of dragging him into it.

Still, Scout will be okay. If anything goes wrong, this will be on me.

"Care to tell me why?"

"I'll tell you on the way. You in?"

He hesitates, but a grin enters his tone. "Sounds like the Dunne brothers gettin' it done."

"Something like that."

He's referencing a time in my life I barely recognize now, a time when he and I were the golden boys, football heroes, and people rolled out the red carpet for us.

It was a time when I thought my life would be so different.

"Can you at least tell me where we're headed?"

"Home." The line falls quiet, but I'm not waiting for a response. "I'll see you in an hour."

Disconnecting, I toss the phone on the passenger's seat and push the pedal closer to the floor.

This is a hell of a car. I've been hitting almost 90 the whole way, keeping an eye out for cops, but the interstates are deserted.

It's weird, like an apocalypse or something. It's perfect for what I need.

Reaching out, I switch on the radio. It's got that satellite service, and somebody left it on a 1970s station. I'm not picky, so I let it go. My mind is a million miles away—or 2,500 miles away to be exact.

Last night, I plotted our route from LA to Charleston. It's a straight line across seven states, from the east coast to the west coast.

Under normal conditions it would be a 36-hour drive. Of course, we'll have to stop, but we should beat that time with no traffic, no construction, no state troopers.

I look out at the sunrise tipping the desert scenery in gold. The windows are down, and the warm, dry air swirls around me. I'm so fucking glad to be out of San Francisco and the cold, damp fog.

Passing a hand over the beard on my cheeks, I think of the other thing driving me across the continent. My little boy Jesse had just turned three when I left that morning. He was on my back holding a football in the air, and we were laughing, pretending like he'd just scored the winning touchdown.

I still see his cotton top, his blue eyes, and Iron Man pajamas. He was just big enough to understand the concept of *I'll be right back*.

Only, I didn't come right back.

I wanted to see him, but the prosecutor called me a flight risk. They set my bail so high, I couldn't go anywhere. I have no idea what my ex-wife Becky told him happened to me. She never even sent me pictures. He'll be five now, starting kindergarten.

My throat aches, and I clear away the thickness.

What Becky did send was a fucking "Dear John" letter three months into my sentence. She wrote how her whole world had changed, how she didn't sign up to be the wife of a felon.

She didn't even question my conviction.

She had the divorce papers served up ready to go in my cell with all our shit neatly divided, like she'd gotten started on it the minute the judge banged the gavel.

My fists flex as betrayal tightens my stomach. I push harder on the gas, when a soft voice behind my shoulder startles the shit out of me.

"Where am I?" A pale ghost of a girl with messy, light-blonde hair rises in the backseat, and I jerk the wheel so hard, the car swerves like we might flip.

She goes flying across the backseat, and I pull the wheel straight, getting us back in the right lane.

"What the fuck?" I shout, but she dives to the open window and hangs out the side.

Her body shudders, and I'm pretty sure she's throwing up.

That does it. I hit the brakes and drive the car onto the shoulder. Whatever's happening right now is about to end real quick.

I've had enough bullshit to last me a lifetime.

CHAPTER
Three

Hope

THE AIR HAS CHANGED.

It whips throughout the car, hot and stinging, and I'm lying on the backseat, rocking side to side like I'm on a speed boat in open water. Blinking against the bright sunlight, I try to get my bearings, but it's like struggling through a fog.

One thing is certain: I am not in San Francisco.

I'm in pain.

My head throbs, and I'm still wearing my thin, flowered sundress from yesterday with my plush, beige coat on top. My feet are bare. Sand is stuck to my toes, and my mouth is so dry…

I must've fallen asleep in Metallicar. Now I'm racing down the highway with The Eagles playing in the background, "Doolin Dalton," and a strange man is driving.

Blinking hard, I try to focus on him. *Who is this guy?*

His profile is chiseled. He has a perfectly straight nose and square jaw covered in a short, dark-brown beard. His hair is dark, but shiny with caramel highlights. It's shaggy like he hasn't had a haircut in a while—*but who has these days?*

He seems angry. His dark brow is lowered, and the muscle in the side of his jaw moves back and forth like he's deep in thought. His heavy, light blue shirt reminds me of a uniform with the long sleeves rolled to his elbows. He grips the top of the steering wheel with one hand, flexing a powerful forearm. Dark ink swirls in a design on his skin, but I can't make out his tattoo.

He's so intensely focused and ridiculously hot. Even in my hungover state, I feel a tingle low in my belly at the sight of him. He's all man, commanding and powerful, and I'm not sure I can look him straight in the eye.

I need to snap out of it. I shouldn't be here—wherever I am… *Where am I?*

Yars is waiting for me at her apartment in Half Moon Bay, but it feels like we're headed south.

Reaching out, I'm wobbly as I clutch the seat in front of me, easing myself to a sitting position. "Where am I?"

Light blue eyes hit mine in the rearview mirror, and it's a jolt of electricity. The car jerks wildly to the right, and I go flying, slamming against the door with an *oof*.

"What the fuck?" He jerks the wheel to the left to get us back on track, and I bolt to the open window.

The entire bottle of wine I consumed last night is making a reappearance.

I hang out the door, as my stomach turns itself inside out, and my shoulders heave. Tears sting my eyes, and I'm so embarrassed.

I whimper, gripping the metal side of the door as the car quickly slows to a stop. I'm sure my face is a wreck, and I pull the sleeve of my coat over my hand, trying to dab at my eyes.

The driver's door slams, and I hear the sharp crunch of boots on gravel just before the passenger's side door jerks open. I almost fall.

"Get out." It's a sharp order, just short of a growl.

He's waiting, and I'm doing my best to breathe normally.

"I'm sorry... I—"

A grip like a vice clamps around my upper arm, and he drags me out of the vehicle, dropping me in the dirt on the side of the road.

"What are you doing in this car?" He isn't shouting, but anger crackles in his tone.

I say the first thing in my mind. "This is my car—"

"No, this is *my* car. I bought it."

"Oh, God." I rock back on my ass facing Metallicar.

He's right, and I'm afraid I'm going to be sick again. I really don't want to puke in front of this wildly gorgeous, hostile man.

It's strangely quiet on the side of the freeway. Instead of cars racing past, the hum of birds and crickets fills the air between us as we breathe fast, facing each other.

Finally, he speaks, his wolf eyes narrowed. "Do you have the virus?"

"No..." I wince. Speaking hurts. "I-I had a bottle of wine."

His hands drop from his hips, and he exhales sharply, stomping back to the car. "You got a phone?"

Feeling around, I find my phone in my pocket. He nods when he sees me lifting it out. "Call someone to come get you."

He slides into the driver's side and the engine roars to life as he slams the door.

Panic seizes my chest, and I jump to my feet, ignoring the flash of pain in my skull. "Wait! Please wait! I can't call anybody!"

My phone is dead, and anyway, there's no one to call.

I grab the open passenger's window, jogging a few steps before he slams on the brakes and glares at me.

"Let go of the car." Dust rises around us, and tears sting my eyes.

"You can't leave me here." My heart beats so fast, and I struggle to breathe normally. "I'm not wearing shoes..."

"Not my problem."

He starts to go again, and I scream. "Wait! Please!"

Again, the tires grind to a stop, and blue fire smolders in his eyes. "I don't have time for this."

"I'm sorry… I'm really sorry, but… you have to find it in your heart…" I'm trembling. My voice wavers. "You can't leave me on the side of the road like this."

Full lips press together, and he looks straight down the road in the direction we were headed.

Seconds like hours tick past. I'm sure he's going to floor it, but instead his shoulders drop. His fist clenches on the steering wheel, but he doesn't look at me. "I'll take you as far as LA. You can get a ride or whatever there."

My eyes slide shut, and I hold onto the side of Dad's black car idling on the shoulder. Then reality hits me. A man I don't even know is driving me to LA. *What then?* I have no money, no phone… No shoes.

"I'm not waiting forever," he snaps. "Get in or stay here. Final call."

I hesitate a bit too long, and the car starts to move.

"Okay!" I scream, and the car jerks to a stop.

Grabbing the door handle, I rush into the passenger's side. As soon as the door slams, he floors it, sending my back against the leather and dirt and rocks flying into the space behind us.

It's quiet inside except for the wind pushing around us. My hands are clutched in my lap, and Los Angeles rises up ahead. The Eagles continue to sing softly on the radio, and I press my lips together in the dry air swirling around us.

"Are you an actor?" My voice is like sandpaper.

The tiny muscles around his eyes flinch. "No."

"But you live in LA?"

He cuts his eyes at me briefly. "No."

We continue powering down the freeway. He's letting

Metallicar eat up the miles, and I feel the power—this car was built for speed. My eyes sting, and my head aches like someone hit it with a sledgehammer. I'd give my little toe for a bottle of water.

"Got anything to drink in here?"

He exhales in an irritated manner. "No."

"Is that all you can say?"

Those ice-blue eyes flash at me, and my stomach flips. "No."

I settle back against the seat, holding the sides of my skirt as I prop my bare feet on the dash.

He reaches over and shoves them down. "Feet on the floor."

My jaw drops, and I catch myself, shifting upright as he rubs his palm over the spot where my feet had been. "Excuse me!"

"You're excused."

His hand returns to the steering wheel, and I cross my arms over my chest, studying his profile. He could be a movie star with that profile. His teeth are straight and white, and I can tell from the way his shirt stretches over his shoulders and down to his waist he works out. He's rough around the edges, but he doesn't look much older than thirty.

"If you're not an actor, what do you do?"

"None of your business."

Shaking my head, I turn to the window, huffing a *whatever*. I've never met someone so rude in my life.

Looking out, I notice the trees sprouting up along the highway are so green, and the high-rise buildings are distinctly clear. It's strange because usually the city is shrouded in a hazy brown mist. It's a beautiful morning.

I look down at my lap, and the shock of waking up here starts to fade. My sadness from last night trickles back. I figure I'll try again.

"This was my dad's car, you know." I say to the open space. "He got it when he was about my age and kept it up all these years."

Mr. Growly doesn't answer. Only Don Henley croons back at me about one of these nights.

"I hope you'll love it as much as he did."

The guy glances at me a bit longer this time. "It's a good car."

"It's a classic." I slide my hand along the passenger door.

We're slowing down, and he hands me his phone. "Can you read these directions to me?"

"Sure…" I'm encouraged by the hint of friendliness. I look around as we exit the freeway. I don't know much about LA or where we are. "Where are we going?"

"I'm picking up my brother."

Looking at the directions on the phone, I realize I have no idea where I'll go from here.

Wrinkling my nose, I look up at him. "I don't know your name."

Another flash of ice blue. "You don't need to."

"Still, it would be helpful—"

"John." His reply is a little too sharp.

"Is it really?" Another glare, and I hold up a hand. "Okay, *John*. I'm Hope. Nice to meet you."

"Don't let me miss my turn."

Nice to meet you too, Hope. I answer for him in my head. So much for friendliness. "It says five hundred feet."

He follows my directions until we're pulling up in front of what looks like an old motel out of the 1960s. It has a pink flamingo painted on the pale blue stucco column in the center, and two long rows of apartments form a two-story, U-shaped structure.

John steps out, slamming the door before walking around and opening mine. "I'll be seeing you, then."

He stands there waiting, and I look down at my bare feet. My fingers twist in my lap. "If you don't live in LA… Any chance you're heading back to San Francisco?"

"No."

So we're back to one-word answers again.

I'm about to argue when a friendly male voice interrupts us.

"Heard you drive up." He pulls John into a one-armed bro-hug. "Good to see you, man… Not looking too worse for wear."

New guy is the same height as John with lighter hair and friendly blue eyes—they're the exact same color as his brother's. He's wearing board shorts and a thin tee that shows off his perfectly tanned, muscular arms. The light scruff on his face doesn't hide the cleft in his chin, and when he smiles, he has a cute dimple in his cheek.

This guy is clearly a movie star. Or a surfer dude.

He's about to toss his bag into the car when he steps back. "Holy shit, where did you get this? It's like straight out of that TV show."

I smile up in response. "My best friend and I used to call it Metallicar."

"Who are you?" He looks at his brother. "You didn't tell me you were seeing anybody."

"I'm not seeing anybody." John seems pissed as he goes to the trunk and opens it. "She sneaked into the car, and I can't get her out."

"Hey!" I frown, looking back at him. "I told you I fell asleep in the backseat."

"She was drunk." John says it like I stole somebody's dog. "Here."

He shoves a bottle of water in my hand, and my eyes widen. I rip the top off and drink it like it's the elixir of life.

"Okay, then!" The brother laughs, sticking out a hand. "I'm Scout. Nice to meet you."

I wipe my mouth with the back of my hand before shaking his. "Hope."

"So you're helping us drive to South Carolina?"

"No." John reaches forward and grabs my upper arm in that vise grip of his, dragging me out onto the sidewalk. "Her part ends here."

Scout's brow furrows, and he looks down at my feet. "Do you have shoes?"

My face flames hot. "I kind of left them at home."

"Where's home?"

"San Francisco. At least, it was before I lost my job."

"It's a six-hour drive to San Francisco." He studies me a beat, but his brother is undeterred.

"Life's tough all over. Say goodbye, Scout."

John walks around Metallicar, climbing in the driver's side while his brother stands in front of the open door, studying me. "You got anywhere to go?"

"We don't have time for this." John looks straight ahead.

"I'll be okay…" My throat is tight, but I force a smile. "I usually land on my feet."

Scout glances at my bare feet again before tossing his bag in the backseat. The frown hasn't left his face.

He starts to get in, then hesitates, standing up again. "You know, he has to bring me back here… If you're not doing anything, you could help us drive. JR wants to be back in a week, but I don't know how the hell just the two of us can accomplish that."

"Get in the car, Scout," barks John… *or JR?*

At this point, I'm ready to take any help I can get. "I don't mind driving. I've never been to South Carolina."

The driver's side door opens and John stands, glaring across the top of the car at me. "You, stay put." He points at his brother. "You, get in."

"I guess it's a crazy idea." Scout shrugs. "You don't know us. We don't know you…"

"Yeah…" I'm standing on the sidewalk watching the only

two people I barely know in LA preparing to leave, and desperation sets in. "But you've got my car…"

"My car," John growls. "Would you come on?"

"Want to use my phone?" Scout steps forward quickly, holding out the device to me. "I haven't left this apartment in two weeks except to surf. It should be safe."

"Thanks!" I take it carefully, tapping in Yarnell's number as John continues to wait. It rings and rings and ultimately her voicemail picks up. "She's not answering."

Dropping my chin, I pass it back to him.

He takes it, pressing his lips together. "Well… good luck, I guess."

"Thanks again." I nod, doing my best to appear brave.

The reality is I'm terrified. *What the hell am I going to do alone on the streets of LA with no shoes and a dead phone?*

I watch as he climbs inside, looking out the window at me, worry lining his perfect face. A breeze pushes the thin skirt around my legs, and the fluffy coat I'm wearing is hot in the LA sunshine.

Metallicar rumbles low as it pulls away, and I lift my hand, waving as they ease from the curb. I step back, walking to the front steps of the Pink Flamingo as the red tail lights grow smaller in the distance.

CHAPTER
Four

JR

"I**T'S NOT RIGHT. WE CAN'T JUST LEAVE HER THERE.**" **MY YOUNGER** brother looks out the window at the waif of a girl standing on the sidewalk in front of his building.

"She's not a puppy, Scout."

"Hell, I'd be less worried about a puppy. At least then somebody might throw her some scraps or take her in. As it is—"

"As it is, we've got to make it to Tucson by nightfall."

I try to fight it, but my eyes drift to the rearview mirror when we stop at the red light. I see her standing there, watching us go in that thin yellow dress with the big beige coat on top that looks like she skinned a teddy bear. She's still holding the empty water bottle, and I can still see her bright blue eyes watching me.

She's too sweet and too damn pretty. "That girl is trouble."

"That girl?" My brother hooks a thumb, laughing at me like I just called her a killer bunny.

"This isn't a joy ride."

"Right. What is this exactly? You get out of the joint and immediately you want to drive thirty-six hours across the country in three days?"

"I want to see Jesse." My throat aches at the thought he might've forgotten me.

I don't include the part where I plan to confront my dad and demand answers—or punch him in the face.

That part makes my blood pressure rise.

The light finally turns green, and I'm about to floor it when Scout grabs the door handle and hops out. "Not on my watch."

I slam on the brakes shouting, "Scout, Goddammit!"

But he's jogging back to where a young guy in a dirty hoodie is talking to Hope. He always has to be a hero. I was like that eighteen months ago—until I learned the hard way heroes just get slugged in the stomach then kicked in the nuts when they're lying on the ground.

The car behind me honks, and I pull out of the lane of traffic, doing a shitty parallel parking job. Stepping out of the vehicle, I watch as Hope shies away from hoodie guy, and I see relief wash over her face when she sees Scout jogging towards her.

My brother doesn't hesitate. He grabs her arm and pulls her to where I'm waiting at the car. Hope's pale blonde hair fans out behind her as she jogs to keep up with him, and that teddy bear coat falls off one shoulder.

She looks too young to be able to own a car, much less sell one and get ditched in Los Angeles alone. Her blue eyes are too round, and her pink lips are like the small roses our grandmother used to grow over the fence in her backyard.

In spite of myself, I take in her slender frame and the heat in my stomach turns to something lustier. I imagine crushing those glossy lips with mine…

Fucking… *What the hell?*

Trouble. This girl is *trouble.*

Scout is talking to her. "I know it's crazy, but these are crazy times. We've just got to go with it."

"You sound like my dad." Her voice is hesitant but curious. "He's always talking about providence and having faith."

My brother holds the door for her. "Sounds like my kind of guy. Get in."

Our eyes meet, and my brow lowers. "This is a bad idea."

She pauses, lifting luminous blue eyes to mine. "I'm sorry, John…"

Her soft voice hits me right in the chest. My jaw clenches, and I swallow the growl rising in my throat.

"John?" Scout closes his door and hops in the passenger's side facing me. "The only person who calls him John is our grandmother."

Her brow furrows like she caught me in a lie, which is ridiculous. "I guess I should be more careful. You never know when people are being honest."

Scout places a hand over his heart. "I vow to be personally responsible for your safety on this trip."

I roll my eyes, looking up at the blue sky. It's a wonder this guy hasn't won a daytime Emmy yet.

Leaning forward, I start the ignition. "You are personally responsible for her. Don't make me regret this."

"Have I ever made you regret anything?"

I pause to think, and no, I can honestly say, my little brother has been the one person I've always been able to count on my entire life.

"Let's go." I shift the car into drive, and we head towards the I-10 entrance ramp.

WE'RE PAST RIVERSIDE, AND I'M ABOUT READY TO TAKE A BREAK. HOPE and Scout have been chatting nonstop, and I've learned she's twenty-three, two years younger than my brother, three and a half years younger than me, and she'd just celebrated the grand opening of her own restaurant Pancake Paradise in the Embarcadero when the lockdown happened.

"It was my dream happy place." Her voice is clear as a bell, a little on the high side but not annoying.

Her jacket is off, and she's in a thin yellow dress with spaghetti straps over her shoulders that show she's not wearing a bra. The sun shines through her wavy, light blonde hair, and she holds a Red Vine to her full pink lips, slipping her small pink tongue out to taste it.

I look out the window, to distract my body from the primal response she provokes. For the last eighteen months, my fist has been my dick's only friend.

"It was like hibachi?" Scout hasn't changed a bit since I saw him last. He's as ready to make friends as ever.

"Mm-hm." She nods. "But with pancakes. You'd get this plastic squeeze bottle like a ketchup bottle but clear. It had your special batter in it, and you could make shapes or write your name or use one of the molds we provided. You could even mix the batters to do like a marble effect."

"What's *special batter*?"

"Whatever you want!" The wind pushes her hair off her soft cheeks, and her nose wrinkles. "Plain, chocolate, vanilla bean, cinnamon, red velvet... we even had whole wheat and gluten-free options. Then once it was done, you could decorate it with whipped cream and sprinkles or fresh fruit or fancy syrups."

My brother exhales a laugh. "I would have never thought of this, but it sounds really fun."

"It was." Her voice goes quiet, sad, and my chest tightens protectively, which is fucking ridiculous. "I invested everything I had in it. Then I lost it all."

"Man." Scout pats her shoulder. "I'm sorry, Hope."

For a minute, she glances out the window, and her full bottom lip disappears into her mouth. It's like when a small cloud passes over the sun on a perfect summer day, a moment of shadow.

Then she shakes her head and blinks quickly. "It's going to be okay! My dad says you're going to stumble when you start to run. The trick is to get back up when you fall."

"He's right." My brother nods. "Hell, I'd just gotten my first callback to be a paid extra in the new Chris Nolan film on March 20, and *bam!* Shutdown."

"Oh…" Her face falls into a sympathetic expression. "Still, that sounds so exciting. It's going to come back, right?"

"I think so. The question is when."

She blinks at him in a way that makes me feel tight and angry. She's curious and cute, and she reminds me of a time when I believed I could do anything, conquer the world if I just got the right chance.

Clearly thoughts of a man who has been driving ten hours straight without a break. "I'm going to pull over and let you take the wheel soon."

"He's alive." Scout looks at me and laughs. "Thought you had mind-melded with the car."

"Like it mattered with you two talking nonstop."

Her eyes meet mine in the mirror again, and again, it's like a sucker punch. She's been doing that the whole drive—glancing at me every few minutes as if she's afraid I'll pull over and leave her on the side of the road again. I should have done it. I should do it now. She's a grown woman, for Christ's sake. As usual, I caved to my little brother, and now I don't know what the hell we're doing with her.

"I blame quarantine." My brother laughs. "After three months of being alone, I'd gotten to where I was stalking the mailman for somebody to talk to."

"Anything's better than being stuck in the house, right?" She smiles, and that little nose wrinkles again.

"Three months alone is nothing," I grumble.

They fall silent, and her eyes drift to mine again. I'm sorry I said anything. We pass a green sign for Joshua Tree National Park, and it informs us the next gas stop is in 47 miles. I glance at the tank. We're good, but I'm exhausted.

Smooth brown boulders rise in prehistoric shapes in the distance, and the spiky shrubs and desert palms rise above the parched earth.

"To think most people just fly over this." Hope looks out the window. "It's gorgeous."

"I read it gets as hot as 120 degrees some days." Scout reaches down and pulls out a bottle of water.

"Give me some of that." He hands it over, and Hope puts her hand on the back of the seat, resting her chin on top.

I'm acutely aware of her proximity to my shoulder. Her head tilts to the side, and she looks at my brother. "I like your name. *Scout.* Where does it come from?"

"Our mom was a librarian." He offers her a water, but she shakes her head. "She named us after her favorite books and authors."

"Scout… from *To Kill A Mockingbird*?" Her head lifts.

"Yep. Bradley after Boo Radley, and Scout. Bradley Scout Dunne."

"That's fun!" She glances at me carefully. "And John…"

"John Steinbeck and Phillip Roth," Scout answers for me.

"John Roth. JR." This time when my eyes met hers, she smiles shyly.

Jesus. It's worse than her fearful looks. Her shy smile is a hit below the belt. Tightening my grip on the steering wheel, I look out the window. No chance of leaving her in the middle of the Mojave Desert.

"I like your name." I can't tell if Scout is flirting or just being his usual friendly self—not that there's a difference. "Hope… It suits you. Is that all there is?"

Her laugh is embarrassed, and she shakes her head. "Hope Eternal Hill."

"Hope Eternal?" My brother's voice goes loud, and I fight a grin. It does suit her. "Let me guess. Old-school California hippies."

She nods, pressing her lips together as her cheeks flush pinker. "We lived in a commune with five other families. We raised all our own food, made our own clothes. We all home-schooled together…"

"Damn." Scout looks at me. "You lived your whole life like that? But what about this car?"

"I didn't live my whole life like that. My dad's family had money. I guess that's why he had the luxury of walking away. My mom's family did not have money, so she wasn't as excited about living like a pauper. She did it for ten years, then she walked away from us."

An unexpected edge enters her voice, and my eyes cut to hers in the mirror. All the fear and shyness have disappeared.

"I'm sorry." Scout is quiet.

"Not your fault." She forces a smile, but their conversation stalls.

We're just crossing the Colorado River, and I notice a gas station off the interstate.

Checking the mirror, I see Hope gazing out at the desert. Her smile is gone, and I recognize the emotion in her eyes—betrayal, anger, unresolved hurt. She tipped her hand a bit, and it's possible we have more in common than I thought.

"Your turn to drive." I point at my brother as I pull the Impala to a gas pump. Looking at Hope, I nod at her feet. "You need shoes."

"If they just have a cheap pair of flip flops—" She looks around the backseat then appears flustered.

I frown. "What?"

"I-I don't have my wallet… I don't have any money."

Or a driver's license, I mentally note. "Don't worry about it. I'll spot you five bucks for a pair of flip flops."

"I'll pay you back!" It's a little chirp I wave away.

"What size?"

"Medium… Seven if it matters."

I grab a paper mask at the door and slip it over my face. The gas station is crammed with western-themed gifts and souvenirs, and I push through the aisles of fake succulents, beer holders, t-shirts reading Chuckwalla Valley Raceway, and Arizona sweatshirts searching for shoes… *Seriously, who needs a sweatshirt in Arizona?*

Flip flops are not on the menu, but I do find a stash of discount cowboy boots I kind of like. Digging through the pile, I grab the only women's Size 7, and pay the man from my cash.

Scout is in the restroom when I walk back to the car, carrying the drinks and boots. I slip the mask in my pocket, and Hope's eyes widen as she looks up at what I'm holding.

"What the… You got me cowboy boots?"

"I didn't have a choice."

She pulls the white ankle boots out of the bag, and her voice goes high. "They're so cute!"

Slipping them on her bare feet, she steps out of the car. They stop just below her calves, and they actually go with what she's wearing.

I feel an unwelcome surge of pride, and my dick reminds me it's been a hell of a long time since I've been near an attractive woman, or any woman for that matter.

Her eyes shine, and she turns side to side. "I can't keep these… I can't afford to pay you back."

"They were twenty bucks. The guy had them shoved in a corner marked clearance."

Her pink lips part, and she looks up at me. "You're kidding?"

"He said you're the first person needing anything but gas in four months."

"Well, I'll be." She turns side to side then smiles at me. "Thank you. I really will pay you back as soon as I get my wallet—"

"Don't worry about it. I can spot you a pair of shoes."

She wrinkles her nose like she does. "In case you decide to leave me on the side of the road again?"

I can't tell if she's flirting with me or if she's fishing for reassurance. Either way, I'm not getting mixed up with my brother's charity case—or whatever she is. I've got one reason for this trip, and it isn't romance.

Clearing my throat, I start for the passenger's side. "You'd better go to the restroom. We're not going to stop again for a while."

"Okay..." She shakes her blonde head at me and rolls her eyes. "*Dad.*"

I watch her sass away in that thin yellow dress with no bra in those white boots, and dirty thoughts come uninvited to my mind. Thoughts that start with her on the hood of the car and end with her on my lap in the backseat... legs spread, hips rolling.

"She's pretty damn cute, huh?" Scout walks out, breaking my pornographic fantasy.

He shoves a mask in his pocket and tosses a football in the air. He throws it to me, and like muscle memory, I catch it.

"I don't care." Looking at the brown leather, I shake my head. "Not interested in this either."

Scout slides in the driver's side, and I climb in the back. "You're just a barrel of laughs these days."

"Nothing to laugh about."

"Getting out two years early sounds like a good place to start."

"I shouldn't have been there in the first place." Lying across the bench seat, I dig in my bag for a ball cap.

"Right." My brother nods, looking out the windshield. "I was thinking you might ask her to stay when we get to Fireside."

"Why the fuck would I do that?"

"Because she's cute as hell, and you're both starting from scratch…"

"When we get to Fireside, I'm sending you both back to California. That's the end of it."

Exhaustion creeps up the back of my neck as I pull the cap over my eyes. I don't even respond when my brother makes some additional remark about life going on. I'm too tired to get pissed again about what happened to me. I'm too tired for much of anything right now.

And as I've already noted, this road trip isn't about romance.

CHAPTER
Five

Hope

"I WALKED INTO THE CONFERENCE ROOM AND SAID, 'HERE'S THE file you needed.' Dustin Hoffman says, 'Thank you, Scout,' and boom. I'm in the union." He smiles, and I can't help smiling back.

"That's amazing. Dustin Hoffman?"

"Yep." Scout is infectious—adorable and open, and so friendly.

Nothing like the dark cloud currently snoring on the backseat. The dark cloud I can't help stealing another glance at... Something about John "JR" Dunne makes my insides all hot and zippy. I want to put my thumb on that full bottom lip and pull it down. I want to bite him... I want him to put his hands on my body and do dirty things to me.

Blinking away that impossible thought, I exhale a laugh, returning my attention to his brother. "It took how long for you to get in the union?"

"Three years…" He winces, looking out the window as if he's embarrassed. "I kind of got off on the wrong foot in Hollywood."

I'm about to ask what happened when Mr. Dark Cloud cuts in. "You can say that again." John sits up in the backseat, and my heart beats a little faster. "Damn I'm starving. Anybody else hungry?"

"Fuck, I could eat a horse!" Scout yells, and I'm glad I'm not the only one starving to death.

All we've eaten today is road junk—Combos, Red Vines, and water. That's following a morning of me barfing up a whole bottle of wine from last night.

"I could eat… if that's okay?" My voice is quiet, because I have no money…

Also, *what the hell am I doing here?* I didn't even have shoes before four hours ago. I was still drunk and hungover when I got in the car this morning, I can't believe I agreed to this trip. My brain is coming back around, and I am very aware I'm driving across the country with two men I don't know.

I blame it all on Metallicar.

And Scout sounding like my dad talking about serendipity and how this year is magical… I'd call this year cursed, but he'd probably argue curses are magical.

Scout shakes my shoulder. "You thought we were going to make you live on sunflower seeds and Chex Mix for three days?"

He's so laid-back, I can't help teasing, "I was hoping for Bugles and beef jerky."

We're just outside of Phoenix, and he exits the interstate. "Check it out… Hopeville. That seems like a good sign to me."

"You're such a little bitch. You haven't even been driving four hours." John's voice is a low grumble from the backseat, but I hear a smile in his tone.

"I've been riding more than eight. We need a break."

He turns in at the Black Bear Diner. It's a long, rectangular building with carved black bears on stumps in rock and succulent beds, and tables arranged under what looks like newly installed awnings. A motel is right behind the restaurant with a huge yellow sign reading, "Rooms $19.95 per night."

"I'm not sure that's a good sign." I shift in my seat, wondering what the plan for sleeping might be.

"We're not spending the night," John snaps.

Scout pulls Metallicar into a spot up front, and we stumble out. My legs feel like Jell-O, and I follow behind as John stalks towards the glass entrance. Reaching out, I catch Scout's arm, pulling him back as his brother goes inside.

"What am I doing here?"

He stops and faces me, grinning like always. "We're taking a road trip to Fireside, South Carolina. The Palmetto State. My hometown."

"Yeah, but what am *I* doing here? I don't belong here. I don't have any money. We don't really know each other—"

"Shh…" He holds a finger just in front of my lips. "You're very important. You provided the car."

"Your brother bought the car. It's his car now. I fell asleep on the backseat after drinking a whole bottle of wine."

"Who are we to question the fates?"

The sun is setting over the desert, and behind us the sky is painted in the most brilliant shades of pink, blue, and purple. It really does feel magical in this moment… And I am a fool for stuff like that. It's because of how I was raised.

"I really need to catch a bus to San Francisco."

He crosses his arms, grinning down at me. "But how will you pay for it?"

Chewing my lip, I look around. He's got me there. "I guess I could ask my dad to wire me the money." If I can get through to him in the nursing home.

"Hope Eternal…" Scout tosses a muscled arm over my shoulders, leading me towards the restaurant. "You have a purpose for being here. I knew it the minute I saw you. It's destiny."

"You've been in California too long." Then I squint an eye up at him. "Are you trying to ask me out?"

His lips tighten, and he stops walking, glancing in the direction his brother went. "No."

Oh fuck, I screwed this up. "That came out wrong. I didn't mean—"

"Hey, no, I'm sorry. I like you a lot! You're really cool and—"

"You don't have to say that." *God, I am such an airhead.*

"Stop. Now listen… I'm going to tell you something." His chin drops, and he rubs the back of his neck. "I kind of have my own reason for making this trip—besides helping JR. I kind of left someone behind in Fireside. And I'm hoping… Well, I don't know if she'll even speak to me now…"

My eyebrows rise. "You have a girlfriend in Fireside?"

"Maybe?"

This is so screwed up. I've been sneaking glances at his brother for the past ten hours, and now I've made things weird with my one ally. "I really should go now."

"I wish you wouldn't." He catches my arms gently, and his blue eyes hold mine. "I don't know why we all ended up in this car together, but I'm serious when I say it feels important. I said I'd look out for you, right? Do you trust me?"

My stomach twists, and this feels so foolish. So stupid and foolish and oh my God, this is nuts. Still, the look in his eyes…

Rubbing my hand over my stomach, I wince. "I guess I never had one of those crazy college road trips people always talk about."

"That-a girl. Now let's get something to eat. Combos and Red Vines are not food."

"I love Red Vines."

JR's sitting in a booth looking at a plastic-covered menu. "About damn time. What the hell were you doing?"

We slide into the seat across from him. "Sorry—Hope was trying to desert us again."

Scout nudges me with an elbow, and I'm terrified he might tell his brother I thought he was going to ask me out. JR cuts those steel-blue eyes up at me under a lowered brow, and I get hot all over. *If I want either of these brothers asking me out…*

That is never going to happen. It's beyond clear John Roth Dunne wants no part of me.

"Welcome to the Black Bear. What can I get you folks?" A middle-aged waitress wearing a paper mask under her nose walks up grinning. Her pale red hair is teased up in a bun, and she has little ringlets at her temples.

John doesn't smile. He doesn't even look up. "This 'Reunited at Last' looks good."

"One New York steak sandwich. And you?" She turns to me, and I order the first thing I see.

"'Let's Catch Up'?"

"Two fish tacos… that just leaves you, honey." She winks at Scout.

He grins and winks right back, reading her nametag. "Heck, Darlene, I can't decide. What's your favorite?"

"Get the 'So Happy to See You.'"

"Works for me." He takes our plastic menus and hands them to her.

She looks around the table. "Arnold Palmers for everyone?"

"Sure." Scout smiles, but JR stops her.

"I'll have a coffee."

"And one coffee." She makes a note, and I'm pretty sure as she walks away, she adds a little wiggle to her strut.

JR glances after her. "This would be a great time to rob a bank with everyone in masks."

Scout leans forward. "It doesn't do any good under her nose."

JR gives his brother a look. "Must you flirt with everyone?"

"Just being friendly." Scout takes a sip of ice water. "You know, every interaction is a little nicer if you make people feel special."

"Oh yeah, how's that working out for you?"

Darlene returns with one coffee and two Arnold Palmers.

I lift mine and take a sip of the half-iced tea, half-lemonade concoction, smiling up at her. "I don't think I've ever had one of these."

Scout stretches his arm across the booth behind me. "What's happening in Hopeville tonight, Darlene?"

"Well, funny you should ask, sugar." She cocks a hip to the side. "Some of the high school kids put together a football team. They're playing some kids from out of town in about an hour."

"You're kidding." He looks across the table, but John is shaking his head no.

She nods. "First recreational thing we've had in months. It's kind of a big deal. Out at the memorial stadium."

"Maybe we'll check it out."

"You do that." She sashays away again, and we're left facing each other.

"We don't have time for a football game." JR's sips his coffee, glaring at his brother.

John and Scout aren't identical. Scout is blond and surfer, while John is dark and stormy... but they have those matching blue eyes, and when they smile, I can tell they're brothers. I can tell they love each other.

"Right, and you were going to tell me why we're driving home like the cops are after us." Scout's tone is serious for the first time all day.

"I told you. I want to see Jesse."

"Yeah, I get that. I believe you want to see him, but I don't think killing ourselves is the best approach."

"Nobody's getting killed." JR says it like he left off the *yet*.

"Who's Jesse?" My voice is quiet, and I say it more to Scout's shoulder than the table.

John answers. "He's my son."

My eyebrows rise, and I swallow the sting of jealousy in my throat. "Oh."

Of course, he's married. I study my drink doing my best to act cool, even though I feel like I just found out there's no Santa Claus.

What's that about? I have no reason to feel disappointed. This guy was going to leave me on the side of the road.

"Have you even talked to Becky since you've been out? Does she know you're coming?"

"I haven't talked to Becky since she sent me divorce papers three months into my sentence." An edge is in his voice, but I'm feeling the tiniest bit better… *Divorce papers.*

"How old is your son?" My voice is still quiet.

"He turned five a few months ago."

"That's a cute age." I give him a little smile, and he blinks at me a second before looking away.

Darlene is back with a teenage guy, and they put the plates in front of us. "Can I get you anything? Refills on your drinks?"

"I'll have a refill." JR unrolls his napkin, and the three of us dig in.

I'm so hungry, I barely even taste the food before I swallow it, doing my best not to groan loudly.

"Damn…" Scout has no such qualms. "I hope you're not planning to starve us every day."

"I hope you brought money," JR quips. "I don't have unlimited resources."

"I have money…" Sitting straighter, I hold up a hand. I don't know why, so I put it down again. "We just have to stop at my bank so I can get a temporary debit card."

"Don't worry about it." JR polishes off his sandwich.

"It's the money you paid for the car, so... I guess if I'm still using the car, it's technically yours—"

His brow lowers. "I haven't made a payment yet."

"Then how'd you get it?" Scout asks.

"They have this seven-day money-back guarantee. Payments don't start until next week."

He looks from me to John then back to me. "Is that why—"

"No," his brother snaps.

My heart beats a little faster, and I think about his comment earlier. *Robbing banks.* "You never said why you were in jail."

"I was set up." He pushes the plate away and digs in his pocket, taking out a wad of cash. "Let's go."

"That doesn't answer my question..." But he's out the door, leaving me confused and a little scared. "Is that why you promised to keep me safe?"

Scout's lips press into a line, and he shakes his head. "JR won't hurt you."

"Why was he in prison?"

The horn honks sharply outside, and Scout slides out of the booth with me behind him. "Our dad owns a gym. One of his suppliers planted HGH in an order of supplements, and JR got caught with it."

"I don't know what that means."

"HGH is Human growth hormone. It's illegal."

I stop walking. "So it was a drug deal?"

"Technically... But not like cocaine or heroin." He walks back to me and catches my hand. "I believe JR when he says he misses his son, but this trip is about more than just a reunion. I think he's trying to get there before our dad knows he's out."

We're at the car, and I'm still feeling nervous. Looking up the road, I don't see any signs of a bus station or any way of getting back to San Francisco. Why didn't I just stay on the side of the road? Or hell, why didn't I stay in LA?

"It's still my turn to drive." Scout leans the front seat forward so I can I climb inside the car. "Climb in. I want to check out that football game."

CHAPTER
Six

JR

THE BLEACHER-LINED STADIUM IS FLOODED WITH LIGHTS AS WE approach. Parked cars ring both end zones, and some spectators have arranged lawn chairs in front of the sparsely filled stands.

"Not sure that's a safe social distance," my brother huffs under his breath, parking at the edge of the field, far from the other cars.

"Not sure they care." I look out the open passenger's window, already growing impatient.

I have no idea what we're doing here, but I step out as Hope exits behind my brother.

The night air is crisp and dry, just what you'd expect in the desert. Kids line up in the middle of the field. They're dressed like any other football team, only they're also wearing black masks beneath their helmets.

"Imagine, one day we'll be telling our kids about this crazy year." Scout leans against the hood, chewing on a Red Vine and tossing that football he bought in the air.

"I'll never forget it." Hope's voice is quiet, and she hangs back by the door.

She's acting nervous again, and I don't like it. At the same time, it bothers me I care about her discomfort. She has no business being on this trip, and I won't let myself get soft around her, no matter how cute she is in those boots with her wavy hair hanging over her shoulders.

A whistle blows, and the starting quarterback falls back. I watch him scan the field, and I'm pulled into a memory like I'm reading his mind. I know exactly what it's like to spot every player, flying through all the potential outcomes in a flash in your brain.

The clock is ticking as he makes a decision, firing a pass like a bullet straight to the wide receiver, who easily runs it into the end zone.

The crowd goes wild, and Scout laughs. "Damn, he's good. Reminds me of how we were."

I watch the people in the stands, waving signs and pom poms. I don't expect the surge of nostalgia it provokes.

"Nothing was like us." I hear it in my voice.

"Come on." Scout hands me the ball. "I'll go long."

I look at the pigskin in my hands, and anger tightens in my stomach. We were kids with dreams then. We stupidly believed people were good. "No."

"Ah, come on. Nobody cares." He jogs backwards. "Show me what you got, old man."

"Old man." My jaw tightens, and I turn the oval ball in my hands.

"Don't leave me hanging," he taunts.

I glance up to where he's jogging in place and pull back, sending the ball in a tight spiral straight into his Velcro grip.

"Yeah!" He throws his arms up, holding the ball high as he

jogs a tight circle before returning to where I'm standing. "The crowd goes wild."

"You're pretty good." Hope's voice is closer now, and when I look back at her, the anger subsides.

Something about her sweetness draws me. She keeps a distance between us, but she's relaxing again.

"The Dunne brothers…" Scout holds up his hand for a high five before placing the ball in mine again. "Getting it done."

He's chanting, but I shake my head. "Not doing it again."

Hope watches him, a smile teasing at her soft lips. "Was that a thing?"

Scout grins, jogging backwards again. "JR was team captain, starting quarterback… Mr. Palmetto State."

I feel her studying me, but I don't look. "That was a long time ago."

"It wasn't that long." My little brother won't stop. "I can catch anything he throws. Even the stinkers."

"I don't throw stinkers."

"He threw some stinkers." He's baiting me, and like an idiot, it's working. "I could read his mind. I knew where he was aiming… I dodged every defensive lineman."

Remembering him slipping past those guys actually makes me grin. "He was like a fucking bar of soap." *Jackass.*

"I bet you were fun to watch." Hope is closer, like a magnetic field beside me. "I never had a sibling. I imagine it must be the best thing to have someone you can always depend on, no matter what."

"Don't build it up too much," Scout yells. "He's still a pain in the ass most of the time."

I look up at the fading sunset. "As fun as this is, we're on the clock. Let's go."

"Come on! One last throw." My brother waves his hands.

I pull back and fire off an intentional stinker—outside and

close to the ground. He pivots into action, springing off the lawn and diving, scooping it up before it touches grass. Just like always.

"He caught it!" Hope squeals beside me, jumping up and down and clapping.

She laughs, grasping my arm, and I shake my head, unable to hold back a smile.

"I knew you were going to do that." Scout's breathless as he jogs back to where we're standing. "Asshole."

"That was a great catch." Hope claps his high five.

"Let's go." I circle around to the driver's side. "I'll take over for a while, see how close I can get us to El Paso."

"I can drive." Hope skips behind me. "I'll use the cruise control. We won't get stopped. I haven't seen a cop the whole way."

"No." My frown is firmly in place. "I'm not taking a chance on this trip. Scout, get in the back and sleep. I'll want you taking over when I'm done."

"Roger that." He hops in the backseat, and I slide behind the wheel, waiting as Hope climbs in the passenger's side.

Having her up front makes her harder to ignore, but I turn on the radio and roll down my window. We don't have to talk.

We're not five miles down the road when my brother sits up. "Tell me, Hope Eternal, you got a fella back in San Francisco?"

I'd tell him to shut up and sleep, but I want to know the answer to this question myself.

"While we're on the subject…" She teases, glancing at me briefly. She's still doing it, and it's like water dripping, wearing me down, making me want to meet her eyes, touch her.

"I told you my story," Scout counters, and she shrugs.

"I was kind of dating this guy in February, but we lost touch after everything happened."

"Isn't that a bitch? Same thing happened to me."

Her lips part, and she looks over her shoulder. "You said somebody's waiting back home!"

News to me. I glance at him in the rearview mirror, but he doesn't meet my eyes. "I said I *hoped.* I don't know if she's waiting."

"When's the last time you talked to her?"

His voice drops, so I almost can't hear it. "When I left Fireside."

I'm trying to figure out who he means, and Hope turns to face him. "You haven't even tried to stay in touch?"

"I felt like I'd be leading her on. Then things got all fucked up, and I wasn't sure she even wanted to hear from me."

Hope's quiet a minute. She looks forward as if she's thinking. "Are you friends with her on Facebook?"

"No."

"Instagram?"

"I kind of got off all social media three years ago."

"That can't be great for your acting career. Everybody's on social media now."

"It's a long story." Shame suffuses his tone. "I'm sort of easing back into it…"

I know the story, and I wonder if he's going to share his shining achievement with her. The "setback" he apparently spent three years trying to overcome.

When he doesn't say more, I decide to throw him a lifeline. "I can't drive the whole way. You'll have to take over in a few hours."

"Right." He drops down on the backseat, pulling my cap over his face.

Hope's full lips press together, and she turns to face front again. We ride for a few songs without talking, then she peeks over at me.

"So you were the star quarterback in high school?" She says it with a little smile.

My hands tighten on the wheel. "That was a long time ago."

"Did you play in college?"

"Some."

She's quiet again. The Eagles are still playing in the background, "Life in the Fast Lane," and I consider changing the channel, but their songs are like cold beer on a hot day. They just go down easy.

"Does it make you angry to talk about it?"

It's a fair question. My mind trips back to those days, even before when we were kids. Dad pushing us to play the game; Mom teasing it kept us from breaking everything in the house.

I played because I was bored, but Scout would sleep with a fucking football for a pillow. It always meant more to him than it did to me. Our dad was determined we would both be stars, but we only played together.

"It doesn't make me angry." It makes me itchy, like a wool sweater on a humid day.

"But you don't like it… Why?" Her voice is gentle, and I think about my answer.

"I guess it was all that came with it. My dad constantly pushing us. People who acted like they cared, but they just used us to get what they wanted. Or to get attention."

She puts her elbow on top of the seat, propping her head on her hand and smiling. It stirs the restlessness in my chest.

"What?"

"That's the most you've said to me this whole trip."

"Wasted words."

"So you let a bunch of selfish assholes spoil something you love?"

"I didn't love it. I did it because I was good at it, and I didn't have a choice. Dad wouldn't let us stop. Scout loved it."

She glances in the backseat briefly then seems to think. "Was the cheerleader one of the selfish people?"

"I don't want to talk about her." I wasted a lot of time being pissed at my ex-wife. Now I just want her to give me my son and go the fuck away. If that's even possible.

"I get that." She nods, shifting in her seat again to face front. "I was in love with this guy once. He wasn't who I thought he was."

"People usually aren't."

Her head tilts to the side, and she gives me that little half-smile. "You don't mean that, do you?"

I look out my window again. "Yeah, I'm afraid I do."

"Are you who you seem to be?"

"Depends." This time I do look at her, straight on. "Who do I seem to be?"

Her blue eyes narrow, and she studies me until I start to feel uneasy. "You seem like a straight shooter. You clearly love your brother... I don't know about the prison part, but besides that, you seem honest. Like a good guy."

My eyes are on the road, and her words are like invisible fingers, tugging on the fist in my chest. It's like she's trying to get it to open, to release the rage. I glance at her again, and she's still watching me, the wind from the cracked window pushing her light blonde hair around her cheeks. *Hope Eternal...*

"I won't ever lie to you."

That sweet smile relaxes her face, and my throat tightens. I push against the way she makes me feel. She makes me want to pull the car over and wrap her in my arms, bury my face in her hair, and just breathe.

I am so fucking tired.

My voice is rough as I flip on the turn signal. "Time to switch drivers."

CHAPTER
Seven

Hope

S COUT HAS ONE ARM ON THE WINDOW AND ONE HAND ON THE steering wheel. The wind pushes his blond hair around his face, and we're flying down I-10, crossing southern Texas. The muscle in his square jaw moves like his brother's when he's thinking, but he seems so much younger.

"An out of work actor, a failed restaurateur, and an ex-con walk into a bar—"

My nose scrunches. "I don't like being a failed restauranteur. I prefer suspended… or temporarily detained…"

"Doesn't flow."

"Frustrated restaurateur…" I suggest.

"Maybe."

"You're *out of work*. Why do I have to be a failure?"

"All actors are out of work."

JR growls from the backseat. "Would you two shut up so I can sleep? We're not going to a bar."

We fall silent as Mr. Dark Cloud turns over on the seat, and I can't resist. "Snarls the grumpy ex-con…"

Scout fake-coughs, "Asshole," and I glance back, catching the ghost of a grin on JR's lips.

It makes me smile. He tries to act so angry all the time, but he likes us. He's talking to me now, and I want more. I want every word he has to say.

I won't ever lie to you…

The simple statement sent a thrill through my stomach. I believe him.

"Who was the first guy you ever had sex with?" Scout glances at me, and my eyebrows shoot up.

"You are so nosy!"

"It's a boring drive. We might as well make it interesting. Tell me your story, and I'll tell you mine."

Mischief is in his eyes, and I chew my lip. Scout is so fun, and I think I like him more knowing we're just friends.

I steal a glance at the backseat, and it seems JR is sleeping…

"Okay." I hold the sides of my dress and rest my feet on the dash. It's how I always rode with Dad, and Scout doesn't seem to care. "Wade Peterson."

"Wade…" Scout says the word like he's testing it out. "That's a name you don't hear much."

"He was one of the commune kids. We lost touch after my mom left, but we met up again when we were seniors. We were at a Young Life meeting, and every time they'd sing 'Wade in the Water,' my best friend Yars would whisper 'Where?'"

The memory makes me grin—my bestie is so crazy.

"So he was cute?"

"He had that California beach thing going, blue eyes, bleached hair, perpetual tan."

"Wait… Isn't Young Life a church thing?" Scout's cheek-dimple appears. "Let me guess… He wanted it, and you didn't."

"Pfft... Hardly."

That makes him laugh. "Teenage Hope was a bad girl."

"That's what he said." I look out the window feeling embarrassed all over again. "I thought... I *think* sex is a natural thing. It's fun."

"I couldn't agree more."

"Wade said sex for fun was *indulging the flesh*." I can still see his eyes, stern and judgmental. God, it's been six years, and I still feel the cringe of shame climbing my shoulders.

"What the fuck?" Scout's brow lowers, and he looks like his brother—pissed and ready to punch somebody. I kind of like this protective vibe he's giving me. It makes me feel safe telling him the truth.

"He said I had a problem. I shouldn't want it so much. He said sex was for procreation."

"So he was gay." Scout relaxes like he's solved a riddle.

"He was... not." Tilting my head to the side, I give it some more thought. "I never thought he was. He was smart and he liked discussing the Bible—"

"Gay." Scout nods like he's an expert. He holds up a hand. "Nothing wrong with that, but he shouldn't have led you on."

A few quiet moments pass, and I think about what he's saying. I think about the things I'd wanted and how dirty Wade made me feel. I tucked those desires away, believing I had a problem. Now I wonder...

Lowering my voice, I lean closer. "I wanted him to say dirty things to me and be rough. Hold me down and take me. You know?"

Scout shifts in his seat. "Unexpected, but okay."

My cheeks flush, and I want to die. "Is that bad? Do you think I need therapy?"

"Shit no." He laughs, running his hand over his mouth and giving me another quick glance. "It's just... Look at you. Then you go and say something like that."

"Wade said it was perverted. He said I must have some deep-seated problem."

"I think your boy Wade had the problem." He gives my shoulder a pat. "I think your shit is hot. I think it's going to make some guy really happy."

Crossing my arms, I flop back on the seat. "Well, I dumped him. He shaved his beard, and I realized he was just a little boy pretending to be a man."

"Good call. Never let some small-minded prick kill your mojo."

"Where are we?" JR's grumpy voice from the backseat makes me jump and put my feet down.

"We're outside El Paso... Socorro."

JR rubs a hand over his face. "I need a shower."

"Me too," Scout says. "I'm getting ripe."

My nose scrunches, but the truth is, I could use one too. I've been riding post-hangover for almost 24 hours.

Scout cuts the speed and leans forward to read the signs. He tosses his phone at me. "See what you can find."

Scooping it up, I tap on the icon for accommodations. "This Deluxe Inn says forty-five dollars a night. Exit... Oh, it's the next exit!"

He immediately puts on the blinker and drives us off the interstate. We take a right and go less than a quarter mile to where a wide, asphalt entrance leads up to a line of ancient cinder-block units painted white.

A big blue sign reading "Truck Parking" greets us at the entrance, and it looks like something out of a low-budget slasher film.

JR seems to anticipate all our reactions. "I'll get one room. If we stay together, we'll be fine. We won't be here long."

I glance out the window and decide beggars can't be choosers, and at least JR is somewhat intimidating. He definitely looks like he can kick some ass if he has to.

Twenty minutes later, I'm in a narrow shower stall with my eyes closed as warm water flows over my face and down my body like rainbows from heaven. I do my best to suppress a groan, but holy crap. After 24 hours of sticky brine from a beach walk followed by sick followed by sweaty heat, this might be the best shower of my life.

Scout went first, because he'd been driving the longest, and he insisted he smelled like ass... *Massive eye roll.* JR said he didn't mind going last, and for his sake, I force myself to cut it short.

Stepping out, I grab a threadbare towel and wrap it around me. Collecting my hand-washed panties, I head into the single-room to dress behind a makeshift curtain he hung around the bed.

"I tried to save you some hot water."

"Thanks." His response is cordial, but he doesn't linger.

The door closes fast, and the sound of water running meets my ears. Scout is sprawled out on the couch in jeans and a t-shirt. One arm is over his eyes, and he's snoring like a lumberjack.

Shaking my head, I look down at my damp underwear. I can't wear them wet. Hanging them on the side of the nightstand, I hope they'll dry somewhat before it's time to go.

I do my best to dry off with the towel, but it's like the material just pushes the water around on my skin. I'm still damp when I go to where I tossed my yellow dress on the bed.

Standing by the desk with my back to a sleeping Scout, I wave my arms trying to air dry a bit more before I put on my dress. JR's shirt hangs from the back of the chair, and I hesitate, glancing toward the bathroom. The sound of water is still going strong, and Scout lets out another snore from behind me.

I trace my fingers along the thick, light-blue fabric. Placing the useless towel on the desk, I lift his shirt and slip my arms in the sleeves, pulling it over my naked body and studying myself in the mirror.

It's too big for me. It stops at my upper thighs, and my small breasts are just covered by the rough fabric. My nipples tighten at the abrasion, and I lower my chin to inhale deeply.

I'm surrounded by his scent, masculine with hints of soap and citrusy deodorant. Closing my eyes, I imagine his large hands sliding up my thighs, squeezing my ass, spanning my waist. I imagine his lips at my ear, that rough voice telling me what he wants to do to me. My eyes squeeze and I picture two thick fingers slipping between my legs, touching my clit.

I imagine his beard scuffing my sensitive neck, moving around to my back, following the line of my shoulders. I imagine threading my fingers in his hair and kissing him hard…

My stomach is fizzy, my core hot and slippery, and I don't realize the water has stopped until the bathroom door jerks open. "Are there any more towels?"

A column of light streams across the room, illuminating me naked, in only his shirt.

"Oh!" It's a gasp, my breasts rising and falling with each quick breath. "I was just… I…"

I don't know what to say.

He hesitates, and his lips part, his dark brow lowers.

My eyes travel down his bare chest, and my head gets light. His skin is tanned and something is inked on his upper chest. I can't read it from here. He has another tattoo on his shoulder leading down to his round, bulging biceps. Deep lines of muscle cut across his torso, and a mouthwatering V disappears into his loose jeans.

Returning my eyes to his face, his jaw is perfectly square, and a cleft is in his chin. "You shaved."

He rubs his face, stepping into the room. "I wanted a fresh start."

His face is strong, manly—with a straight nose and high cheekbones. My fingers curl with wanting to touch him. "It's perfect…"

Without thinking, I take a step closer, ad his shirt opens, giving him a view of everything.

His eyes flinch, and I see the struggle, the flex in his jaw. "What are you doing?"

I glance down. "Trying on your shirt."

Desire crackles in the air around us and ice blue eyes blaze at me. "You're playing with fire, Hope. I haven't been with anyone in almost two years."

"Neither have I."

His eyes slowly move down my body like a caress, lingering on my breasts, my hardened nipples, drifting to my stomach, my bare pussy. His throat moves with a swallow, and my whole body is on fire. I want him to kiss me, touch me, *anything*...

"Give me the towel." It's a rough command.

"It won't do any good." A high, soft reply.

"I'll decide that." He snatches up the soggy scrap of terrycloth and returns to the bathroom, closing the door fast.

Scout lets out another loud snore, and I step back to sit on the foot of the bed, trying to breathe, trying to calm the trembling in my stomach, the raging fire in my veins.

JR Dunne is the sexiest man I've ever seen, and oh boy, I would've done anything just now for him to touch me.

CHAPTER
Eight

JR

I WANTED HIM TO SAY DIRTY THINGS TO ME. I WANTED HIM TO BE ROUGH... Her words taunted me as I lay on the backseat of the car pretending to sleep.

Now I'm gripping the crummy sink in this cheap motel bathroom, fighting the urge to go back out there and take her.

Opening the door, I was pretty sure I'd go blind when I saw her standing in the shaft of light wearing nothing but my light blue shirt. God, she's a walking wet dream.

Her pink lips parted, and her body... Small breasts rising and falling, dark nipples tight, peeking at me from inside the fabric. It took every single ounce of will power to keep myself in one place. My hands shook... My hands are still shaking.

My dick is a steel rod, aching for her tight body. *Fuck*. I step into the shower, flicking on the water and grabbing the tiny bottle of cheap conditioner. Closing my eyes, I rest my forehead on my arm. I imagine bruising her pink lips with mine, turning her to the wall and pushing in from behind.

Her soft voice transforms to moans as I slide my hands from her stomach up to her breasts, kneading and caressing, tweaking the hardened tips. One hand would go between her thighs, stroking and circling her clit until she's begging for more.

She likes it rough. I need it rough. After this long, it'll be hard to stop. I see my large hands covering her soft ass, squeezing and lifting her. I see her small feet rising onto her toes with every thrust, and it doesn't take long before orgasm snakes up my thighs, centering in my cock, and pulsing into the stream, disappearing down the drain.

Coughing to hide my groan, I stay there until the water is no longer warm, and I'm able to leave this tiny bathroom without thinking about touching her. She's right about the towel. It doesn't dry me off for shit, although it doesn't help I'm the third person to use it.

Snatching up my jeans, I jerk them over my hips before opening the door. I move slower this time, quieter. Scout's still sawing logs on the couch, and I scan the room for her. She's curled on the bed in that thin yellow dress. Her eyes are closed, and she seems to be sleeping.

My blue shirt is on the chair with a Deluxe Inn notepad on the table in front of it. *I'm sorry* is crawled across the top sheet.

I study her a moment. Her light hair is wavy against her cheeks, and her face is relaxed. Her skin has the slightest gold tone, like she's been in the sun, and her nose tilts up at the end. Her lips are full and pink, and damn, I want to kiss her. I want to fuck her hard, but I want to kiss her softly, pull her lips with mine, touch her nose.

Stepping away, I scrub my hands over my face, forcing these thoughts to stop.

I don't know where this is coming from. I don't even know this girl. I'm exhausted and frustrated and too much anger is driving me. I have to stay in control. The last thing I can afford to do is make a foolish mistake with this dreamy-eyed girl, this innocent who stumbled into my path and doesn't belong here.

Going to the other chair, I set my phone alarm to wake us in two hours and try to get comfortable. We've got to get on the road and make up for lost time. The sooner I get to Fireside, the sooner I can take care of business—and put both of them on a bus back to California.

CHAPTER
Nine

JR

IT'S A LONG DAY DRIVING ACROSS TEXAS, WITH A WHOLE LOT OF nothing to see except miles and miles of flat, brown desert dotted with cacti and, I imagine, rattlesnakes.

My brother seems to have caught up on all his words. He's quiet in the backseat most of the day, watching out the window with a Red Vine in his mouth. Hope seems withdrawn, and I guess it's because of our moment. She leans against the door, and I think she's asleep.

I'm pushing us hard—mostly because every time I glance at her, I still see her blue eyes looking up at me so open and needy. I'll probably never forget the sight of her small breasts, nipples tight, beneath my shirt.

I have to forget.

We've been driving since morning, stopping only for gas and snacks. At this point, we've gone ten hours on Red Vines, Slim Jims, and sunflower seeds, but I want to get through Texas. We switched from I-10 to Interstate-20 several hours ago, and we're on the other side of Dallas, closing in on the state line when my brother comes to life.

"Come on, man, we've got to stop for food," he groans, shifting in his seat. "I can't eat another Red Vine."

"Can you make it to Shreveport?" I glance at him in the mirror.

"Only if you let me drive."

"Deal."

We make one last pitstop in Longview to gas up and switch drivers. Hope hangs back, looking cute in that dress and those boots I bought her, sneaking glances at me as we stand around, stretching our legs and waiting on my brother.

Walking over to where she's hanging by the car, I put a hand on my hip. "It's okay."

"Okay?" She smiles, barely meeting my eyes before looking away again.

"Yeah." I feel like I ought to say something more reassuring, so I tell her what I've been thinking about all day. "What you told Scout about that guy… Wade?"

Her eyes go wide as pink fills her cheeks. "You were listening to that?"

"I'm not deaf when we're in the car together."

"Oh, my God."

"Anyway, I've known guys like that—who can't be honest about themselves for whatever reason."

Her slim brows furrow, and she looks up at me curiously. "You have?"

"I'm from South Carolina." She frowns like she doesn't understand, and I explain. "It's pretty religious there."

"Ohh…" Her chin lifts.

"Guys like that can be cruel—especially to people who *are* sure of themselves. Like you."

She blinks up at me, wrinkling her nose in that sweet way she does. "I'm not always so sure."

We're right back to where we were last night with her looking at me in that way that feels like an open invitation. I'm starting to wonder what the fuck is wrong with me. She had pulled back. She was giving me space. Why can't I leave well enough alone?

I clear my throat, backing away from her like she's an electric fence. "Well, that's all."

Scout jogs up, and I'm glad to let him take over the conversation. "Everybody ready?"

"Yes." The gruff is back in my voice.

Climbing in the car, I take the backseat, determined to keep her at arm's length before I forget what I reminded myself this morning. This girl has no business in my world, especially considering what I'm doing, what's waiting at the end of this journey.

We're less than an hour down the road, forty-five minutes of Scout and Hope singing along to 1960s satellite radio, when blue and red lights flashing ahead pull us up short.

"What the hell?" Scout lets off the gas, and we ease back.

"Get off here." I grab his shoulder. "NOW."

He hits the brakes hard, exiting fast onto a state highway headed north. "What the fuck, JR?"

"That was a roadblock. Put on the news and see what's happening."

Hope fiddles with the dial, but we can't find anything useful. It's all national news. Nothing local.

"Use my phone." Scout hands it to her, giving me a worried glance, and she taps for several seconds, swiping and reading.

"Here!" Her voice goes loud. "Road blocks at the border to keep sick people from entering the state."

"Damn..." Scout exhales. "Should I circle back?"

"No." I have my phone out, charting a new route. "We'll cut over through Arkansas."

"Arkansas?" Scout groans loudly. "When are we getting food?"

"We can stop here… in Magnolia."

It's dark as we slip across the border from Texas to Arkansas on a two-lane highway in the middle of nowhere. The Impala headlights cut through the dark night in white columns, and The War on Drugs blasts on the radio.

None of us speak, and Scout keeps glancing at me like he knows I'm hiding something. I'm not getting into it with him.

We're getting closer to Magnolia, and I see golden arches. "Just stop at the McDonald's."

"Fuck that." Scout cuts his speed through the small town. "I want real food."

We're crawling up the four-lane strip leading through town, but other than the usual fast-food restaurants, everything appears closed.

"It is Sunday." I look out the window not seeing any other options.

We're on the other side of town when a big tent rises like a circus in a large, open field. It's white and enormous, and lit up like it's some kind of festival.

Scout turns the Impala onto a dirt drive leading up to it. "Let's check this out."

I sit forward. "We don't have time to stop."

"Miracle Tent Crusade…" Hope reads the big white sign above the chain-length fence. "Lose your sins and find your savior."

Her expression is playful as she looks to my brother. "I don't know…"

"I'll praise Jesus for a plate of fried chicken." My brother pulls up next to a parked station wagon, but I have a bad feeling about this.

"Let's just get McDonald's."

"No way." He shoves it into park and gets out, me right behind him.

Catching his arm, I pull him back. "This doesn't feel right."

"That's your guilty conscious talking. You need to get some chicken and lose some sin." He gives me a wink and takes the keys, striding in the direction of the mob with confidence. "We've been driving for ten hours, and I need a break. Christian people aren't going to hurt you."

My stomach is tight. It feels like famous last words.

Hope glances at me like she's not sure what to do.

A voice echoes through the tent, extending out to us in the parking lot. "Come in, brothers and sisters, come in…" It's a voice like urgent singing. "Find your seats. We've got a special guest for you tonight. God's man of faith and power, Brother Bob Gantry, all the way from Colorado Springs, Colorado."

I tear my eyes off the giant white canvas and look at Hope. "I guess we're going in."

"LET ME HEAR YOU SAY *YES!*" THE MAN WITH THE MICROPHONE HITS THE *yes* hard.

Brother Bob has a big white grin and even bigger white hair. It's brushed back from his face, but a curl falls down on his forehead like one of those old-timey preachers.

The air inside the tent is hot, making my mask uncomfortable. Industrial-sized round fans are situated on both sides, blasting air through the space, and bugs swoop and dive at the lights far overhead.

People in masks stand in small clumps throughout, swaying in time with the music, arms raised overhead.

"Yes!" They cry in response, filling the air with their muffled voices.

"Yes!" The man shouts louder, this time with a touch of vibrato.

"Yes!" The congregants echo.

I catch up to where my brother's holding a long paper plate loaded with fried chicken, mashed potatoes, green beans, and two dinner rolls.

"Yes, Lord!" Rings out over my head.

"What are you doing?" My voice is sharp at Scout's ear.

"Yes, Lord!" He shouts in time, grinning behind his mask. "Grab a plate and let's dig in."

I watch him go to a group of long picnic tables lining the perimeter, but I don't fix a plate. Hope is close at my side watching the people moving in time with the organ music.

"Is it okay to eat the food if we're not planning to stay?" She looks up at me, but I shake my head.

Some people close their eyes and do a dance where they're hopping back and forth on each foot. The atmosphere is charged, and I can't decide if it's a good charge or something more ominous.

"I'm not hungry." My stomach's too tight to eat, and I lead her to where Scout's sitting.

The best thing I can say is the table where he's sitting is a safer distance from the crowd. The sides of the tent are open, so we can run if we need to. Also, it's a little cooler here, the air is fresher.

Scout is at the end of the long table, and I take a seat beside him facing the stage. Hope sits at my left.

"Why didn't you get any food?" My brother shovels a plastic fork full of green beans into his mouth and shakes his head. "Mmm… Somebody cooked these with bacon."

Ushers in black masks stand in locations throughout the crowd watching. They're big guys, and I can only see their eyes, which has me on guard.

I'm sure it's residual defensiveness from being in prison. Still, I'm not sure we're going to get out of here without making some kind of commitment.

"Must be five hundred people in here."

Scout nods. "Big crowd."

"It's like we're crashing a wedding." Hope leans forward, her mask hanging off one ear.

Scout hands her his extra roll, and she pinches off a piece.

"I'm sure it's fine if we don't stay long." I say it to them as much as to me. "They prepared all this food. They probably meant for people to eat it."

"People who are here to *praise Jesus!*" Scout's voice goes louder, and he holds up a fork.

I can't tell if he's making fun, and I wish he'd keep it down. Maybe this isn't our flavor of church, but I don't believe in ridiculing others—no matter how strange their style comes across.

Also, they have us outnumbered.

The man on the microphone grows solemn. "How many of you are afraid tonight?"

The organ does a loud flourish, changing from dancing to solemn just that fast.

"Amen!" Somebody shouts from the crowd.

"How many of you are in the *grip* of anxiety?" He says it like *anxi-uh-tay.*

It's all drama—his heavy breathing loud in the mic and lines of sweat tracing down his cheeks from temple to jaw.

Scout raises his eyebrows like he's having the best time. "I didn't know they still did shit like this."

"Don't swear in the tent revival." Hope's voice is barely audible over the din.

Glancing at the faces, it's a mixed crowd, mostly white folks. They're not well-dressed, and some of them are in serious need of dental work. All of them have hungry eyes, sad eyes, mistrustful eyes.

My throat grows tight. "I think people are ready to try anything to appease this year."

"I'd love to play a character like him in a movie." He polishes off the chicken, wiping his fingers with a paper napkin.

A woman steps to the center of the tent, right in front of the stage and begins to wail and shake her hands over her head. Her back arches, and she spins in place like one of those whirling dervishes.

"Yes, Lord!" Brother Bob hops off the stage and strides to her. "Release that spirit, yes-ah. That spirit of *tor*-ment. That spirit of fear." He smacks his palm on her forehead, giving her a firm shake as he shouts. "Release her!"

The woman goes down, and several ushers surround her, easing her to the grass as one covers her legs with a blanket.

Hope sits higher in her seat, straining to look. "He shoved her down!"

"It was the spirit." Scout leans forward. "Or was it?"

"I don't like this." I shift in my chair. "Are you done? Give me the keys. We're leaving."

"Hang on." He holds up a hand. "This is great research!"

"For a movie you're not in. Let's go." I stand, and the man with the mic locks eyes on me. *Shit.*

"When Paul was on the island of Malta…" Brother Bob's voice changes to storytelling-style. "The Bible says a serpent came out of the fire and latched onto his hand." He paces back and forth on the grass in front of the stage. I don't like his eyes on me.

"Dammit, Scout." My jaw is clenched, and I want to sock my little brother in the nuts. *If this guy tries to shove me down, I swear…*

"The apostle shook it off into the fire, and the men said he was a *god!*" His voice goes loud on *god* and voices in the congregation echo with amens. "Paul said the Spirit of the Lord *is upon me…*" More amens. "I can touch the deadly thing and *it will not hurt me!*"

Brother Bob pauses in front of the stage, and two ushers enter from the side carrying a flat wooden box.

"I said the deadly thing *will not hurt me!*"

The congregants cheer a loud chorus of amens.

"This is about to get crazy." Scout is way too excited as he jumps to his feet.

"Touch the deadly thing!" The lid is off the box and Bob reaches inside, swooping out a thick, beige snake with black markings.

"Oh, shit." Hope rises beside me, slipping her small hand into mine.

Apprehension beats in my chest, and my fingers tighten over hers.

"What is that?" Scout's eyes flare. "A copperhead?"

A tray begins circulating the crowd, and people throw money into it. I see crumpled twenties, fifties. I don't know how these people can afford it.

"We're leaving." I pull Hope closer to my side. "Give me the keys."

Scout is mesmerized, and I'm all too aware this ringleader is slowly edging closer to where we stand. It's in that moment, Brother Bob turns his glittering black gaze on my brother.

"I see there are some of you in our midst needing deliverance… *Let him come forth!*" His eyes blaze as he watches Scout.

My jaw is tight. "I said let's GO."

"Men struggling with the sin of *sodomy!*" He lowers the snake into the box, leveling his gaze on my brother. "For God has said it is a sin for a man to lie with another man as with a woman…"

My grip tightens on Scout's arm when I notice his expression has changed. His jaw is clenched, and he's seething. "This guy recognizes me."

Looking around, I see people looking around, searching for the offender.

"Come kneel at my feet and *repent!*"

"This guy's a fake." Scout's voice rises, and I pull him harder. "We're fucking outnumbered. Let's go!"

"He's a *liar!*" Scout shouts even louder, drawing attention of the people around us.

"What's happening?" Hope clutches my arm in both her hands.

"Stay with me." I grab my brother's arms and muscle him to the perimeter of the tent.

He struggles against me, but I'm using my size advantage to get us to safety. We're outside in the darkness now, heading toward the parking lot, and I reach for Hope's hand. She quickly slips it into mine again.

"Come on." I hold Scout ahead of me as we walk quickly to the Impala.

He looks over his shoulder, back at the tent, his jaw still clenched. "He's lying to those people, taking their money... We've got to expose him."

"We're not going back in there."

"I don't understand." Hope's voice is quiet at my shoulder.

I'm still holding her hand, and I reluctantly let it go to unlock the car. "Get in. I'm driving."

"How you folks doing tonight?" The muffled voice pulls me up short, and I spin around to see three of the beefy, black-masked ushers have followed us out.

Scout answers fast, stepping forward to meet them. "Not so great, considering that Brother Bob in there is a fucking liar!"

"Start the car." I toss the keys to Hope and step up beside my brother. "We're not looking for any trouble. We're just leaving."

"Sounds like your friend is doing the devil's work."

"He's my brother," I correct the tank of a man. "He just doesn't like snake handlers."

I put my hand on Scout's arm. "Let's go."

"I don't like liars who preach they hate homosexuals when they're secretly into it themselves." Scout steps towards them, not following me to the car.

"Is that so?" The big guy's jaw clenches, and I see a cruel gleam in his eye. "How would you know something like that, pretty boy?"

Adrenaline spikes in my veins, and I lower my hands, clenching my fists. *Here we go...*

"Brother Bob seemed to recognize me." Scout flexes his elbows, bringing his fists together under his chin. His blue eyes are leveled.

The car engine roars to life behind me, and I can't help thinking, *Good girl, Hope.*

I try one more time. "We're really not looking for any trouble."

"You're not going to cause any either." The other two guys step closer, and I turn, putting my back to my brother's just in time for the first punch to fly.

Scout's fast, and I hear him grunt as he absorbs the big guy's gut punch, turning and pulling him forward. The guy across from me goes for my face, but I didn't spend two years in prison not to learn how to dodge a thug.

I catch his wrist, pulling him closer and drive my knee upward into his stomach. He pitches forward with a groan, and Hope turns the car around, facing the exit.

She pushes the passenger door open and yells at us. "Get in!"

I hop over the guy's fat body to the car. "Come on, Scout!"

He's close to me when the middle guy catches him with a right hook to the cheek.

"Fuck!" My little brother starts go down, but I grab him under the arms, shoving him into the front seat with me right behind him.

"Floor it!" I yell, slamming the door, and Hope punches the gas.

CHAPTER
Ten

Hope

MY HANDS ARE SHAKING, BUT I GRIP THE STEERING WHEEL AS I FLY out of the dirt and gravel parking lot onto Highway 43.

Rocks scatter and one of the huge men attempts to chase us a few feet. He doesn't make it far. I'm breathing fast, as I check my mirrors. We're leaving this little city, speeding into the night.

"You okay?" My voice is shaky as I glance at the guys.

"Yeah," JR groans, sliding over the seat into the back. "Those guys were more fat than muscle."

Scout's in the seat beside me holding his cheek. He's looking at the side mirror, and his voice has an edge I've never heard in it. "We've got to report that guy. He's stealing those people's money."

"Report him to who?" JR's voice is equally sharp, but I don't feel afraid.

I saw the protective fire in his eyes when he took my hand in that tent. He kept me by his side the whole way to the car, and I never felt safer.

"You're lucky you got away with just a sock in the face," he barks. "You were messing with their hustle."

"I hate bullshit like that." Scout's so mad. I don't know what to think. "He's a fucking hypocrite."

"Good luck trying to prove it." JR stretches back, exhaling deeply.

"Anybody care to tell me what just happened?" I glance at Scout.

The car falls quiet, and music plays softly, The Chicks singing about truth. I keep driving a little longer, then I laugh, shaky with nerves.

"Seriously? You're not going to tell me?"

I glance in the rearview mirror, and JR's eyes meet mine. "Not my story to tell."

Scout only stares out the window, and the muscle in his jaw moves. "It's not that big of a deal."

My eyes are on the road, but I steal another glance at him. "It was big enough to get us chased out of a tent revival."

"Because that guy's a con man. Handling snakes and talking about evil spirits."

Pressing my lips together, I'm not sure what to say. I try to trace back over what happened. One minute we were sitting at the picnic table eating and joking around, then the snake came out, and the brothers jumped up for a closer look... Heck, we all did, except I was safely behind JR's shoulder.

Another glance at Scout, and I think about everything that's happened. I didn't really press him too hard for details on the person he left behind in Fireside. He said it was a girl, but I guess sometimes gay guys call each other girl... I think. *Do they still do that?*

"Well, I grew up in San Francisco, so 'love is love,' I always say." My voice is confident, reassuring. "If you think you have to hide your truth from me, I hope you know—"

"What?" Scout winces at me. "I'm not gay, Hope. Shit. Not that there's anything wrong with that… It's just not me."

I frown at him. "But… that guy back there was talking about Sodomites, and you lost your shit."

"Because I have gay friends. I don't like them being treated that way."

"But you said he recognized you…"

He doesn't answer. He looks out the window and quiet fills the car, except for now it's Taylor Swift singing about cardigans and getting on busses.

JR sits up, touching me on the shoulder gently. "You're going to take the next right to get on I-20. See it?"

As frustrated as I am with Scout, I can't help warming at JR's touch. His hand on my shoulder makes my stomach all tight and fizzy. He was such a badass back there beating up those thugs and holding me close to his side.

"Thanks." I'm pretty sure I sound like a crushing teenage girl. And I'm very aware this is a silly way to act, but there it is.

Following the road, I get on I-20, and my stomach growls. I can't help thinking Scout's the only one who got a real meal tonight.

"Want me to stop at a McDonald's?" I glance back at JR, who's watching the lights pass out the window. "You never got to eat."

His ice blue eyes meet mine. "You only got a roll."

I smile. *He noticed.* "I don't want to spend your money."

"It's no problem."

I wish he'd suggest we stop at another motel, maybe we all need to shower again. After the way things played out tonight, if I had another chance, I wouldn't wait for him to make the first move. I'd close the space between us and kiss him myself.

WE'RE BACK ON THE ROAD, HEADING ACROSS THE TOP OF LOUISIANA.

JR got a cheeseburger and fries, Scout got a super-sized cup of ice for his cheek, and I got an Egg McMuffin and small coffee. I hope I can drive for several hours now that I'm in the seat.

I switched the radio station, and it's back to the 60s on 6. "My dad loved this station."

I'm halfway through my egg sandwich, taking a sip of my coffee when Scout blurts, "I'm a gay porn star."

Blazing hot liquid sucks into my mouth, and I cough, swerving on the highway.

"Jesus!" he shouts. "Don't wreck the car!"

Blinking hard, I cough again. "What did you just say?"

"Rammin' Rod. *Dreamboys.*" He looks at his lap, and I hear a chuckle from the backseat.

I'm not sure if I should laugh. "You're a gay porn star?"

"Print media only." He says it like that somehow changes things.

"So like... you're in magazines? For gay guys?" I glance at him.

"Just one. And alone. I mean, it was just me alone. One time."

"How..." I don't even know where to begin to start asking questions.

"I guess I should've known when I went to Ultimate Sensations Photography Studio something was up."

"The studio was called *Ultimate Sensations*? That sounds like a brand of condoms."

More chuckles from the backseat.

"Shut up, JR." Scout casts a glare at his brother. "I had just arrived in LA. I didn't know anybody, I didn't have any fucking money, and every audition required a headshot."

"Let me get this straight. You went in for headshots and came out a gay porn star?" My eyes narrow. "How does that happen? Don't you have to sign a release or something? Get paid?"

"Apparently it was part of the paperwork I signed. The headshots were so cheap because I agreed to let him use my image."

"But... you said you went for a headshot. Why were you naked?"

Scout pushes his feet against the floor, squirming in his seat. "He had this whole spiel... ten professional poses, including headshots."

"Including *nudes*?"

"He said I should do a few nudes in case the casting directors wanted to see me naked. Like for R-rated movies like *Fifty Shades of Grey* or something. *History of Violence*. Hell, even Bruce Willis has his dick out in *12 Monkeys*."

Squinting at him, I'm trying to understand. "You fell for that?"

"He was a really nice guy. He had me hold a football. Apparently, I have an appealing cock. He said I should do art photos for magazines."

"So you're a natural blond."

JR laughs more, and Scout cuts his eyes at me. "Alcohol."

My eyebrows shoot up. "He got you drunk?"

"I want alcohol. I'm not having this conversation without whiskey."

"We're not stopping." JR snaps from the backseat. "Keep driving, Hope."

Scout turns in his seat. "Look, I know you've been in the joint for two years, so you've forgotten what it's like, but if I'm describing my biggest fuckup in Hollywood, I want whiskey."

I look at the green sign approaching. "Hold that thought. We're twenty-four miles to Vicksburg."

We pull off at a Pack n Save and gas up. Scout grabs a bottle of Jack Daniels and two paper cups. Back on the road, we're both in the backseat, paper cups in hand with JR at the wheel. So much for me driving.

"It was six months before I knew what had happened." Scout leans his head back.

My feet are up on the seat in front of us. "What happened?"

"I went for a callback on this TV show, *Mighty Thunder*. It was about stock car racers who fight crimes. I was going to get to race cars."

"Never heard of it."

"Yeah, it didn't make it through pilot season." He slugs the rest of his whiskey and pours us both more, even though I've barely taken a sip. "We were standing around, and this one guy kept checking me out. I get that a lot, so I just ignored it."

I take a sip of the burning amber liquid and squint. "Was he a gay porn star too?"

"No." Scout gives me an annoyed glare.

"Sorry!" I hold up a hand and bury my nose in my cup. "Jeez…"

"After my take, he asked if I was the guy from *Howard's Other End*." I can't help snorting, and Scout shakes his head. "It's funny. I know. I told him I'd never heard of it. The day went on, and this other guy, one of his friends apparently had been Googling me all day. He made some comment about how he questioned the integrity of the production. When people asked why, he said they hired porn stars to be in it."

"Oh, no." My voice is quiet.

"The casting director asked why I hadn't disclosed I was Rammin' Rod from the December issue of *Dreamboys*." He exhales heavily. "I tried to explain I didn't authorize it, I didn't even know about it, but it didn't matter. Apparently having a porn star in the cast kills your ratings. I was asked to leave."

"I'm sorry." I put my hand on his shoulder.

"It took three years for that shit to go away. I'm not sure it's completely gone. It probably still keeps me from getting called for things. But six months ago, this new casting director gave me a shot in that Christopher Nolan film. Then everything shut down."

JR isn't laughing anymore, and I feel bad. I also feel fuzzy and warm from the whiskey.

"I bet when we get back, it'll be even more ancient history than it was before. You'll see."

I'm not sure I'm making sense, but Scout doesn't seem to mind. He leans back and gives me that disarming, dimpled grin. "Hope Eternal, thank you."

He's a bit wobbly when he holds up the half-empty bottle, but I shake my head. "No more for me."

He drops it on the floorboard and sits up, pressing his fingertips lightly on his cheek. "My face stopped hurting."

Leaning closer, I inspect the damage. A red line is at the top of his cheekbone, but the skin isn't broken. "I don't think you'll have a black eye."

Catching my neck, he pulls me in for a rough kiss to the top of my forehead. "You're the best." Then leans against the door and goes to sleep.

I sit back and look at the half-empty cup in my hand.

JR's eyes meet mine in the mirror. "It's lucky he's so good at football."

I check the bottle he dropped on the floorboard. The top is sealed tight, so I climb over the seat into the front.

"Hollywood is hard." I pull my knee up and set my chin on the top, facing him. "We always heard stories from people who went and came back."

"Yeah, that porn thing's just a setback. He'll be fine. People love working with him."

Tilting my head to the side, I study his square jaw and striking profile. "It's not that way for you?"

Ice blue eyes flicker to me, sliding down my neck and back. "No."

It's probably the whiskey, but that brief, hot look gets the blood simmering in my veins.

I shift in my seat, lowering my knee and tracing my finger along the back of the seat towards him. "You've got qualities."

His eyebrow arches, and he glances at me. "Qualities? Like what?"

"Like back there, the way you stood up for your brother." I want to say it was sexy as fuck, but I might need another shot of whiskey.

JR exhales a laugh. "He didn't give me much of a choice."

"What would you do if you had a choice?" My insides are all sizzling, and I scoot a little closer.

The muscle in his jaw moves, and I want to touch it. "I thought I'd work with my dad."

"Running a gym?" My eyes are on his full lips.

"I thought I'd take over when he was ready to retire... Maybe open a second location closer to the coast."

"You don't want to do that now?"

His brow lowers, and that anger is back. "Now I want to know what he knew about San Francisco."

Chewing my bottom lip, I think about this. "You think your dad set you up?"

"He made the deal. He sent me to do the pickup."

"Was that different?"

"I was married with a little kid. My dad is a widower with two grown sons—one he could've visited in Los Angeles." His fists tighten on the steering wheel and he exhales, looking out the side window. "His favorite."

We're quiet again and Taylor Swift is back singing about love stories. I don't know what to say.

"Does Taylor Swift just write the same song over and over?" he growls, turning down the radio.

Reaching forward, I switch it to the original station. "My dad liked the 60s, but I prefer the 70s. It's old, but it's better for a road trip."

He doesn't answer, and this isn't going how I'd hoped... not that I have any idea how else it might've gone with him driving. "I'm sorry I didn't help more."

His brow relaxes, and he gives me a half-smile. "You helped a lot. He needed to get that off his chest. It's hard to lose control of your reputation."

"Like what happened with you?" My eyes are heavy, but I don't want to lose this moment. JR never talks this much.

"People back home think I'm a drug dealer, a felon." His voice is quiet. "I've got to clear my name... for Jesse."

"And for you."

Scout snores loudly from the backseat, and I glance over my shoulder. "He really should get that checked out. Snoring is bad for you."

"Pull his arm down."

I give him a glance before leaning over the seat. It takes me a minute of struggling to catch his brother's forearm, which is tossed over his head, but once I do and pull it down, he stops snoring.

"You were right." I'm a little breathless when I drop into the seat again, and I notice we're slowing down. "What's happening?"

"Taking a break." JR turns the car, pulling off at an exit for Livingston. "I need to clear my head."

CHAPTER
Eleven

JR

HOPE'S LITTLE ROUND ASS WIGGLING IN MY FACE AS SHE WRESTLES TO get my brother to stop snoring is the final straw.

My blood's been hot since we fought those thugs outside the tent. Having dinner, listening to Scout confess what a dumbass he was when he first moved to Los Angeles relaxed me a bit, but once he passed out and Hope slid into the seat next to me, leaning closer, blinking up at me with those bright blue eyes...

I had to take a break.

The rest stop is dark with no big trucks in the lot. It's strange, but welcome. I put the car in park and kill the engine under a massive live oak tree, but I leave the key on so the headlights shine.

Stepping out, I walk around to the front, reaching to the side to ease the tightness from the fight. One of those fuckers caught me in the kidney, and it's aching.

"Want the rest of this?" Hope comes to where I'm standing.

She's holding what looks like two fingers of whiskey in a paper cup, and I frown, taking it. "How much did he give you?"

"He kept pouring, but I can't drink that fast. I'm not used to whiskey."

I shoot it and toss the cup in the trash. "We'll set an alarm and nap a few hours. Then we can get on the road again."

She nods quietly. Her chin is down as she walks away.

The air is thick and humid, and a giant streetlight shines behind her. It lights up her hair like a halo and turns her thin dress transparent.

I can see the silhouette of her slim body as she walks, flat stomach, nipples high and tight. My cock stirs in my jeans, and I realize shooting the whiskey might've been the wrong call.

She stops at the car and watches me like she wants me to do something. The radio plays softly, and she's waiting, studying me.

It makes me angry... or fuck it, maybe I'm just pissed at everything right now.

"What?" It's a rough sound.

"I was just thinking..." A smile lifts the corner of her mouth.

"Are you going to tell me?"

"I wonder how my life would be different now if I'd gone into the house instead of climbing in the backseat of this car that night."

My hands are on my hips, and I walk slowly to where she's standing. "Why did you?"

"My dad said this would be the year of perfect vision." I'm standing in front of her now, and her pale brows pull together. "I've been trying to make sense of it all, you know, see it clearly... but it's not working. Everything feels pointless and cruel."

I don't know what to say. I've been struggling with the feelings she's describing for almost two years.

"But when I look at you..." Our eyes meet, and she steps closer.

An old JT song about making promises surrounds us. She puts a slim hand on my chest, and her eyes close as she smiles. "Would you dance with me?"

It's a mistake, but I can't seem to stop myself. My hands slide around her waist, learning the shape of her curves. Her body presses against mine, warm and soft.

Lowering my face, I inhale the side of her hair. She smells like flowers and coconut, fresh and sweet as a summer day.

She exhales a sigh. "Remember when people used to go out to bars and dance?"

My eyes close briefly, and I'm in this space of memory with her. "I haven't danced in a long time."

We sway side to side, holding each other.

"You're still good at it." Her chin pulls back, and she blinks warm blue eyes up at me.

Our gaze tangles and heats and she rises on her toes. Her fingers curl in my shirt. "I'd like to kiss you."

Heat flares in my veins. I've wanted to kiss her for two days, but I've been fighting it. "Hope…"

Hope Eternal Hill is light and pure, and I can't be the black storm that smashes all her dreams with my quest for revenge.

"It's been too long." She whispers, sliding her nose along my cheek. "For both of us."

Her fingers trace behind my neck, into my hair, and it's like a match striking. I push her back against the door. Cupping her cheeks, I cover her full lips with mine and devour them.

She makes a little noise, and I kiss her deeper. Her mouth opens, and I slide my tongue against hers, tasting her sweetness.

She's syrupy whiskey mixed with a hint of coffee.

Her arms are around my neck, and her soft breasts crush against my chest. Sliding my hands up her torso, I cup them through the fabric, squeezing them and circling my thumbs over the hardened tips. She moans, and my dick is an iron rod in my pants.

"God…" I lift my chin, and her lips move to my throat.

Her tongue slides along my skin, and I'm fighting. I want to fuck her. My whole body craves it, the satisfaction I know is waiting between her thighs. It would be so easy to lift her leg and plunge deep… again and again.

Her hand is on my waist, tugging at my shirt, and I catch it. "Wait."

Her brows clench as she looks up at me. "What's wrong?"

Our eyes meet, and I'm hanging on by a thread. "You don't know me."

"I know enough." She leans up again, putting her hot mouth against my jaw. "I know you didn't touch me last night when I was naked in your hotel room. I know you ran into danger to protect your brother. I know you're fighting what's happening right now…"

"You have no idea."

Her lips are at my ear. "Haven't you ever been reckless?"

My hands tighten on her shoulders, and Scout's prediction is in my ear… when we get back, you'll ask her to stay. *No.*

"I'm sorry." I have too much unresolved shit to drag her into it.

The rod in my pants will have to take a rain check. I made this mistake once, and it almost broke me.

She blinks a few times, dropping her face into her hands and exhaling a frustrated noise. "I think I must be doing this wrong."

Stepping away from her magnetic field, I shove my hands in the sides of my hair. "You're not doing anything wrong. Trust me."

Squinting up at me, she smiles. "Then what are you afraid of?"

"You're going to wake up in the morning and realize this is not what you want." Stepping back, I open the door. "And if it's not then, it will be eight hours later, when we're in Fireside."

"I think you're wrong." Her chin lifts.

"I think you're drunk, and you're seeing what you want to see."

"I'm not drunk, and I see you better than you see yourself."

Shaking my head, I lean the passenger's seat forward and climb in across from Scout, who has managed to get his arm over his head again and is roaring like a grizzly. "We could go on like this all night. I need to sleep."

Hope stands for a moment with her hands on her hips then shakes her head, climbing into the front seat. I pull Scout's arm down before rolling up my jacket and putting it on my brother's hip, doing my best to get comfortable.

"Would you pass me my coat?" Her voice is soft and so tempting.

I'm a fucking pussy is what I am. I should've given her what she wanted. What we both wanted...

Swallowing the fire in my throat, I grab the teddy bear skin off the floorboard. "Lock the doors."

She does it and rustles around in the front a few seconds before finally getting still. It's quiet in the car. The noise of cicadas grows louder. I can hear the chirp of frogs, and I'm pretty sure a screech owl is mixed in there. I wonder if I'll sleep.

I'm too pent up to sleep. The shot of whiskey only fueled the fire in my veins.

Rolling onto my back, I look out the window at the stars flickering through the tree branches.

"You awake?" Her voice is soft. I'm pretty sure it wouldn't wake me if I was asleep.

Still I hesitate.

"Yeah." I finally respond—clearly, I can't do what's right.

"Tell me about your little boy."

My chest warms. I close my eyes, and I see his towhead, his blue eyes.

"I don't have much to tell. He was only three last time I saw him." A fact that twists my stomach. *What does he think of me now? What have they told him about where I am?*

"He's five now…" Her voice is thoughtful. "You must've been young when you had him."

That makes me laugh softly. "Just finishing college. He was a surprise. The one time I was reckless."

"Too bad for me." A grin is in her voice.

"I like to think I've learned from my mistakes."

"So tell me about him."

We're quiet a bit, and I picture my son. His sweet little voice and happy eyes relaxes the anger in my chest. It's what used to get me through the nights in prison, thinking about the day when I'd be out and go home to him.

"People said he looked like me." I'm a little embarrassed to sound so proud, like one of those doting parents that buttonhole you in the supermarket. "He was already a little bruiser. He loved to play football."

"I bet he did." Hope's voice is warm and full of smiles.

It draws me to her, makes me want to climb up front and kiss her again. It makes me want to hold onto her.

Damn, this girl.

"I don't remember what I looked like as a kid. I thought he looked like Scout."

"You look alike. Haven't you seen pictures?" I can't see her face, but it sounds like she's being sincere. "I'm sure he looks just like you."

"I don't know what he's going to do when I see him." My stomach is a mixture of anticipation and anxiety. I want him to be happy, but I worry he might be angry… Or afraid of me.

"He's going to be so happy to see his dad. You'll see."

Tomorrow.

God, I can't worry about it now. We're almost home.

Closing my eyes, I think about holding Hope in my arms, pressing my lips against hers. She's like a warm, dry blanket on a frigid, San Francisco day. She smells like warm coconut and fresh flowers, and her body is soft against mine.

She felt so good leaning into me, wanting so much more. I can't decide if I'm an idiot or a wise man, but I know for certain next time it won't be so easy to hold back.

Which is why there can't be a next time. This is a road trip, not a romance.

Hell, it's starting to sound like a mantra.

CHAPTER
Twelve

Hope

"**S**O ULTIMATELY BEING A GAY PORN STAR WAS A GOOD THING?" I bite off the end of a Red Vine.

Scout's behind the wheel, not seeming too hungover after his whiskey binge last night. JR's still asleep in the backseat, and I've been stealing glances, alternately reliving the intensity of his kiss, his hands on my body… and swooning over his adoration for his son.

"I mean, yeah." Scout nods. "I learned being an ally means more than partying with gay guys at Mardi Gras or Halloween—or not being weirded out when a guy thinks I'm hot. It's about stepping up when it's inconvenient or awkward."

"Basically, being a good human." I tuck my windblown hair behind my ear. "That's very evolved of you."

"Maybe." His lips press into a frown. "There's also the other side, where being a gay porn star is a career killer. Any porn star, for that matter."

Propping my feet on the dash, I hold the sides of my skirt. "Yeah, but don't you think we fetishize wealth too much in this country?"

"What do you mean?"

"Like we treat people better because they're rich. Like making a lot of money means someone is good or admirable, whether or not they really are."

"Oh, yeah." He nods, sliding his hand up the steering wheel. "Or not taking a job that might help somebody because it won't make you a lot of money?"

"Sure. Or thinking people aren't so good because they don't have a lot of money." My eyes drift out the window to the big green sign telling us we're almost to South Carolina. "You know who didn't have a lot of money?"

"Who?"

"Jesus."

"Yep." Scout nods.

We're quiet a minute, thinking. The tires hum on the road and Heart sings softly about Dreamboat Annie.

Scout glances at me and winks. "I still want to make a lot of money."

"Me too." Grabbing another Red Vine, I contemplate our dilemma. "Maybe *knowing* we fetishize wealth too much is enough?"

"How did I sign up for Philosophy with the Blonds?" JR groans, sitting up in the backseat.

Shifting in my seat, I rest my chin on my hand and smile at him. "Sleep okay?"

"No."

My lips press together, as I try to stop a laugh. He's such an old grump. "Maybe tonight will be better."

"Doubt it." He rubs a hand over his face. "Where are we, Scout?"

"Just past Augusta, closing in on the state line."

"Three more hours."

I glance out at the mixture of pine and oak trees flying past. They're a blur of deep, forest green almost black and shimmering pine needles almost yellow. It's so different here from California, where it's all palms for days.

Speaking of California, as soon as my phone came back to life, it blew up with texts from Yarnell.

"I really should call home. My friend's probably wondering why I never showed up at her place."

Scout glances in my direction with a smile. "Won't bother me."

"Maybe I could get in the back?" I look to where JR is focused on the window.

It's down, and the strong breeze musses his golden-brown hair, making it flop over his brow. It's shiny and thick with a slight curl at the ends, and it's so soft.

I remember threading my fingers in it, giving it a tug... I imagine doing it again, with him on top of me pressing me into the mattress.

Ice blue eyes level on mine, sending a flush through my body. "What?"

"I just need to make a phone call... I was thinking I'd get back there so I'm not talking in Scout's face."

"You want to switch places?"

"Is that okay?"

He scoots to the side, and I climb onto my knees before diving over the bench. My dress catches on my knee, and the top pulls down, exposing the top of my bare breast. Finding my seat, I pull it up quickly, but JR's eyes are on me, hot as a brand.

He doesn't say anything, but his expression is fierce as he slides into the front. I know he saw it. I know he liked it, and it's a thrill low in my stomach even if he's fighting it.

Pulling out my phone, I tap Yarnell's number and wait for the ring.

She answers fast. "Hope? What the hell? I was about to drive to your house, start a search party, drag the shoreline for your body—"

"I'm sorry!" I cry, trying not to be too loud.

"You called me from the bridge and said you were coming here, then you never showed up! I texted and texted…"

"I know! My phone died, and I just saw—"

"Don't ever do that again!" She's shouting in my ear, and I hold the phone away, smiling and feeling like I might cry at the same time.

My emotions are so twisted, and I miss my friend so much.

"Where are you?" She demands.

"I kind of took a road trip."

"A road trip? But I thought you sold Metallicar?"

"I did." My eyes are on the side of JR's face. "I kind of met the new owner, and… it's a long story. He needed help driving."

"You're on a road trip with a complete stranger?" Her voice goes loud again.

"And his brother."

"Do I need to call the police?"

"No! Like I said, it's a long story, but it's kind of fun. They're nice." My eyes drift from scowling JR to relaxed and happy Scout. "We're getting to be friends."

Yarnell's voice is worried. "Things are strange right now, Hope. People aren't making the best decisions…"

"I'm fine, Yars, really. We've been driving pretty much non-stop, but I didn't want you to worry."

"Too late." Her voice is sarcastic.

"It's going to be okay. We're almost there, and then…" My heart catches in my throat, and I can't say it.

"Then you'll come home?" She finishes for me.

"Yes." It's a quiet reply.

"Good. And I want you to check in when you're on the road headed back."

"I'll text you."

Sadness like ice water trickles through my chest as I disconnect. My eyes drift back to JR, and I wonder what the heck I'm doing.

This journey was impulsive and crazy. Scout said it was meant to be, but meant to be what? A three-day trip where we shared our darkest moments, escaped a crazy tent revival, talked about our dreams… *And kissed?*

My eyes slide shut. JR's kiss shook me to the core. So aggressive and demanding, so much pent up passion and need and hunger. I felt it all the way to my toes.

I want to do it again and again.

"Everybody okay at home?" I blink out of my daydream to find Scout's eyes on mine in the mirror.

"Oh, yeah. Yars was worried, but it's all good."

"I'm sure they miss you." JR's voice is quiet.

"Thank you." I can't tell if he meant it as a compliment, but I'm going to take it as one.

I give him a smile, and he shifts in his seat, looking away.

That hurts.

"Should be there in two hours," Scout says. "What's our first stop?"

"Becky." It's a flat reply.

My stomach should not twist unpleasantly when he says his ex-wife's name. I shouldn't care that she's the first stop he wants to make.

But I do.

"Home it is." His brother nods.

"No…" JR frowns at him. "I want to see my son first."

"Wait…" Scout cuts his eyes. "You don't know?"

"Know what?" It's more like a growl.

Scout looks like he swallowed a goldfish, and I lean back against the seat. I'm afraid to hear what he thought his brother knew. It doesn't look good.

He forces a reassuring smile. "Maybe we should stop for breakfast, stretch our legs."

"Maybe you'd better tell me what you thought I knew."

Scout's chin dips. "She remarried."

My heart beats faster, but to his credit, John nods as if he doesn't care.

"I expected as much. Hell, I figured she was seeing somebody when she sent those divorce papers so fast."

His brother's expression is somber, almost like he's waiting.

Home. Scout said *home…*

John glances at him and then appears to have the same realization I have at the same time. "If she remarried, why is she at our home?"

"I think we should stop and get some coffee."

"Would you stop acting like an old lady?" JR's voice is sharp.

His brother's eyes drop again, and the car slows. We exit at a blue interstate sign that says Prizzy's Diner. "I bet they have good coffee at this place."

"Are you going to tell me?"

He keeps going, and in less than two minutes we're pulling up to a Route 66-style roadside diner. I half expect waitresses in poufy skirts and roller skates to greet us.

Exiting the vehicle fast, JR is right behind his brother.

"Scout?" JR pulls his arm, and Scout meets his eyes.

I climb out slower, watching with wide eyes, not sure if I should wait or follow.

"It's Dad, man. She married Dad."

CHAPTER
Thirteen

JR

AIR LEAVES MY LUNGS AS MEMORIES FILTER THROUGH MY MIND. How long was this going on? Were they together before I left? Was this why he set me up? It's a kaleidoscope of moments in my mind, and anger is a ticking time bomb in my chest.

I leave Scout and Hope at the car, and step inside the glass-walled diner.

A petite, brown-skinned woman in a kitten mask greets me. "Welcome to Prizzy's! Table for three?"

I nod, and she grabs three huge, plastic-covered menus, leading us to a booth in the middle of the restaurant.

Scout and Hope slide into the seat across from me, and a waitress quickly walks up.

"Three coffees?" Her voice is bored and muffled, but I don't look at her.

Scout answers. "Yeah, thanks."

"I'll give you a minute to look at the menu." She's gone,

and I stare at the oversized pictures of eggs, bacon, and toast on plates.

Scout and Hope are looking at me. "You okay, bro?"

The whirlwind of memories of times when we were all together starts to dissipate, and in its place comes something strange. A cold band of iron tightens across my chest, and my throat feels hot. My brain feels a little loose, and I can't decide if I want to punch someone or flip the table.

"Three coffees." The waitress reappears setting the thick mugs in front of us. "Have you decided what you want or still need a minute?"

The menu is in my hand, and I haven't even looked at it.

I look at her name tag. "Heidi, is it?"

"Yes, sir!" Her eyes meet mine, and her chin pulls back. I think she sees I've lost it a little bit.

"I want you to bring us everything on the menu. Can you do that?"

"I don't understand…"

"We want it all." My voice rises a bit louder. "Bring us one of these Western frittatas… and some of these… Huevos rancheros, and what's this? Chipped beef on toast? That sounds good. And wow, eggs Benedict. Fancy. And pancakes. Check it out, Hope. They have pancakes. We can do a comparison taste test."

"I don't want pancakes." Hope's voice is soft, her eyes round with worry.

"She doesn't want pancakes." I look up at Alice again. "How about you bring her the chicken and waffles. Scout can try the blueberry pancakes."

"So you want the Western frittata, the huevos rancheros, chipped beef on toast, eggs Benedict, blueberry pancakes, and chicken and waffles?" Heidi reads her pad back to me so fast, I'm impressed.

"And one of these mixed fruit plates. To be healthy."

"You got it, sir. Can I get y'all anything else?" She looks at Scout and Hope, who are both staring at me with wide eyes and parted lips.

"Ah, no." Scout quickly takes the menus and pushes them towards her. "Thanks."

I take the cloth-wrapped silverware off the table and unroll it, putting the napkin in my lap and the flatware beside my mug.

My brother's voice is low. "Are you okay?"

"Yep."

"You ordered everything on the menu."

I nod slowly, my eyes on the fake wood tabletop. "You said you were hungry. Hell, we haven't had a decent meal in three days."

"Eating everything in sight isn't a decent meal. It's more like… a binge." He's still watching me. Hope hasn't said a word… other than she doesn't want pancakes. "What are you thinking right now?"

His question makes me think, which makes me want to laugh. "What am I thinking?" I lift my chin and meet his eyes. "I'm thinking about my last day in Fireside, the morning I left for San Francisco almost two years ago…"

Jesse ran into the bedroom in his Iron Man pajamas, and Becky exhaled some complaint. She was lying on her side with her back to me. We hadn't slept together since he was born. She was always too tired or not in the mood or she had cramps.

My jaw tightens, and I realize she wasn't sleeping with me because she was sleeping with…

"Here you go!" Heidi's voice cuts my train of thought. A stout Latino busboy is with her, and he starts unloading plate after plate. "That there's the frittata… and we have the huevos rancheros, the eggs benedict… We were out of the beef tips on toast, so I substituted corned beef hash. I hope that's okay…"

Plates fill the table, and I finally dare to look at Hope. Her eyes are still round, but the shock is gone. Now she's looking at me in a way that makes my chest tight and my appetite disappear.

Heidi straightens, putting her hands on her hips. "Can I get you anything? Coffee refills?"

Scout holds up a hand. "I think we have enough. Thanks, Heidi."

We all sit in front of the feast, staring at the steaming plates of poached eggs covered in bright orange hollandaise or red-brown corned beef with green peppers and bits of potato.

The scrambled eggs in the frittata are a sunny yellow, and the waffles are thick and fluffy with dark fried chicken on top. Heidi even brought us buttermilk biscuits.

The scents blend together, and I feel slightly nauseated.

Taking up my fork, I scoop up a bit of the corned beef and put it in my mouth. I quickly stab the huevos rancheros and put a forkful in my mouth. I cut the side off a blueberry pancake and shove it in as well.

My cheeks are full, but the food has no taste. My throat is tight, but I force myself to swallow. All this food. All this food and all this hate and all this anger and all these lies…

So many lies.

Pushing back on the table, I take one last look at the massive spread and slide out of the booth.

I reach into my pocket and dig out the rest of my money, hoping it's enough to cover all this. I toss it on the table and turn, heading for the doors.

Scout calls after me, but I'm moving fast. The windows of the Impala are down, and I lean through the passenger's side, swiping the half-empty bottle of whiskey off the floorboard and heading for the sparse forest.

Thin pine trees rise around me, and we're close enough to the shore that sand is under my boots. I don't know where I'm going. I need to get away from everything so I can breathe.

I don't know where I am or even how far I've walked. I'm in

the middle of nowhere, and the trees are thicker, their branches coming together to form a dim alcove. I stop and put one hand on the trunk of a tree before sliding down to sit on the ground.

Pine needles cover sand here. I bend a knee and pull the cork-lined top off the whiskey. Putting the bottle to my lips, I tilt it up and take a long pull.

It burns like fire going down my throat. My eyes squint shut, and I exhale a growl. *Damn, them.*

I do it again, taking a longer pull, and this time when my eyes open, I see her standing there. Like a beam of sunlight or an iridescent angel, Hope steps quietly through the trees in those white cowboy boots I bought for her.

She comes to where I'm sitting and lowers to a squat, taking the bottle from my hand and replacing the cap. She puts it on the ground beside me and reaches out to slide her fingers through my hair, moving it off my forehead with her thumb.

"Are you okay?" Her voice is gentle.

I don't answer her right away. I gaze at her blue eyes so warm, so full of concern. Her light hair falls in gentle waves around her cheeks. She's so pretty.

My voice is dry when I speak. "No."

"You have every right to be upset."

I think about it. I do have the right to be upset. My father stole my life. He kept me away from my son…

"Are you still in love with her?" Hope's voice is quiet, tentative, and my eyes lock on hers.

"No." I say it with conviction.

Any love I had left for Becky died when those divorce papers showed up. Learning she's with my dad just makes my reasons for coming back more specific and more focused.

I couldn't give a shit about them. I only want my son.

Her hand moves from my hair to my shoulder. "What are you feeling?"

Lifting my eyes, I feel hot blood in my veins, and I feel tired of fighting.

"Come here." Reaching out, I catch her by the waist, pulling her onto my lap in a straddle.

She doesn't fight me, resting her slim arms on my shoulders. I pull her closer, resting my face against her neck like I've wanted to do so many times, and just breathe. God, it feels so good.

Soft lips touch my brow, and I'm surrounded by coconut and flowers and *hope eternal*.

With my eyes closed, I slide my hands around her waist, pulling her closer against me, her soft body flush against my hard chest. Her knees rock forward onto the soft sand, and I lift my chin, searching for her mouth.

She cups my cheeks, and our lips seal together. It's a match striking. Pushing hers apart, I'm hungry for her kiss. Our tongues meet and curl. She tastes good like fresh coffee mixed with the sharp sting of whiskey.

My hands drop to her thighs, and I slide them higher, under her dress to the line of her panties. I grasp her soft ass and squeeze, dragging her slowly up my lap, over my hardened dick in my pants.

"John…" She gasps, kissing my cheek, my temple.

It's all the encouragement I need. Moving my hands to her hips, I rip her panties away then push my fingers between her thighs, circling her clit as she rises higher, panting in my ear.

"Oh, God, oh…" She moans, riding my hand.

I've got to get these jeans off.

I reach down to unfasten my pants. She quickly unbuttons my shirt, grasping and pushing the fabric away. Her palms slide over my chest, followed by her lips.

We're driven by lust and need and hunger. My jeans slip down and her fingers wrap around my cock, not quite touching.

Blue eyes rise to mine, and her nose wrinkles. "So big…"

Her head lowers to my lap, and I groan loudly as her hot little mouth closes over my tip, sucking and pulling.

"Oh, fuck." I twist and writhe, doing my best not to thrust it down her throat.

Her head bobs fast, and her tongue slides up and down, teasing the ridges. She comes off with a pop, while her fist pumps my shaft.

Her smile is naughty, and her hair is messy, her full lips swollen and glistening.

"Wait…" I'm going to come too fast at this rate.

Digging frantically for my wallet… why didn't I think of this before? I don't even know if I have a condom. Shit.

"Hang on." She sits up on my legs and pulls off her boot, turning it over. What looks like a gold coin drops out, and she scoops it off the sand, cleaning it with her dress.

My eyes are wide, and my dick is aching. She's gotten me right to the edge. "What are you doing with a condom?"

"I bought it at the gas station." She peeks up at me. "I thought I might get lucky last night… But I didn't."

Grabbing her waist, I pull her against me again, rougher this time. "You're about to get lucky now. You're about to get fucked hard."

Her eyes flare, and she grins. "You weren't supposed to be listening to that."

My hands slide to her shoulders, raking those straps down her arms so I can palm her bare breasts. They're perfect handfuls, her nipples tight and straining. Pulling one into my mouth, I give it a firm suck while I tweak the other with my fingertips.

Her back arches as she threads her fingers in my hair, rocking her hot little core against my aching cock. "Mmm… yes."

"Give it to me." It's a rough order.

She puts the coin in my hand, and I twist it apart, quickly

rolling it on as she traces her lips along the top of my ear, against my neck. Sizzles of pleasure race through my shoulders.

Lifting my chin, I capture her mouth with mine, gliding our tongues together as I lift her, lowering her onto my rock-hard erection.

"Oh!" She lets out a startled cry, and my mind blanks. Jesus, she feels so good, so damn tight.

For a minute, I'm afraid I hurt her. She's breathing fast, and we're still as she takes a moment. Then she starts to move.

Her hips roll forward like a dancer, sliding back and forth, picking up speed, and I close my eyes, tracing my fingers up the skin of her thighs. I'm certain it couldn't feel better, then she rises on her knees, bringing me all the way to the tip and dropping again fast.

"Fuck…" I choke out, and she does it again.

I almost can't focus. She's so tight, bouncing on my cock, her small breasts teasing at my mouth. Leaning forward, I catch one in my lips, giving it a firm pull that causes her sweet little pussy to clench tighter around me.

It's been so long, and this girl feels like heaven, drawing me to the edge with every unexpected movement. Clutching her soft ass in my hands, I grab her, moving her faster on my dick.

"Yes…" She murmurs, moving with me. "Keep doing that."

I couldn't stop if I wanted. My hips rise up to meet her, and she's riding me, her moans growing more frantic. I can't hold out much longer, and she slams her knees into the sand rising up as her body breaks into spasms. Her pelvis bucks with every move-ment, and her inner muscles clench and pull.

It's so intense. My head drops back against the tree and I let go with a low groan. I'm driving higher, holding onto her like an anchor to the ground. My orgasm shakes my thighs, lifts me off the Earth and sends me to the stars.

I'm weak as I start to come down. Hope's cheek is against

my forehead, and our chests are flush, skin against skin. It feels so good. Her arms are around my shoulders, and a bead of sweat traces down my neck.

Sliding my hands slowly up and down her back, I chuckle. "Why the hell did I wait so long to do that?"

Her body tightens with her laugh, and I reach between us, catching the edges of the condom before slipping out. I quickly take care of it, putting it aside before pulling her to me again.

"It was worth it." She props an elbow on my shoulder, meeting my eyes. "I think the anticipation made it hotter."

"So we should wait three days again?"

Her lips press into a small smile, and she looks down. "I don't know. A lot can happen in three days."

Reaching up, I cup her cheek in my hand, pushing her soft blonde hair behind her ear. I know what she's thinking. It's the same thing I'm thinking. We've reached our destination. This is where the journey ends.

Only… it's not that simple. My part in all of this is more complicated than a three-day road trip, and I've got forces pulling me in both directions.

Curling my fingers in her hair, I guide her lips to mine for one more hit of my new favorite drug. It's soft and sweet, with the faintest hint of whiskey.

Our eyes meet. "I hope we don't." It's the best I can say at this point in the story.

Her smile is bittersweet, and I hate it.

I want to make promises. I want to tell her we never have to part, but I promised I'd never lie to her.

I have to follow this path to the end and deal with my shit before I can start fresh. If that's even possible anymore.

This beautiful girl is way more than I bargained for that early morning halfway between San Francisco and LA, and I don't know what to expect when we reach Fireside.

CHAPTER
Fourteen

Hope

JOHN ROTH DUNNE JUST BLEW MY MIND, AND NOW HE'S BREAKING MY heart.

I'm sitting on his lap with my dress around my waist still aching from that incredible ride on his massive cock, and all I want is to do it all again.

He said he'd never lie to me, and I know he means it. Still, when he kisses me that way, I feel more than I've ever felt in my life. What's happening here is special.

"Seriously, guys? Where the fuck are you?" Scout's voice breaks our moment, and I'm off JR's lap in a flash, pulling my dress up and removing my destroyed panties.

He's right beside me, jerking his jeans over his hips and buttoning his shirt. Warm hands cover mine, and he takes my underwear, slipping them into his pocket.

Arching an eyebrow, I step into my boots. "What are you planning to do with those?"

"Refresh my memory." His gaze is wicked, and it curls my toes... just as Scout breaks through the trees.

He takes one look at us and shakes his head. I'm sure it's very clear what just happened. My hair is a wild mess on my head, and I've got sand stuck to my legs. JR's shirt is untucked, and he's doing his best to bury the evidence.

Scout pivots, returning the way he came. "Time to get on the road, people. Let's go."

My bottom lip is between my teeth, and I cover a snort with my hand before JR grabs my wrist, leading us through the woods to the car.

A LARGE, BROWN PAPER BAG IS BESIDE ME ON THE BACKSEAT, AND THE WIND whips through the car as we fly towards Charleston.

"What's this?" I pull the top open.

"I got Heidi to box up all the food my insane brother ordered then walked out without touching."

"You think it'll keep?" JR glances back.

"Hell, I don't know. But children are starving in Africa, and I'm not letting that much food go to waste."

"I'm glad you didn't. I'm starved." Reaching inside, I take out a foil container and remove the cardboard lid. "Jackpot!"

Lifting out a piece of fried chicken, I take a big bite, exhaling a groan.

"Hand me one." JR shifts around, and I grab the next container down.

"Glad to see you worked up an appetite." Scout cuts his brother a look as JR cracks open the corned beef hash and takes a big bite.

"I kind of had a moment back there." He sounds apologetic, but his brother derails that train.

"Fuck, yeah, you did. You deserved to. I wish I'd known you didn't know." He gives JR a glance. "You still want to go home first?"

JR exhales heavily. "I still want to see my son."

"Home it is."

The closer we get to the coast, the narrower the roads become. The trees are spaced out more, and palms fill the shoulders of the road now. We might be close to Charleston, but Fireside is a small town.

Entering on Main Street, a large banner hangs over the road reading "The Palm is Sacred."

"Looks like they still haven't changed the town motto." Scout laughs, and JR shakes his head.

"I bet Alice is still circulating a petition."

"Who's Alice?" I slide forward on the backseat.

"Our grandmother." Scout exhales a noise. "She's a trip. She's an awesome grandmother, don't get me wrong, but she's a trip."

Leaning my head on my hand, I study him. "In what way?"

"She was our mom's mom, and she taught at the high school until she retired. Then she because the town historian, and…"

He doesn't finish. "And?"

"She says the town was founded by some cult." JR shakes his head, looking out the window. "She's harmless."

"Was it?" I look from one brother to the next, and Scout only shrugs.

"I don't think there's any definitive evidence. The town council has always maintained it gives the place color."

"It's ancient history." JR's demeanor changes the farther we get into town, becoming more surly.

Another sign reads Welcome to Historic Downtown Fireside, and Scout stops at the only red light. When the signal changes, he takes a right into what looks like a historic neighborhood.

The houses are large and pretty with white front porches and lots of wood details. The yards are well manicured with large gardenia bushes and tall crepe myrtle trees. Palms are everywhere, and some of the houses have the state flag on them, that palm tree with the crescent moon. It's very Americana, and my heart beats a little faster when we pull into a driveway. I've heard so much about these people. Now I'm going to meet them.

Scout kills the engine in front of an enormous house with a mixture of live oaks and palm trees in the front yard. Ivy climbs all over the red-brick wall lining the sidewalk, and a large fountain is in the center. The two-story, white-wooden house seems very grand and very old.

"Ready?"

"As I'll ever be." JR steps out of Metallicar, pausing with his hands on his hips as he surveys the place.

His brother opens the driver's side door and steps out as well, and I wonder if I should wait in the backseat or follow them.

It doesn't matter as the front door opens and a pretty blonde woman walks slowly out onto the front porch. She pauses, crossing her arms, and a slight breeze pushes her long, straight hair over one shoulder.

I'm not sure what I was expecting of Becky, but this wasn't it. I expected a more hapless young person, a former cheerleader who dated the high school football star and accidentally got pregnant in college. A young woman who was stunned by her husband's arrest and imprisonment and perhaps rushed to get a divorce out of fear.

The actual person looks like she's never been afraid a day in her life. She knows exactly what she's doing. She's only a few years older than me, but she's dressed like a much older woman in navy slacks and an ivory twinset. A strand of large pearls is around her neck, and she's clearly not happy to see her ex-husband.

Her thin lips press into a line, and her voice is low, almost like she's a smoker. "What a surprise. You're home early."

"Actually, I'm eighteen months late." JR isn't smiling. His expression is grim. "Where's my son?"

"You always did have such a charming personality. I should've known you wouldn't care how I've been."

"I've heard how you've been, not that you ever told me."

"I don't have to tell you anything. We're not married anymore."

"You didn't tell me anything when we were married."

I'm on edge listening, analyzing every word they say for any hint he still has feelings for her. I hear none.

He drops his chin and exhales slowly. "I didn't come here for you. I came to see my son."

"Hello, Scout. You're looking well, considering you're an utter embarrassment to your father."

My jaw drops. *What a bitch!*

Scout only laughs. "Damn, Becky. I didn't think it was possible for you to get any more obnoxious. Guess I was wrong about that, too."

"You're usually wrong about everything." Her arms are still crossed, and she turns to go back inside the house. "Your father isn't here. He's at the gym."

JR starts walking to the house, and my heart hammers in my chest. "I want to see my son."

Becky spins on her heel, and her voice is a sharp command. "Don't you step foot on this porch, or I'll call the sheriff."

I'm surprised her threat actually stops JR in his tracks… then my mind drifts to his strange behavior when we saw the roadblock in Texas.

He lifts his chin, his ice blue eyes scanning the enormous house. "Jesse?" He calls loudly. "Jesse?"

Becky rushes to the top step holding out her hand. "Stop shouting. What will the neighbors think?"

"I don't give a shit." JR snaps, yelling again. "Jesse!"

"He's not here. He lives with Alice now. Bill said he'd already done the daddy thing and isn't interested in doing it again."

She's still speaking, but JR has signaled Scout, and they're jogging back to where I'm waiting in Metallicar. They jump in on both sides, and Scout turns the key. It's the first time I've been so proud of the way it roars to life like a true muscle car.

Scouts slams it into reverse and backs out of the drive. He gives the gas a little pump, and it makes a loud roar as we leave the Ice Queen standing on the front porch clutching her pearls.

He shakes his head. "That girl's only a year older than me, right?"

"She's aging in dog years." JR grumbles, and I can't resist.

"Because she's a total bitch?"

Scout lifts his chin and exhales a laugh. "I get it. Bitch, dog years. Good one."

He holds his palm back, and I slap it. JR doesn't smile, and I feel a little guilty. I don't normally dump on ex-girlfriends... or ex-wives, but that woman is the worst, from what she said to Scout to how she spoke to JR.

He's silent the rest of the drive, and my stomach is in knots. Our moment in the woods was so hot and amazing, and to me, it felt like it meant something. It felt like we connected in a deeper way, a real way.

Now he's right back to where he was the first day we met—angry and withdrawn and not looking at me at all. I know he has so much pressing on him, he's learned so much so fast... Still my heart aches with longing for him as I watch the scenery change outside the window.

The houses are growing smaller and closer together on this end of town, with shaggy wisteria draping over the trees. The yards aren't as pristine, and I don't see a single brick wall or ivy-lined fountain.

Finally, we pull into the driveway of what looks like a

two-bedroom, red brick house. It has a white front door and a single-car, concrete driveway to the side. White, floral cast-iron columns stand on each corner, and the front door flings open right when Scout kills the engine.

"Oh, my gracious! My word!" A small lady in a red blouse and white pants with a teased helmet of white hair scuttles out the door. Both her arms are stretched over her head, and her face is beaming. "Both my boys are home at last! It must be Christmas!"

"Hey, Gran." Scout leans down and picks her up in a hug, making her squeal.

"Bradley Scout! Put me down before you crush me."

He gives her a shake side to side instead, and she fusses more. "Put me down! My old bones can't take all this man-handling."

JR cracks a grin, and it makes me smile from where I wait beside the car. His brother finally releases their tiny grandma, and she fusses, straightening her shirt and patting her hair.

"That boy, I swear." Then she sees her other grandson and clasps her hands under her chin. "Oh, my John. Thank the Lord you're home! Come and give me a hug, my sweet boy. How are you?"

"I'm fine." He goes straight to her, bending down to hug her gently. "How are you feeling, GA?"

"Well, I got this reflux giving me trouble. The doctor says I might have to have my gall bladder removed, but my gynecologist thinks it's an overreaction."

Scout calls from the front porch, "Don't talk about your gynecologist, Gran!"

She waves at him. "You're a grown man, you know about these things. Anyway, I wasn't talking about my female parts." Her blue eyes land on me, and she grabs JR's arm. "Who is this angelic creature? Is she with you, John?"

Warm embarrassment floods my cheeks. "Hi, there." I do a little wave.

"Well, come here, young lady, I can barely see you that far away." She squints at me, smiling, then her eyes go over my shoulder. "Although I can see that gorgeous car you're driving. Scout is that your car?"

"It's mine, GA, and this is our friend, Hope." JR waves me closer, but my stomach sinks. Their *friend.*

"Well, you'd better snatch her up quick." The little lady pulls me into a hug. "You're just as pretty as a picture, Hope. What are you doing with these wild boys?"

"She helped us drive from California, Gran. JR bought the car from her. Or her dad."

"Good gracious, did you three drive all the way from California?" Her wrinkled, spotted hand presses to her chest again. "You must be absolutely exhausted! Come inside, and I'll make some sweet tea."

"Now tell me, Bradley, have you met that RuPaul fellow yet?" She takes Scout's arm. "I just love him. He is so funny!"

"I'm not a drag queen, Gran."

"I know that, but isn't he part of your audience?"

"Gran!" Scout cries, as she leads us into the tiny house.

"I'm not saying there's anything wrong with that, Bradley Scout!" She leaves us in a small living room with plastic on the backs of the furniture. "I just don't like you taking your clothes off for money. If you were my granddaughter, I'd say the same thing."

The sound of glassware clinking comes from the kitchen, and JR is scanning the place. He goes to a short hall and looks down it.

"The good Lord makes us the way he makes us, and it's up to us to do what we will with the talents we're given." She returns to the room carrying a tray with four tall glasses of iced tea on it.

"I'm not gay, Gran. I thought I was taking headshots, and things got twisted."

She straightens, making a disappointed face. "Now, Bradley

Scout. I might be old, but I know a thing or two. You don't take your clothes off for a headshot."

"GA?" John slides his hand onto her arm. "I really want to see Jesse. Is he here?"

"Oh…" The old lady's eyes warm, and she smiles at him. "He is just the most adorable thing. It's like having you all over again."

"Can I see him?"

"Well, of course you can!" She hands her eldest grandson a glass of tea. "You have to wait for him to get home from kindergarten."

"He's at school?" My eyes go wide. "And he lives with you?"

"Oh, don't you fret dear. You know those St. Johns have always been a bit…" She sits on the couch, raising her eyebrows and looking away, which I take to mean snotty, bitchy, pretentious. I couldn't agree more. "But his mamma has him in this very small group of kids. Learning pods, they're calling it. It's supposed to limit their exposure, but it might end up being better than regular school."

"When does he get home?" JR sets his glass of tea on the tray.

"What time is it?" She looks up at the clock, and I hear a car pulling up out front.

A sharp honk of a horn, and a young woman's voice calls.

"That's Trudy now… You remember Trudy Barnett? She picks the kids up after school…"

JR's grandmother is still speaking as the door opens, and the cutest little boy-voice shouts into the room. "Hey, Gran! I'm home!"

My eyes flicker to JR, and his brow is raised. His lips are parted, and when I see the mist in his eyes, mine fill with tears.

CHAPTER
Fifteen

JR

WHEN I WAS IN THAT FUCKING CELL, AS MUCH AS I HATE TO ADMIT it, there were times I wondered if I'd been a bad husband. Maybe I was too gruff or not sensitive to Becky's needs or whatever women say.

When she walked out on that porch looking as old as her mother and equally as bitchy, I almost thanked her. It was the closure I'd needed for fifteen months.

My dad was always preoccupied with the St. Johns and the stuff they had, the trips they took, and what they were doing...

What did Hope call it? Fetishizing wealth?

I couldn't have cared less.

When she turned up pregnant during my last year of college, I didn't care what those people said about her trying to hold onto me or whatever, and it didn't matter if it was a boy or a girl. I just wanted to be a dad.

Now I'm standing in my grandmother's living room, and my heart is beating out of my chest.

Jesse James Dunne runs in, looking just like my brother always did.

His hair is darker blond now, but his eyes are clear as the blue sky. His voice is little-boy cute. It'll drop once he hits puberty and has to deal with all that shit, but right now, he's still a boy.

He's innocent and sweet, and I wonder if he's still into football.

It's been eighteen months, and I want to scoop him up in my arms. I want to hug him close to me and smell his hair.

I want to touch his face like I did when he was a baby and tell him all the cool things we're going to do when he gets bigger.

Now he's a lot bigger.

And I don't want him to be afraid of me…

"Jesse, there's somebody here to see you." GA stands, looking from him to me.

I'm not sure if I should go to him or stay where I am or bend down… None of it matters.

"DADDY!" He shouts so loud, my heart skips.

Like a streak of light, he runs across the room, and I drop to my knees.

I catch him under the arms and lift him to me, holding his small body tight, blinking away the heat in my eyes.

He feels the same but bigger. He feels like my son. He's sturdy and strong, and he smells like he's been playing in the grass and having fun.

"Jesse." My voice cracks.

So many emotions flood my chest, I'm doing good to hold on, and that's just what I do. I hold onto my little man.

"I MADE THIS WHEN I WAS IN LATIN CLASS."

"Latin in Kindergarten?" I look to my grandma, and she just shrugs. "That's amazing, J."

"Did you know the gladiators spoke Latin? Mr. Perkins told us that. He even has a real gladiator shield. He let us touch it. Then he showed us how you use it to protect yourself if somebody was coming at you with a knife."

"Lord have mercy, Jesse, take a breath!" GA puts a plate in front of my son with a cookie and a glass of milk. "You're going to hyperventilate."

"It's okay." I smile up at her. "I want to hear it all."

I've missed so much. I want to hear everything he wants to tell me. My hand is on his little back where he stands in front of me at the coffee table showing me all his school work, and every few minutes, I lean forward to kiss the back of his head.

"Look what I got for my birthday!" He takes off running to the back of the house, and my grandma shakes her head.

"He spends the whole day running. He has so much energy." Then she chuckles. "But it's just the one. Not like the two of you."

"You loved it." Scout pushes off the wall where he's been leaning with his arms crossed. "You were always on the front row decked out in all our team colors."

"I was also fifteen years younger!"

"Does somebody need another hug?" My brother starts towards her, and she lets out a little holler.

"Bradley Scout! Don't you pick me up again. You'll break my back!"

"Check it out, Dad!" Jesse runs in the room carrying a football as big as him. "Poppy got it for me. He said it's regulation size!"

I choose to ignore the bitterness in my throat at the mention of my father. Instead I focus on this little guy between my legs with one arm around my neck doing his best to hold an adult-sized football under his arm.

"Want to play with me, Dad?"

"Heck, yeah, I do." Scooping him up, we start for the door, where Hope hasn't moved.

She's watching us, and her eyes are shining. When they meet mine, my chest tightens, and I want to put my arm around her and pull her into this twosome. A sensation deep in my bones says this would be right. Would she change her life for this mess I'm facing?

"He's adorable." Her voice is soft, and her cute little nose wrinkles with her smile. "I was right. He does look just like you."

"He looks like my brother." My voice is different, gentler.

"Who looks just like you."

Jesse is restless on my hip. "Come on, Dad!"

I know it will eventually get old, but right now I love it when he shouts that in my ear. "Hey, Jess, I want you to meet a friend of mine. This is Hope."

"Hi-ya, Hope!" He waves a hand over his head, and I laugh. "Who taught you that?"

"Hi, Jesse. It's really nice to meet you. Your dad's told me a lot about you."

"Did he tell you we play football?" I'm not sure why my son is shouting, but I don't care.

My brother swoops up beside us and swipes the ball from his hands. "Give me that."

"Hey!" Jesse bucks on my hip, and I let him go.

He charges out the metal door right behind my brother into the yard, and I shake my head. "I've missed a lot."

"You'll get it back." Hope Eternal is standing beside me. "He's so happy to see you."

"I never let him forget you." GA is at my side sliding her arm around my waist. "I showed him your picture every night and told him you were thinking about him, praying for him... I told him you were coming back."

It hits me hard to hear her say those words. Turning, I pull my grandma into a firm hug, my eyes burning.

"Thank you, Gran. You have no idea…" My voice breaks.

"Dad!" Jesse yells from the yard. "Come on!"

"Now get out there." My feisty grandma pats my back and pushes me to the door. "That little guy's going to rupture something if you keep making him yell."

That makes me laugh, and I head out into the yard where Scout is tossing him easy passes. Every time Jesse catches it, he runs straight to my legs and gives me a hug. I bend down and hug him back.

"Help me throw it to Uncle Scout!" He hands it to me, and I drop to a knee, taking the ball in one hand.

"You ready?" I look up at my brother, and he spreads both hands.

"When am I ever not ready?"

Rearing back, I pass it then give my son a nudge. "Go get him, J!"

He takes off running at top speed, which isn't super-fast for a five-year-old. Still, my brother slows down and lets Jesse catch him. He even pretends to fall and they both roll around on the ground, making Hope laugh.

"Come on, Hope. I'll teach you to pass the ball."

She walks to where they're tussling, and I step up beside my grandma, who's watching them with a big grin on her face as well.

"She's a doll." GA glances up at me with one eyebrow raised. "She sure gives you a lot of loving looks."

"I haven't noticed." It's a lie. I've noticed. "I can't drag her into this mess."

"Drag her? Looks to me like she's walking towards it."

I can't argue with my grandma, so I don't even try. "Is he here with you full time now?"

"Pretty much." She exhales a deep sigh. "It was clear after the honeymoon your father didn't want his grandson around every day."

The fist of anger is back in my chest. "I'm going to see him."

There's still so fucking much left undone. It's all I can think about.

"Did you see me, Dad?" Jesse runs with all his might to where I'm standing beside my grandmother. "I caught it! Uncle Scout threw it, and I caught it!"

"I saw you, little man." I drop to my knee and return his hug. "You're amazing."

He holds me a little longer, turning his face to my ear. "I love you, Dad."

My heart splits as he takes off running back to where Hope is talking to Scout. I'm torn between wanting to hold him no matter what that means and wanting to smash everything so we can be together again.

"Where are you three planning to sleep?" GA calmly takes out her iPhone. "Scout can stay here. I think Regina's entire BnB is empty if you and Hope want to stay there. No breakfast, of course."

Rubbing my hand over the back of my neck, I'm all twisted up inside. "I need to take care of my business first."

"Your business can wait a few hours. Have dinner with your family tonight, spend time with your son. Talk to your father tomorrow."

"I don't have much time." What I've done hangs over my head like a sword waiting to fall.

If I'm discovered here, it would ruin all my plans and possibly my life. I'd never see Jesse again... Still, watching my little boy showing Hope how to run out for a pass, and Scout laughing and throwing the ball at her, as painful as it is, I want to linger a little longer.

"The day's almost over. Give us one night?"

"One night is all I have left."

CHAPTER
Sixteen

Hope

"IT'D PROBABLY HELP IF YOU TAKE OFF THOSE BOOTS." SCOUT HOLDS the football at his shoulder, waiting as I toe off my boots. "Now go long."

Hesitating, I look side to side. "What does that mean?"

"It means run!" Jesse grabs my hand and starts running to the other end of the yard, dragging me behind him.

He's really the cutest thing, and no matter what JR says, he looks just like his dad. The only problem is I can't chase him across the yard, and I definitely can't roll around on the ground like he's been doing with Scout.

The ball spirals towards me, and I squeal, holding both hands over my head and ducking.

Jesse jumps up beside me, but he doesn't catch it either. The ball bounces wildly and flies in the opposite direction.

"What the heck was that?" Scout jogs up to us laughing.

Jesse takes off after the ball. "She's not on my team."

That makes his uncle laugh louder, and my jaw drops. "I've never played before!"

Scout tosses an arm across my shoulders and gives me a reassuring shake. "Just a tip. You're not going to catch anything throwing your hands over your head and screaming like a girl."

Looking around, I lean into his ear. "I have a problem.

He steps back, curling his lip at me. "Aunt Flo? But you and JR were just—"

"No!" I push his arm hard. "Not that. I need a shower, and I need... Leaning forward I try to say it without moving my lips *urhnderwhuur*."

"Who's Aunt Flo?" Jesse is back beside us, carrying the football.

Scout's eyes narrow as he tries to figure out what I murmured.

I quickly answer Jesse. "She's a friend of mine."

"Why do you call your friend your aunt?"

"I mean, she is my aunt." I struggle, trying to think of anything. "She's also my friend. Or not. She's not a very good friend."

"Oh, shit!" Scout's eyebrows shoot up, and I see he's finally figured out what I said. "Hey, Jesse, run this to your dad. I need to help Miss Hope with something."

"Okay!" he yells, running to where JR is talking to his grandmother. "Catch, Dad, catch!"

Scout takes my arm. "Come on."

We head into the house, and he goes straight to the back room. "They're probably going to be the size of a tent."

"I can't believe we're doing this." I wait in the hall, watching the door. "You think she'd mind if I took a shower?"

"I think she wants you to stay... Oh, hell no."

"What?" I whisper, looking into the lavender room.

The windows have lavender chiffon curtains with dark purple butterflies that appear hand-painted.

"I did not need to know this about Gran." He holds up an egg-shaped device, and my eyes go wide.

"Is that a…"

"We-vibe," he reads, and my hands fly over my eyes.

"That's none of our business! Focus, Scout!"

"Kinky grandma." He quickly shoves the vibrator back in the drawer and lifts out a pair of white panties. "I don't know, but I don't think they'll fit you." He holds them up high between us. "They're as big as my head."

"I'll make it work." I snatch them from him and head into the bathroom. "Make an excuse for me."

Stepping into the pink bathroom, I close the door and cringe when I see myself in the mirror. My hair is in desperate need of a wash. I've been in this same dress for three days, but at least we did all shower halfway through the drive.

Ten minutes later I'm clean, hair washed with honeysuckle shampoo, which actually smells amazing, and I'm quietly searching under the sink. I manage to find travel size deodorant, a toothbrush, and toothpaste, but there is not a safety pin in sight.

I do find a pair of scissors, which I use to cut the waist down from under my armpits, then I cut the sides apart. Stepping into the massive, white-cotton undies, I make two little snips on each side and tie small knots, top and bottom securely on my hips.

"Dang," I whisper, turning side to side in the mirror. "That's not half bad."

While I wait for the world to begin again, maybe I can host a YouTube channel for wardrobe emergencies. Knotted panties could totally be a thing.

Giving my dress a sniff, I decide it's not too bad to wear again, like I have a choice. All I have is this dress, my teddy coat, and my iPhone. It's equipped with Apple pay at least—not that I have much money to spend.

Exiting the bathroom, I hear rattling coming from the

kitchen. Following the sound, I find JR sitting at a small, yellow Formica table across from Jesse. They're playing Uno while Scout stands beside Alice at the counter, slowly cutting thick slices of bread.

It's such a homey scene. It makes me so happy. "I can help!"

When Alice sees me, she smiles big. "There you are! Were you able to find everything you needed?"

Scout grimaces. "How'd it turn out?"

I want to pinch him. "Good! All good! I'm sorry I didn't ask you first. We were playing, and I suddenly realized how long it had been since I'd showered."

"Nonsense!" Alice waves a hand at me and returns to the pot where she's stirring what looks like Marinara sauce. "But you're wearing the same dress. John, why don't you get Hope's suitcase out of the car?"

"Suitcase?" He looks up just as Jesse yells *Uno*.

"Oh," I jump in. "I, um… I didn't bring a suitcase."

Alice draws back confused. "But you've been driving for three days! You didn't bring a bag or anything?"

I'm panicking, looking from Scout to JR. "You're not going to believe," I exhale, putting a hand on my hip. "I didn't realize we were taking such a long road trip. JR told me, but, you know…"

"Yeah, we, ah, got our wires crossed, Gran." Scout jumps in as Jesse lays his last card down.

JR groans at his handful of cards, but his son laughs loudly.

"Sometimes I don't listen." I do my best to look contrite. "JR's always saying I should listen better."

JR hasn't said a word. He's leaning back in the chair studying me in a way that makes my stomach squeeze and tickle. We know I'm lying, and he's not helping me at all.

"Well, don't you worry. You're here now." Alice pats me on the arm. "I'll ask Regina if her daughter has anything you can borrow."

Regina? I look at JR. He's shuffling the cards for Jesse's demanded rematch.

"My friend Regina Winthrop owns a bed and breakfast in town." Alice continues. "She said you could stay there as long as you need."

"That's so nice…" I start to ask more when she takes my arm.

"Now come sit and have your dinner. Boys, put away those cards."

Scout carries a bowl of fettuccini pasta while Alice produces a platter of mouthwatering marinara with fresh boiled shrimp. It's spicy and delicious, paired with the crispy, warm French bread and generous glasses of red wine. It's the nicest meal I've had in a long time, months probably.

An hour later, we're stuffed and Jesse is asleep with his head on his daddy's shoulder. Scout's turning back the bed in Alice's guest room, and I look around, wondering where JR is going to stay.

"Regina said she left a few things for you to have if you want them. She said coffee is in the cabinet, but the fridge is empty. You'll have the whole house to yourself."

JR is still at the table holding a sleeping Jesse. His large hand is on his little boy's back, and he hasn't stopped hugging and petting him since we arrived. They've both been so attached, it almost hurts to watch, knowing how they were separated for so long and without any warning.

"Give him to me." Alice reaches for her grandson, and the reluctance in JR's eyes makes my chest ache.

He stands as she takes him. "What time does he leave for school in the morning?"

"Seven, but he'll be home at three. You'll see him every afternoon."

He winces ever so slightly. I might not have seen it if I hadn't been watching his face all evening. Alice steps into the hall, and I go to where he's now standing. I want to slip my hand in his like I did in the tent, but I'm not sure he wants it.

"Are you okay?" My voice is quiet.

He looks at me for the first time since dinner, and when our eyes meet, he seems to relax. Still, something is troubling him.

"You two get going. Regina said there's a bottle of wine in the refrigerator." Alice gives me a wink, and my cheeks heat.

We're both staying there? Alone? My bottom lip slips under my teeth.

JR goes to his son's room, and I follow quietly, waiting at the door. The room is all little boy stuff, with Iron Man illustrations and football stickers on the walls. Jesse is the cutest thing sleeping all tucked under his Iron Man covers. It's so clear how much he's loved.

JR slides his hand over his sleeping son's head, checking the blankets around him, making sure he's completely comfortable.

Alice watches with a smile. "He's good. Time for you to get some rest."

Reluctantly, JR steps away, and when our eyes meet in the yellow light of the hall, his expression worries me. It's like a warm hello and a sad goodbye all mixed up in one.

"Ready?" He takes my hand, and a niggle of hope squirms in my chest.

Maybe things haven't changed between us? I just wish I knew why he seems so grave.

"SHE LEFT COOKIES." I STOP AT THE TABLE JUST INSIDE THE KITCHEN OF the gorgeous old home where we're spending the night. "They're still warm!"

The kitchen is all stained pine and red and white checked everything. It's very farm-country, with a tin rooster in one corner and a milk churn in the other. A note on the table reads, *Enjoy your stay!* And a bouquet of colorful flowers is beside it.

"Regina has owned this place since I was a kid." JR steps up beside me, lifting the note and reading it briefly.

He was quiet the whole drive over, and my body is tight with desire, worry, anticipation… and so many questions. What's going to happen now? We were spectacularly together this morning… Is he sorry?

He's been so focused on his son, and so distant since we got here. I mean, he should be focused on his son—they haven't seen each other in almost two years…

But why this distance?

Ugh… I wish he'd talk to me.

Of course, when has John Roth Dunne ever been chatty? Once on the entire three-day drive?

He touches my shoulder, and I jump out of my thoughts. "Oh… Sorry, what?" I exhale a nervous laugh.

He lifts his chin towards the stairs. "We have our pick of the rooms. Which do you want?"

My heart sinks, and I blink away the disappointment heating my eyes. He doesn't want to share a room.

"That's not right. I'm the stowaway. You pick the one you like."

We walk slowly towards the stairs, where the biggest calico cat ever is lying on the fourth step like a cuddly distraction just for me.

"Look at you!" I drop to my knees to pet him, and he slowly lifts a head like he's used to strangers fawning over him. "Who is this big guy?"

JR smiles, taking a knee beside us as well. "This must be Cosmo." A crooked grin splits his cheeks, and my heart melts. "I can't believe he's still alive."

"He's just a big ole boy." My lips pucker out as I talk to him in my kitty-voice, scrubbing my fingers around his ears. Cosmo closes his eyes and purrs. "Yesh, you're just a big ole cutie boy."

I'm shaking my nose close to the cat's when JR stands, going to the top of the stairs. He pauses on the landing, inspecting the second floor. "This looks like the master suite."

Rising from the Cosmo love-fest, I slowly walk the rest of the way and stop beside him. "You want it?"

His shoulders drop, and he takes my hands in his. "You can have it if you want."

As much as I hate being the only one doing the chasing in this relationship, my dad once told me if I wanted something, I had to go for it.

"We can share it." It's a cautious suggestion, coupled with a sweet smile.

He doesn't answer, but his hands tighten around mine. "Hope…" He says my name on an exhale, almost like a prayer. He's so heartbreakingly sexy.

Lifting my eyes, I meet his. "That's my name. Don't wear it out." It's meant be playful, but it comes out a little sad.

I guess I'm not as great an actress as I'd like to be.

Releasing my hands, he cups my face, lowering his forehead to mine. "I can't drag you into this mess of mine."

"It doesn't look like a mess. It looks like a family."

"You have no idea." His thumbs move against my cheeks, and he lifts his head to meet my eyes.

I stretch higher, touching my lips to his jaw. "Either way, I'm here."

"Hope…" It's a rough whisper.

"Kiss me, John."

It's all it takes.

He lowers his mouth with a groan capturing my lips with his. Fire shoots through my veins as his tongue finds mine, curling and teasing.

Raking my fingers along his neck, I thread them in his hair, pressing my body against his.

His kiss is rough and beautiful. My core tightens, and I ache for him to satisfy my need.

He lowers to sit on the foot of the bed, putting his face at my waist. Reaching down, he slides his hands up the back of my knees, lightly up my thighs, lifting my dress.

I hiss as electricity flames higher with his touch. Reaching down, I pull the thin garment over my head, baring my body for him, all except for the makeshift undies.

His blue eyes darken, studying my breasts, my tight nipples, the air rushing in and out of my lungs.

He holds both of my wrists behind my back, not letting me move. It's thrilling and it shifts my body closer to his face.

Tracing his nose along my bare stomach, he pauses at my underwear. "What's this?"

"What's what?" My eyelids lower, desire burning in my veins.

"Your panties are in my pocket." His mouth forms a hot pucker on my hip, and he pulls the skin, touching me with his teeth.

Wetness floods my core, and I gasp. "Scout stole some of Alice's underwear—"

His grip on my wrists tightens, and he pulls me back. When our eyes meet, his twinkle. He's almost laughing. "You stole my granny's panties?"

I exhale a laugh. "I didn't have a choice."

"They're sexy." His face returns to my hip, and he pulls another little bit of flesh between his teeth.

Oh, God. My chin drops back, and my eyes roll. It's just what I want. I want him to take me, hold me down, fuck me hard.

I'm breathless. "I'll take them off."

"I will." His ironclad grip on my wrists loosens, and large hands cover my hips, sliding the cut and knotted panties down my legs.

He takes his time, and I think I'm going to dissolve in front of him. When they're at my ankles, he glances up at me and I see all the hunger burning in my stomach reflected at me.

Straightening again, he slides his nose along my lower stomach. "You are so beautiful."

"I think I'm going to combust."

I'm lovestruck standing in front of him, swaying to the movement of his lips across my flesh, the scruff of his new beard against my sensitive skin. I want him inside me. I want his body sliding against mine, firm and hard. I want his massive dick in my body.

"How is this possible?" He slides warm hands up the back of my thighs, cupping my ass.

"What?" I manage to inhale.

"You're so damn sweet, so innocent… and you hypnotize me. I'm completely at your mercy."

My hands are free now and I thread them in his soft hair. "What makes you think I'm not at yours?"

Leaning forward, he covers my bare pussy with his mouth, roughly sliding his tongue across my clit, turning my knees to liquid.

"Oh, shit…" Gripping his hair, I can barely stand. He's holding me up, and his mouth moves faster, tongue lapping hungrily, and my legs begin to tremble. "John…"

Another kiss, another suck, and currents of orgasm race through my thighs.

"I'm going to come." It's a broken cry.

He slows down, giving me a little grin. "Not so fast, beautiful."

Gripping my waist, he turns me to lie back on the bed and he stands, pulling the shirt from his jeans. Stormy blue eyes survey my body, moving from my lips to my neck to my breasts, to my hands sliding lower on my stomach. It's a heated caress, turning my skin to chills.

I'm mesmerized at the sight of his ripped body disrobing in front of me. His tattoos are on full display. My knees rub together, and I'm sizzling inside reading the quote on his upper chest. *This much is true.*

I will have this man, I complete the thought in my mind.

"Will you touch yourself for me?" His voice is thick.

"I'll do anything for you." I don't even care how that makes me sound.

His eyebrow arches, and a tease of a smile is on his sexy lips. "I'll keep that in mind."

Those loose jeans are the last thing separating our bodies, and I can see his massive cock, pushing against the thick fabric.

God, I want him naked.

Now.

A swift push, and they're on the floor. He stands, and his cock rises in all its glory. I want it inside me, stretching and filling, but he's more focused than I am. Reaching for his jeans, he pulls out a condom.

My eyebrow arches, and I do my best sassy. "What are you doing with a condom?"

"I thought I might get lucky." He rips the foil painfully slowly. "Apparently my brother has several."

"Lucky him."

"Lucky me."

JR rolls the shield on slowly, and he's like a god, shoulders broad, muscles rounded, hands fondling his dick. I'm in my wildest fantasy watching him.

As soon as it's on, he places a knee on the mattress, climbing over me slowly, like a predator, thrilling my insides.

"I'm going to hold you down." He dips down to kiss my stomach. It's shockwaves through my limbs. "Then I'm going to fuck you hard."

He's at my breasts, and he slides his tongue around my tight nipple before pulling it between his teeth. It's a charge direct to my throbbing core.

"Is that acceptable to you?" His face is right above mine, and the muscle in his jaw moves as he waits.

My thighs readily part for him. "I will allow it."

Lifting his chin, he looks up at the ceiling. That ridiculous dimple appears in his cheek—the one that just pushes all of his amazingness over the top. "This girl…"

He exhales something like a laugh, and I lean up to lick him.

My tongue touches the top of his chest, and I raise higher, dragging it to his neck. It's as far as I get before his mouth covers mine fast, hard and demanding. His lips shove mine apart, and it's all wildness. Tongue pushing into my mouth, swiping away the saltiness of his skin on mine.

He's ferocious, and I'm writhing in the sheets, wanting more, wanting everything.

Our hands collide between his legs. Together we guide his cock to my pussy, and he shoves in so violently, my breath catches.

"Oh…" My back arches, and I can't stop a gasp of surprise.

We were together only this morning, less than twelve hours ago, but he's still a shock to my senses. I'm so full.

Despite his declaration, he pauses. A large hand smooths my hair back from my forehead, and our eyes meet.

"Are you okay?" His brow is lowered, concern in his lusty eyes.

I close my eyes as my body quickly accommodates his size. "Yes…"

Rotating my hips, I'm better than okay.

It's enough. Pulling back, he thrusts harder, faster. He's focused, working out his own needs, scooting me higher in the bed with every plunge. My eyes flutter shut, luxuriating at the heaviness of his body, the press of his frame, holding me against the bed, claiming me, taking me.

My knees are bent, rising rhythmically with every thrust. My hips buck higher to meet his, and deep inside, I feel the tingling of something new. He's touching a part of me that curls my toes. Sharp waves of pleasure lift my hips, clench my core.

"Hope…" He groans loudly, lifting up and clutching my ass.

Dragging me closer as he pushes deeper, my hands slap the mattress as my body tightens. I've never felt pleasure like this. I'm shaken to my core.

He leans down to pull sharply on a hardened nipple, and I break, wailing and shaking. It's an experience I've never had.

His head drops back, and he groans low and loud, tingling my entire body. I feel him pulsing deep inside me again and again. Our rhythm is primal and perfect. Our bodies are one in this release.

As we come down, his grip on my skin relaxes. Quickly disposing of the condom, he returns to the bed and gathers my now-boneless body to his chest. We don't speak, yet he holds me so close.

Warm lips touch my brow, and I'm so satisfied. I'm so happy to be wrapped in his arms, safe in his embrace. He's the grumpiest, sexiest, most divine man I've ever known.

He's the most amazing thing I've ever held in my life, and it terrifies me.

What will I do if he tells me it's time to go?

CHAPTER
Seventeen

JR

'M ROUSED BY THE GOLDEN GLOW OF THE SUN BREAKING THROUGH ivory lace curtains. Hope's little body is against mine, her perky, round ass close to my morning erection.

Damn, I've got to get out of this bed before I fuck her again. Why didn't I ask Scout for more than one condom?

Truth is, I wasn't sure she'd want to sleep with me again. I was a little drunk when I took her in the woods yesterday morning. I don't remember if I asked. I only know I saw her beautiful body shining like an angel, and I couldn't fight anymore.

Now we're at the end of our journey. She says she was a stowaway, but I can't help feeling like a kidnapper. I felt like a shit and a half when GA told me to get her suitcase.

She doesn't have a suitcase.

Hell, I tried to leave her barefoot on the side of the road between San Francisco and Los Angeles. The memory stings my stomach so bad.

Today I have to do the right thing. It's going to hurt like hell, but I can't ignore the truth any longer.

"Hmm... Hey, grumpy." Her soft voice fills my chest with warmth.

Her slim hand traces along my neck, threading in my hair. Reaching up, I pull her fingers to my lips. "Good morning."

"Why are you leaning over me scowling?" Her eyes aren't even open.

"How do you know I'm not smiling?" Leaning down, I kiss her shoulder.

It rises, and she grins, blinking awake. "That doesn't sound like the John I know..."

Our eyes meet, and her voice trails off like she wants to say more. I want to say more, but instead, I turn away, moving the covers aside and going to the bathroom.

Closing the door, it takes a minute, but I'm able to use the restroom, put on some clothes, and mentally kick my own ass. I can't do this with her now. The timing is wrong, and shit, speaking of timing, my time is up.

When I return, the bed is empty. The sheets are pulled over the mattress, but her dress, sexy granny panties, and little white boots are gone. I quickly jog down the stairs to the scent of coffee meeting me halfway.

Hope's opening and closing cabinets in the kitchen. "She has coffee, but there isn't any food here. Besides the cookies."

My phone buzzes in my pocket, and I slide it out. "GA made breakfast. Let's go."

She looks around. "I guess I don't have anything. Let's go."

"WHERE'S YOUR DAD NOW?" SCOUT RIPS OFF A PIECE OF TOAST AND sticks it in his mouth.

"Shady Rest." Hope leans closer to him, and I push against the irritation.

My brother likes hearing people's stories and asking questions. Of course, she's drawn to him. Not that it matters.

He scowls, talking with his mouth full. "Is that a funeral home?"

Shaking her head, Hope takes a sip of coffee. "It's a short-term nursing home facility. He had to have his knees worked on, and we thought February would be a good time. I had no idea he'd end up trapped there. They won't even let me visit!"

Gran places a hand on her chest. "My goodness! That's terrible."

"Yeah, but I call him all the time. He's in good spirits." She finishes the last of her oatmeal. "Dad's a Buddhist, so he believes everything works together towards the greater good."

"That's not just a Buddhist philosophy." GA nods, standing and collecting plates.

"Let me help you!" Hope jumps out of her seat, taking the plates from my grandmother.

"You sit right back down. You're company." Scout and I both stand at the same time, and she looks at us. "Look at my boys. They're going to help."

She hands each of us the dirty dishes and takes Hope's arm, leading her into the living room. "Tell me more about your family."

"There's not much to tell…"

Scout and I look at each other, and he exhales a laugh. "I guess we're doing the dishes."

"Too bad she never bought a dishwasher. I'm drying."

"Jerk." He snatches up the rag and switches on the hot water.

It doesn't take long to wash the few dishes we used. I dry the plates and stack them on the counter.

"Good night?" He cocks an eyebrow at me, and I shake my head.

"Not going there."

He frowns. "But you slept with her, right? Or should I say slept with her *again*?"

"I'm not talking about her to you."

He's quiet a minute, rinsing the soap off the last plate. "Are you going to ask her to stay?"

"No."

"Dammit, why not?" He tosses the dish cloth on the counter. "She's perfect for you."

Is she? Things are pretty great, but in my experience, perfect can go bad fast.

"Bad timing."

My stomach is tight. I don't want to have this conversation with him. It was hard enough having it with GA then asking her to loan me money. She was cool about it, saying she had plenty, but if that were true, why is she still living in this matchbox sized house?

"Look, I get it. Becky is a bitch, and finding out about her and Dad is enough to make anybody give up on love, but you've got to look at what's right in front of you."

I turn my back to the counter; I can't help wondering how this happened. How have I gotten to the point where I have no control over my life? So many things I want, I can't have.

Exhaling deeply, it's time to level with him. "I'm getting on a plane for San Francisco in five hours."

"What?" His voice is hushed. "Why?"

"I violated my parole coming here. I got that car, hoping I could make it back before I have to check in with my parole officer on Friday. If I don't... If they catch me, I'll go back to prison for the rest of my sentence. Possibly longer, depending on the judge."

His eyes widen, as his lips part. "That's why you freaked at the roadblock... That's why you backed down when Becky threatened to call the sheriff—"

"I can't take any chances. I'm going to see Dad, then I have to get back to California. Fast."

"Jesus… Why didn't you tell me?"

"I don't know. I didn't want you to worry."

"Worry, hell. You're risking everything coming here. Why?"

Scrubbing my fingers against my forehead, I think of all the reasons. "I couldn't sit in that dead city and wait. I had to see Jesse. I had to come here and confront Dad. I had to find out why he did it and make him fix it."

"What made you think you could do it without getting caught?"

I look out the window at the sunny neighborhood street.

It's completely empty.

"I read this article about the Cannonball Run. Some guys set a new record last month… Twenty-seven hours."

"That's the race from New York to LA?"

"Yeah." I remember reading the story, and the plan unfolding in my brain. "They talked about the empty highways, no state troopers… I thought, if you could help me drive, I could do this."

"We did make pretty good time." He turns to lean beside me against the counter. "But now you're flying back? Isn't that just as dangerous? What if you pop up on a watch list?"

"I don't think they'll be looking for me flying into California. Anyway, it's more risky to drive, possibly get held up."

His lips tighten and he exhales deeply. "How can I help?"

Gratitude swells in my chest. I expected him to be shocked. I expected skepticism, possibly disappointment, but he's only supportive.

I pull him in for a brief hug. "Thanks."

"It's the least I can do." His voice is quiet. "I'm sorry I couldn't be there for you when it all went down."

"Hey, you were dealing with your own shit. I know."

"I guess I thought Dad would take care of it."

I can't answer that. I know he knows what I'm thinking. We both expected too much of our dad. We always have.

Which brings me to this, the part that's going to hurt me the most. "You can do something for me. If it's not too much to ask."

"Ask away."

"Stay here with Jesse. Until I'm out of the woods. I don't want him to worry, and I think you'll help him."

"I can do that." He nods. "Hell, I'm going to be freaking out until I know you're okay."

"Join the club."

"Well, I think that's just wonderful." GA walks slowly into the kitchen with Hope right beside her. "I hope it works out for you."

"I hope so, too." Hope lifts her crossed fingers.

I don't know what they're talking about, but she's adorable. Then she turns to me, and her expression warms. She's still smiling, but her pretty eyes are so full of questions.

A bitter ache twists in my chest, and I know as much as it hurts, I've got to let her go now, too.

"Can we talk for a minute?" I feel Scout stiffen at my side.

"Sure." Her voice is soft, and I step forward to catch her hand.

He turns behind her holding his hands over head and pointing as he mouths, *Marry her.*

I shake my head. Leading her outside to the waiting car, I think about what I'm going to say. I don't want to tell her the truth, that I violated my parole and if I'm caught, I'll go back to prison. It's still hard grappling with the fact I was even in prison. The lies, the fact my father never came to my defense, still burns in my stomach. Add to that, I have no idea if I'll ever be able to clear my name, get my life back.

I don't want her worrying like my brother.

We stop at the driver's side door, and she looks up at me expectantly. "What's up?"

The wind pushes her wavy hair across her pink cheeks, and her blue eyes are so bright. For a minute I can't speak, I can only gaze at her loveliness, wishing things were different.

Last night was everything. She smelled like honeysuckle and tasted like the ocean. She was electric, melting into me, fueling my desire. We made love until I wasn't sure where I ended and she began. It was so good. It was everything I needed. It was like coming home.

It felt like my brother is right...

It felt perfect.

"I want you to keep the car." My voice is low.

Her eyebrows shoot up. "But you paid for it."

"I never paid for it. I used the seven-day trial period to get it." I can't tell her I never planned to keep it.

"Don't you need it?" She reaches up to move a silky lock of hair off her face.

My fingers curl with wanting to do that. It'll only make this harder. "It's your dad's dream car. You need to hang onto it."

A sad little smile lifts her lips, and she glances down at her boot-clad feet. "I don't know how much longer I can. I don't even know what I'm doing here... Am I staying? Going back?"

My eyes squeeze shut, and a knot is in my throat. Still, I have to say it. "You can decide what you want to do. I'm flying back to San Francisco tonight."

Her lips part, and she pulls back. "Tonight?"

"I've got unfinished business, and if I don't get back—"

"So that's it? You're leaving me here?"

I can't tell if she's angry or hurt. Or both. And I hate it.

"Hope..." My chest tightens. "We knew from the start it would end this way."

"End?" She blinks fast, and the mist in her eyes guts me.

Reaching forward, I pull her to my chest. Her body is tense like she's fighting me. Still, I wrap my arms around her, holding her tight to my heart.

"If I could change things…" My voice is rough.

We don't speak, and gradually she starts to relax. Her hands are on my waist, her cheek against my chest. I want to kiss her…

Releasing her, I step back, sliding a hand in my pocket. "Your dreams don't deserve to wait on me and my shit."

Her head is bowed, but she squints up at me. "This year has taught me I can wait on a lot of things."

This girl. "Hope Eternal… You're always so positive. So wise. How do you do it?"

Shaking her head, she blinks away from me. "I have a dream. I just hold onto it."

"What is it?"

She looks across the top of the car at the blue sky. "It's doing what I love. It's being with someone who loves me as much as I love him."

Her words resonate in my soul. The truth of what she and I have shared is undeniable, but is it possible?

Stepping forward I grasp her waist, drawing her to me. I can't resist her. I lower my mouth to hers, parting her lips.

Her arms wrap around my neck as our tongues slide together, and her body presses against mine. It's magnetism and chemistry and friction. It's all the elements coming together. It's completion.

I kiss her cheek. I trace my lips to her eyebrow, inhaling one last time at the top of her head. I'll never forget her scent.

Lifting my chin, I focus on the blue sky above, the only thing we have for sure. "Goodbye, Hope."

"Goodbye?"

Taking her hand, I look into her eyes. "I said I'd never lie to you. I can't make a promise I can't keep. I don't know what's coming next, but if there's any chance—"

She steps forward, placing her fingers lightly to my lips. "I'll wait for that chance."

CHAPTER
Eighteen

JR

I park GA's ancient Chevy pickup outside my father's grand estate. It's a beat-up old orange step side, but my grandmother says a truck is the most useful vehicle on the road. When I suggest she could at least upgrade to a more recent model, she accuses me of ageism.

"I know all this ole boy's quirks. I'm too old to start over with a younger model."

Who am I to argue with her?

It's a conversation that soothes the gaping hole in my chest. Hope refused taking money from me. She said her phone had Apple pay, whatever that means. She'll find the envelope of cash I tucked inside her teddy bear coat.

She climbed in that Impala and drove away, and I felt like a chain had been hooked to my heart, my lungs, my stomach. All three were ripped out, dragging along the road behind her like beat up old tin cans.

Now I'm standing on the front porch, waiting to confront my dad. Three days ago, this moment was the only thing on my mind. She's right… this year has taught us a lot.

The door opens, and Becky crosses her arms as she surveys me. "So you're back."

It's not a question. She's dressed in mom jeans and a green sweater. Her straight, white-blonde hair is smoothed into a high ponytail, and even though it's a young look, that severity in her eyes makes her look so cold. I can't help wondering… Did I ever love her? I loved Jesse from the moment I saw him, purple and red and screaming his head off.

But her?

"I'm here to see my father." My voice is flat.

"He's not seeing people right now. He's working on the books."

"He'll see me." I've lost too much getting to this point to walk away.

Her hip cocks to the side, and her eyebrow arches. "He said he didn't want to be disturbed."

Consequences be damned, I push past her into the foyer. We grew up in this house, but it was never decorated like this. It looks like something out of one of those British movies. The ones with those old ladies in frilly dresses with pinched up faces squawking about tea time.

"Dad?" I shout, looking up the polished-oak staircase. "Dad?"

"Stop shouting, John."

My eyebrows rise, but I don't care to ask since when she calls me *John*. I don't have time. "Tell me where he is."

"I already told you—"

"It's okay, Rebecca." My dad's polished voice interrupts. "The prodigal returns. Unexpected, but isn't everything these days?"

He looks strangely younger than he did two years ago. His

hair seems less gray, and his skin a bit tighter. He's always been fit, even when we were young. Today he's dressed in a navy Adidas track suit, and he holds out his arms like I'm fucking going to hug him.

Anger blazes to life in my chest. "Cut the crap. You know why I'm here."

Lifting his chin, he laughs, but it's not merry. It's controlled laughter.

"My boy. Always the straight-shooter." He lowers his gaze on mine. "And why are you here, John?"

When I was a kid, I remember grown men being intimidated by my dad's leveled gaze.

I'm not intimidated. "Tell me why you sent me to San Francisco." Energy rises in my chest with every word. "Tell me why you had me meet a supplier we'd never worked with. Why I had to go alone. Was it all for *her*?"

His eyes soften, and he dares to act like I'm amusing him. "Come. Let's talk in the study."

Holding out a hand, he motions towards the short hall leading under the stairs. I follow him into a wood-paneled room lined with bookcases filled with all sorts of books—fiction, nonfiction, hard- and soft-bound. It smells like a library. I would sit in here to do my homework when Mom was still alive. Otherwise, Scout and I were relegated to less fragile parts of the house.

Going around a green leather wingback, he takes a seat behind the desk. I sit in a matching chair across from him.

"You insisted I go alone." I repeat, ready for his confession. I've had almost two years to think about all the ways he set me up, then never showed up to defend me.

"Let me get this straight." He rocks back, and his voice drips with sarcasm. "You came all this way to make what you did my problem?"

"I came to make you confess. I spent eighteen months locked

in a cell, not knowing what might happen from day to day, not able to see my son ..." I have to stop there.

If I think of Jesse, I'll lose control.

Focus.

"Did you do it all for her?"

If he says yes... *What a waste.*

I'm a completely different guy than I was when I left here that morning, and I know for sure I'm not in love with the woman standing in the foyer. I wonder if I ever was.

"I didn't do it for Rebecca." Leaning forward he levels his gaze on mine. "I didn't like Clyde. He was twitchy and suspicious, and I didn't trust him. I figured if anyone could handle him, it was you."

"So you knew." It's not a question. It's an answer. "You set me up."

"I did not set you up." His voice rises. "I sent you to see if the guy was legit."

"But you didn't tell me. You were hoping I wouldn't come back."

His eyes cut to the desk, and he doesn't dispute me.

Rage spikes in my veins. "When did you start sleeping with her?"

Blue eyes, same as mine cut through me. "Yes, I wanted to fuck her." It's a lusty rasp. "Rebecca always made my dick hard in that short little cheerleader skirt, flirting with her eyes at me."

My throat tightens. "You're sick."

"Come back in a few years, and we'll talk." His eyes narrow. "I was forty-two when you were a senior. Your mother had been dead ten years."

"You didn't answer my question."

"I never touched her before your divorce." He taps the mahogany with his middle finger. "That's the truth, John."

Shifting in my chair, I decide to let that part go. "If it wasn't a setup, why didn't you help me? You let them convict me when you knew I was innocent."

"I didn't know anything. First your brother goes to California and becomes a porn star, then you head out there and start dealing drugs. I couldn't pollute the brand any further with your behavior."

Slamming my palm on his desk, I stand and lean closer. "You knew I wasn't dealing drugs." My voice is low. "You knew what happened."

If he's intimidated, it only lasts a second. He's on his feet just as fast. "I'll tell you what I knew. I knew you got an offer to play with the Chiefs, and you turned it down. I knew you had the chance I never got and you walked away from it for what? To work at a gym?"

I'm momentarily thrown. "What the fuck are you talking about? Becky was pregnant. I didn't want to play for the NFL. I wanted to be a father. I wanted to be here with my family."

"Everybody needs money. And with a wife like Becky, you needed a lot of it."

It's like the rug is jerked out from under me. I take a beat to catch my breath. "Are you honestly standing there saying... You really fucking believed I was dealing drugs for money?"

"A lot of guys in this business do it."

"So you turned your back on me just like you did Scout, who for the record is not a porn star. He's a dumbass, but he's not a porn star."

"Yes." He doesn't even hesitate to admit it.

Standing here across from him, I remember how I thought I'd react in this moment. I thought I'd grab him by the neck and shake him. I imagined yelling in his face what a son of a bitch he is. I planned to rail at him for the time he stole from me with my son, the memories I lost.

And that was before I knew he'd married my ex-wife.

I never expected this.

Shaking my head, I step over to the bookcase where a framed photo sits of Scout and me holding a football, so young and innocent. It's all he ever cared about. "We're your sons, and you fucking don't know us at all."

Turning back, I study *my father*. He's my height, fit and muscular, and he looks like a very small man. Fifty-three and dressed in a track suit, married to a shrew who's probably only interested in his money.

I pity him.

"If I was wrong, I apologize."

"You were wrong."

"Well…" He nods, and something like regret crosses his face. "I apologize."

"You're going to do more than that." Returning to the chair, I lean forward. "You're going to help me clear my name. You're going to give me my son full-time, and it's not going to be a discussion. It's going to happen."

His eyes remain on the desk in front of him. "I have no interest in starting over as a dad at my age."

I go to the door and stop. He's still sitting there looking defeated. I'm done with him. "You're not the man I thought you were."

Becky is waiting when I return to the foyer. I'm not interested in talking to her either, but when our eyes meet, her thin lips press together.

Her chin lifts, and she shakes her ponytail back. "John?"

I pause, curious about what the fuck she might have to say to me.

"I never meant to hurt you." Her fingers twist, and she almost seems nervous. Almost. "We married too young. Your dad was here. I was lonely."

Is this how she's rewriting history? "I was always here. If you were lonely, that's on you."

"You were here, but you were playing with Jesse or going to your grandmother's or doing things with Scout. You weren't here with me. I was alone. Bill was the only person who found me interesting."

After what he just told me, I don't want to think about why my father found her interesting.

Relaxing my stance, I don't want to fight. I just want her to go away. "Look, you can let yourself off the hook. I'm not hurt. I only want my son."

She has the nerve to look concerned. "What does that mean?"

"It means, he's not staying with Alice. He's moving in with me."

"And I don't get a say? He's my son, too, John."

"Are you pretending to care?"

"I'm not a monster," she sniffs. "I don't mind if he lives with you full-time, but I like visiting him every week."

"I have no problem with you visiting him."

"You're not going back to California?"

Her question makes me hesitate, wondering how much she knows or how much she's been able to put together. "I'm going back tonight."

"It's out of the question. You're not taking my son to California." Her eyes flash, and she steps forward. "Are you even supposed to be here?"

"No, but I'm working on it."

She hesitates, realizing she has an advantage. "What would happen if I picked up this phone and called the parole board right now?"

Anger flares in my chest, and I step forward, looking down my nose at her. "If you do that, you'd better pray they put me away for life."

Her defiance holds a moment before she backs down, scampering from the room. "I'm going to speak to your father about this."

"She's not calling anyone." My father's voice fills the room.

Becky makes a surprised noise and stops. I'm momentarily

taken aback, but I can only hope what I said put a crack in the stone where his heart should be. "Thanks."

Becky pipes up from beside him. "Don't ever threaten my family again, John Roth."

I'm annoyed at her using my given name like she's my mother, but my father puts his hand over hers. "Do what you need to do, son."

Glancing at the clock, I'm out of time. "I'll be in touch."

"I'VE ADDED YOUR NAME TO THE PRAYER CHAIN, JOHN." GA'S HAND IS IN the crook of my arm as we walk slowly towards airport security. I'm still amazed I got a one-way ticket for less than a hundred dollars. "We've faced worse orgies than this, and the Lord answers prayer."

"*Ogres*, Gran." Scout's voice is low, and he glances over his shoulder around the small space. "The word is *ogres*."

She frowns at him. "That's what I said. We've prayed against worse orgies than the California judicial system. God will provide."

My brother gives up trying to correct her. "What orgies have you prayed against worse than this?"

"Don't be rude, Bradley," GA scolds. "Regina's cousin Gwen had a spot on her lung last year, and Regina put her on the prayer chain. When Gwen went for her follow-up appointment, the doctors couldn't believe it. The spot was gone."

Scout makes a skeptical face.

"Don't you question the power of prayer, Bradley Scout!"

He throws up his hands. "I'm not questioning. Y'all pray."

Their banter does little to ease the ache in my chest.

Jesse is on my hip. His arms are around my neck, and his head hasn't left my shoulder. I've waited as long as I could to go through security. Now I have to leave.

"But you just got home." His little-boy voice is at my ear.

Hugging him tighter, I rub his back. "I know. I wish I could stay."

"Last time you were gone a long, long time."

"This won't be like last time."

"Come to me now, Jesse." GA puts her hands on his waist, but his arms tighten around my neck.

"I don't want you to go."

Bending my knees, I set him on his feet, holding him in front of me so we can make eye contact. "I have to fix something. They made a mistake last time. It's why I was gone so long. Now I've got to fix it so we never have to worry about it again."

"I can help!" His eyes light. "Mr. Perkins says I'm a good helper. I'll go with you."

My throat aches, and my stomach is in knots. "I wish you could, little man. You've got school."

A crystal tear appears on his bottom lash. "Don't go, Dad."

Closing my eyes, I hug him. I knew this would be hard, but our last separation is still so heavy, it's almost unbearable.

Thickness is in my throat, and I clear it away. "Can you be brave for me?"

"I don't know."

I cup the back of his head, kissing him right on top. "Uncle Scout's going to stay with you until I come back. Or until you can come to me. Does that sound good?"

"Yeah, buddy." My brother squats beside me. "It's going to be great. We'll play football. I'll show you how to skateboard. How does that sound?"

Jesse's eyes are red-rimmed and watery, and he looks at me with so much trust. "You'll be back soon?"

Nodding, I blink away the mist in my eyes. "Soon."

"You won't even notice he's gone." Scout gives him that grin everybody loves.

"I'll notice."

Reaching out, I pull him close for one last hug, closing my eyes so I can memorize the feel of his sturdy, little body, so different from last time. "I love you, Jesse."

His arms tighten around me once more. "I love you, Dad."

I hold him until I can't anymore, then I reluctantly let him go, standing to hug my grandmother. "Thanks for this. For everything."

"Don't you worry, John Roth. Everything's going to be fine. It's going to be better than fine. You'll see."

"I'll take care of him." Scout hugs me roughly. "Get back here as soon as you can."

I don't attempt to speak. I hold my son's hand one last time before turning to head to the gate.

CHAPTER
Nineteen

Hope

"**H**E JUST LET YOU GO?" YARNELL SMOOTHS MY HAIR BACK FROM my face.

My head is in my bestie's lap, where I'm camped out on her sofa. "More like he didn't try to stop me."

Or take me with him.

Tears were in my eyes as I pulled away from Fireside, leaving JR standing there, his lips a warm memory on my fingertips.

Tears streamed down my face as I drove as hard as I could to Half Moon Bay, stopping only for gas and to crash at motels along the way. I was through Atlanta when I found an envelope with five hundred dollars in cash tucked inside my coat and a note from JR. *Pay me back when you can.*

It made me start crying all over again.

I cried the whole way home. I wasn't sobbing, but the tears wouldn't stop streaming from my eyes. I couldn't stop seeing his face when he looked at me and asked me how long I'd wait.

Now I'm utterly exhausted. "He was so cryptic. He didn't tell me anything, only that he wouldn't lie to me."

She exhales deeply. "What are you going to do?"

I've thought about that question over the past three days. "Check on Dad. Try to get a job. Get on with my life."

Inhale, exhale.

Take one step, then the next.

Keep walking until the pain is a ghost in the rearview mirror.

"We're short-staffed at the Lodge. I could ask if they'd let you on in housekeeping. It's not the greatest job, but the place is practically empty."

"Yars!" Sitting up fast, I dive into a hug. "You're the best friend I've ever had! Could you?"

"I'm your very best friend, and of course I can. It's like the Wild West these days, anything goes. I'll vouch for you."

Sitting beside her, I lean my head on her shoulder. "Do you think it's because of my mom?"

"What?" She picks up the remote and starts cycling through Netflix.

"The reason I can't seem to hold onto a guy?"

Slapping the remote beside her on the couch, she shifts to face me. "Nothing is wrong with you, Hope Eternal Hill. You dated a self-righteous zealot—"

"Scout said Wade was probably gay."

Yarnell tilts her head to the side. "That actually makes sense. His parents were super religious and controlling, and he was doing his best to be exactly like them."

"He was cute, though."

Shaking her head, her stern tone returns. "You dated a self-righteous zealot who was possibly closeted, and now you've spent a week with an ex-con. How does any of that add up to something is wrong with you?"

I think about what she's saying. "So the problem is my

picker? JR is so hot, though. You should see him. Rough, angry, and that bod…"

I can't help a shiver, remembering his lined torso, the tattoo on his chest. *This much is true…* He has the hottest body, and he has such a good heart behind that grumpy exterior.

"He's good, Yars. I know he is."

"Of course, you do!" Placing her hands on my arms, she gives me a little shake. "You're a believer. You only see the best in people. It makes you the best kind of person, but it also makes you susceptible to the wrong kind of guy. That is not a flaw. You have to be more careful. Don't let your hormones get the best of you."

She scoots around again, putting her back against the sofa and retrieving the remote. I return to cuddle at her side, watching a collection of aspiring British bakers doing their best to roll cake.

Memories of JR and Jesse flood my mind, the way they hugged each other like they were making up for all those lost days. Not everybody gets a dad who'll do anything for them, one who is so in love with you, he'll do whatever it takes to make sure you're happy. I have one. JR is one.

A hot tear hits my cheek, and I swallow the thickness in my throat. "He isn't the wrong kind of guy."

"How do you know?" Her voice is flat, disbelieving.

"I know."

"I know you're going to work with me in the morning, so get some sleep. Sonny will hire you on the spot if I tell him to."

"Because you're a boss bitch."

"Yes, I am." She leans down to give me a hug, and I hug her tight.

"Thanks, bitch."

"Now let that shit go and don't make me kick your ass."

Warmth comforts the ache in my chest. "I won't."

The Half Moon Bay Lodge is like that resort in *Dirty Dancing*. The main hotel is in the center of the property with twenty-four rooms spreading out in two stories on each side. Then smaller cottages branch out into the hills.

Housekeeping is a team of six—one laundry assistant, one supervisor, who doesn't seem to do much besides eat chips and watch TikTok, and the rest of us who clean the rooms.

Two weeks later, and I still kind of suck at this job. It's not that I don't clean well, it's more I take a really long time… I just don't care.

Standing in the middle of the narrow, two-bedroom suite, I watch Rubí Perez doing her best to get out of the poverty of her university life on Netflix. It's in Spanish, so I miss a lot of the story when I look away from the subtitles. Still, everyone is so beautiful and earnest.

Lifting my phone, I touch the number for Dad.

"Hey, sunshine!" His voice always helps me forget my worries.

"Hey, Dad! When am I ever going to see you again? I've forgotten what you look like."

Walking around the brown and gold room, I pull the thick white sheets off the mattresses. I always hated making beds. How is it possible I've landed a job where I do something I hate more than anything?

I should be in charge of laundry. I could sit and watch *Rubí* and switch loads in and out for days.

"My hair's a little longer these days, but isn't everybody's?" My dad's jovial voice is so good to hear.

"Longer?" My dad is sort of a mix of Sam Elliot and Keith Carridine, and I imagine him as *Road House* meets *Deadwood*.

Shaking away the distraction, I press on. "When can you come home?"

"Well, I don't know," he hedges. "I thought you were staying with Yarnell until things got back to normal.

"I am, but I miss you, Dad." Sitting on the foot of the king-sized bed, I switch the show to *Schitt's Creek*, so I don't have to read.

"I miss you too, sunshine…"

I feel like he's not telling me something. "How are your knees?"

"A lot better. I've started taking a yoga class, and you wouldn't believe the benefits. It improves respiration, which right now is major, and it relieves anxiety…"

My eyes narrow. "Dad, you're a Buddhist. You already beat anxiety."

"I don't know if I'd go that far. I mean, with all the decreased social interactions. Do you know how important physical touch is to mental wellness?"

Oh, trust me. I know. I struggle with the memories of JR's hands on my breasts, his lips between my thighs. *Focus, Hope.*

"So you're able to do yoga with bad knees?"

"Well, I can't do all the poses. I'm mostly doing it for the meditation. It's very calming."

"You're always very calm." It would be impossible for me to be more suspicious.

"Now I'm even more so. The instructor is very good…"

Bingo.

"Dad? Are you sleeping with your yoga instructor?"

I won't lie. A week ago, I might have been weirded out by this, but after all we went through on the road, learning about JR's dad, and finding Grandma Alice's vibrator, I'm pretty sure there's nothing that would surprise me now.

"Hope Hill, I'm not having this conversation with you."

"Are you?" I'm not convinced.

"Of course not. She's probably ten years younger than me."

"You're only fifty-five dad. It's okay if you are."

"I've got to go. They're ringing the bell for small group time."

He's trying to get rid of me. I'm pretty sure Shady Rest isn't that worried about whether or not their temporary residents show up for group.

"I love you, Dad."

"I love you, too, daughter."

We disconnect, and I study my phone. My mind drifts to JR. I remember waking up in the back of Metallicar, and sitting up to see the angriest, sexiest man alive driving us south to Los Angeles.

And immediately barfing out the window.

He almost crashed. Then he almost left me on the side of the road.

Walking away from the unmade bed, I step into the bathroom, where an array of expensive-looking cosmetics is spread out on the counter. They're beautifully packaged in glass jars with sparkling accents. I pick up a jade green bottle with a pink lid, turning it in my hand. It says it's some kind of plumping acid.

Plumping. I stick out my tongue and put it down.

We never bought cosmetics when I was a child in the commune, but one of the moms made homemade soaps and lotions to sell. She'd buy raw shea butter from the drugstore and mix it with coconut and essential oils.

She made a lotion she called Egyptian Spice that smelled like sandalwood and coconut and exotic flowers. I loved it so much, I still order it from her today.

A bright golden-yellow plastic bottle with *Brazilian Crush* on the label looks fun and summery. I slip off my mask and pump it into the air. It smells like salted caramel and pistachio and the beach. Closing my eyes, I lift it over my head and spray it again, stepping through the falling mist so it can cover my body.

After so long being stuck inside in the cold, then being so close to the warm summer beaches of South Carolina, my one regret is not taking a detour and crying my heart out at Myrtle Beach or the Outer Banks or somewhere soothing like that.

Of course, I have no idea where I would've stayed in any of those places. I also didn't know I had so much cash tucked into my coat. *JR, what are you doing to me?*

Exhaling a sigh, I stand in front of the mirror in my light blue housekeeping uniform. How in the world does he expect me to pay him back? I don't even know where he is right now. My eyes close, and I see the muscle moving in his square jaw, the emotion in his eyes.

He didn't want to say goodbye, I have to believe he didn't.

Even when he did.

If there's any chance…

I'll wait for that chance.

I'm struggling with my emotions when a shrill voice yells, "What the hell are you doing?"

Jumping around, I see an older woman with a wide stripe of gray down the center of her jet-black hair scowling at me.

"I was just—" My heart is beating out of my chest.

The television is blasting *Schitt's Creek*, the bed is unmade, and I'm standing in the woman's bathroom holding her body spray, mask off…

I am so fired right now. "I'm sorry!"

"Are you stealing my cosmetics?" Her voice is loud and slightly hysterical.

"No!" I quickly hook my mask over my ear again, moving towards the door with my back to the wall. "I'm sorry. I was just scenting—"

"I'm calling the manager! You were stealing, and I intend to press charges!"

She reaches for my arm, but I spin out the door before she can catch me. We're in the hotel, so I don't have a lot of options. I dash down the hall with her standing outside her door still yelling.

"Stop, thief! Manager! Someone call the manager!"

It won't be hard for them to figure out it was me. There's only six of us for God's sake. Running from door to door, I turn the knobs, searching for somewhere to hide, until one of them opens, and I fall inside.

The room is dark, but I don't go any farther than the entrance. I hold a crack in the door as hotel security runs past, headed in the direction I came.

Ten heavy breaths later, or ten seconds… twenty? It's quiet. My heart is halfway back to normal, and I decide it's safe to creep out. My plan is to jump in Metallicar and drive all the way back to our beach shack in San Francisco.

I'll call Yars and explain it was all a misunderstanding—I'll be damned if I go to jail over Brazilian body spray.

"Hold it right there." A sharp male voice from behind makes me squeal and spin around. "Who are you, and why are you in my room?"

A tall man in a tan suit stands over me. I can tell he's rich because his suit is so smooth, it almost has a sheen, and unlike everybody else these days, his hair is neatly trimmed. He's very handsome, and very scowley.

"I'm so sorry, sir." Ducking my chin, I actually do a little bow. *Why am I bowing?* "I didn't mean to disturb you. I'm with housekeeping… I—"

"What is that you're holding?" His eyes are on the bright yellow-gold plastic bottle in my hand.

I didn't even realize I still had it. I guess I did steal her toiletries.

Lifting it slowly, I can't resist. I press the top, sending a clear arc of spray fanning into the room. Even masked, I remember the lovely scent.

"Hm…" He nods, studying my name tag. "That's nice, Hope. Hope what?"

"Hill, sir."

His chin lifts, and he turns, as if contemplating what to do with me. "Why are you bursting into my room, Hope Hill?"

"Well, I was… I was just…" *Busted watching Netflix and sampling the lady in Room 218's toiletries—one of which I stole.*

"You're not a professional maid, are you." It's not a question.

"No, sir."

"What is your profession?"

I'm not sure why I feel like I'm on trial before this man, but I do. He has dark hair and piercing green eyes, and he doesn't smile.

Still, unlike JR Dunne, this man's sternitude is more like his usual manner, rather than something thrust upon him by life and a double-crossing, wife-stealing father.

Clearing my throat, I answer. "I'm a restaurateur." Blinking down, I figure I should correct that. "Actually, I saved all my money, drew up a business plan, found investors, rented a prime location in the Embarcadero, hired a publicist, and had a huge grand opening for my first, dream restaurant… on March 13."

He goes to the brown leather chair positioned in front of the window and takes a seat. "Not so lucky Friday the 13th." He's not really being mean. I've thought the same thing myself. "And?"

"And I lost it all." It's still a hot poker jabbed in my chest when I say it.

"I'm sorry."

Oddly, he actually seems to mean it.

"What's your name, sir?"

"Stephen Hastings." He crosses an ankle over his knee. "Tell me more about this restaurant, Hope Hill. What type of food did you serve?"

"Pancakes." His eyebrow arches, but I quickly describe my quirky, fun, Pancake Paradise, where parents and kids of all ages could come together and have quality time, learn to cook, play, celebrate milestones, or simply pass the time.

Bittersweet warmth fills my chest as I tell him about it,

remembering how excited I'd been, how I imagined being the Barefoot Contessa of the San Francisco waterfront, welcoming regular customers and new ones with weekly specials and samples of our latest pancake creations.

I had such big dreams, and they were all coming true.

This was going to be my year…

Until it wasn't.

He watches me closely. "Would you say it was a children's restaurant?"

"Not at all!" My voice is high. "Of course, we were kid-friendly—very kid-friendly—but we also had savory options, omelets and sandwiches. We offered mimosas and other cocktails, wine and beer. Pancake Paradise was going to be a neighborhood hangout."

"If you were lucky. Restaurants have obscene failure rates—something like 75 percent or more fail in the first two years."

"I wouldn't have failed." I'm not letting him cloud my dream.

"You said you lost everything?"

"I still have a few things." I trace my fingers along the edge of the mahogany credenza. "I have the lease on the space for two more weeks. And nobody wanted industrial-sized bags of flour and cinnamon. Nobody could use them."

He leans forward, resting his forearms on his thighs and clasping his hands. "I think the location was a poor choice."

"It was an excellent choice. Our research showed—"

"I think your idea has promise." That shuts me up. "I think it would be better suited to a boutique location, like Monterey. Somewhere with a large population of wealthy young professionals with young families. A community where people hold gatherings, where you could develop regulars. San Francisco is too transient for what you have in mind."

"Monterey is pretty far—"

"It's an hour and a half."

Crossing my arms, I face him. "What difference does it make to you?"

He shifts in the chair, flicking his blazer. "I don't say this often, but I have a very large bank account."

"Everyone who stays here does."

"Mine is bigger than theirs." It doesn't even seem like he's bragging, more just stating a fact. "I invest in companies, mostly military tech and healthcare initiatives. I'm here for that very reason, but the fellow I met with this morning didn't have his numbers in order. I had to say no."

Tilting my head to the side, I study him. "You want to invest in my restaurant?"

"Maybe." He stands and reaches into his coat, taking out a slim phone. "Restaurants are a horrible risk. The timing couldn't be worse. Still, I'm a bit of a gambler, and I have the capital. I like your passion and your drive. Do you have a phone?"

"Of course." Reaching into my skirt pocket, I take out my iPhone.

"If you're willing, unlock it, and I'll give you my secretary's number."

My heart jumps, and I quickly unlock my phone and hand it to him. "You want to be my partner?"

"We would *not* be partners." His tone is firm as he quickly types on my phone. "I would be an investor only. I'd loan you the capital to reopen, then you'd pay me back with interest."

I know how investors work. I also know the current business climate. "How long would you be willing to wait?"

"I'll give you until things are back on track." He escorts me to the door. "If it's still something you want to do, update your business plan, incorporate my recommendations regarding location, and send me your proposal when you're ready. I'll share it with my business partner, Remington Key, and he and I will discuss it. We usually trust each other's instincts."

My heart is beating so hard now. He's talking about my restaurant like it could actually happen. This man could make it happen. I think about my song. *I believe in angels.*

Picking up the small bottle of body spray, I decide it must be lucky.

Slipping it in my pocket, I pause at the door. "Why are you doing this? You don't even know me."

"I can tell good people when I meet them." His brow furrows like he's sorting a riddle. "We'll get through this time, but we can't lose faith in each other."

"I wasn't sure people still had faith."

"Of course, they do." Placing his hand on my upper arm, he gives it a squeeze. "I think you've got what it takes, Hope Hill. Don't let me down."

My brow furrows, and I smile carefully. "I don't want to let you down."

That makes him smile, and pride warms my chest.

"I'll look forward to hearing from you."

CHAPTER
Twenty

JR

"**P**ISS TEST." A YOUNG WOMAN IN A NAVY UNIFORM AND BLACK mask with a name tag reading *Blank* claps a plastic cup in front of me. She has short brown hair and brown eyes, which never meet mine. "Place it in the window. Come back here when you're done."

Taking the small cup, I go to the bathroom and fill it, following her instructions. It has a label bearing my name on it and a lid. Washing my hands, I swallow the fresh anger at being in this system—peeing in a cup, being forced to ask permission to go home to visit my son.

I sit in the metal chair across from Deputy Blank and study her thin face, thin wire-framed glasses. Her uniform seems designed to make her appear bulkier. A pistol is on her hip, and she looks like she just graduated from high school.

"Have you applied for work or secured full-time employment?" She reads the sheet on the clipboard like a drill sergeant.

"No." My eyes are focused on her hands, bare, short fingernails.

She hesitates a moment. "Did you try?"

Blinking up at her, I sit straighter. "There aren't a lot of options right now."

Also, I'm a felon.

Her jaw moves as she chews her gum. "I'll give you that." Her eyes return to the clipboard briefly. "Dunne."

I shift in my chair. "I was wondering, Deputy Blank, I have a son in South Carolina. What do I need to do to be able to see him?"

She blinks up at me, and my request seems to piss her off. "You might have thought of him before you started dealing drugs."

Tightening my lips, I swallow the burn. "I don't deal drugs. I was set up."

Her eyebrows quirk as she returns to the list. "Not what the judge said."

"Maybe not, but it's the truth."

"Sure it is." She's not interested in my story, so I don't press it.

"Anyway, what do I need to do to be able to see him again? I'd really like to get permission to relocate, or—"

"Relocate?" The corners of her eyes crinkle, but it's more of a wince than a smile. "What do you think this is? Summer camp? You don't go home. Your butt's staying right here in San Francisco where it belongs." She mutters under her breath. "It belongs in jail, but that's not up to me."

My throat is tight. I want to argue. I want to snap back *I didn't fucking do it.*

I don't.

I swallow those feelings and force a smile. "I'm sorry. I just miss my son."

"How about you answer my questions, and we'll take it one week at a time."

One week at a time.

I promised Jesse I'd be home soon.

I said *soon*.

Walking from the precinct to the studio apartment I'm renting on Divisadero Street, I think I should have punched my dad when I had the chance. I called one of those rocket lawyers, and she said the only way to get a conviction overturned or "set aside," is to find new evidence—DNA or some kind of written or verbal confession.

I almost laughed in her ear. Then I almost threw the phone across the room. How the fuck am I supposed to get something like that? For all I know Clyde Shaw is long gone by now.

For all I know...

Standing in the street, looking up at the ancient, second-floor apartment, I decide I've got nothing to lose and nothing but time.

I dig a metro card out of my pocket and hop on the bus, taking it all the way out to Golden Gate Park. It's late afternoon, so I'm not expecting much. Still, I want to retrace my steps.

Fog clings to the mountains and dark-green ivy climbs all over everything. It's cold and foggy all the time. I never liked San Francisco. I only came because my dad was diving deep into supplements as a new source of income.

He claimed this *shilajit* would put us on the cutting edge of adaptogens. Supposedly the goop gave you more energy, improved sex drive, better memory and focus. It all sounded too good to be true to me. *Snake oil.*

Still, Clyde Shaw was a top distributor of the resin, which he claimed was sourced directly from small farmers in the Himalayas and thoroughly tested for heavy metals and pollutants. He claimed to be a holistic guru-type. I thought he was a creep. Clearly, I underestimated him.

The bus stops, and I trot down the steps, nearly colliding with a girl with long, pale dreadlocks. She has a bandanna over her face and ratty clothes, and she carries a longboard. I watch as she drops it and skates down the promenade without a word.

This is the weird part of town, where everybody smells like pot and dresses like they're homeless. I remember wondering what the hell I was doing meeting a supplier here.

Rainbow Falls is right in the middle of the park. Clyde said it was part of his daily meditation ritual. He really sold the whole package.

I left my rental car parked on the street while he told me about the benefits of controlled breathing, the way you could slow your heart rate by breathing in for five seconds then breathing out for six.

Standing in front of the giant stone cross, I can't believe I didn't see through that guy. Old anger starts to heat my chest, but as I look up at the cross, an idea forms in my mind…

Clyde Shaw counted on me trusting whatever he said. When I got busted, he vanished like a ghost after Halloween. At the same time, I have no reason to believe he's not still in the city.

He was well connected. Shit, the day we met, two burnouts buzzed by and bought pot from him. Why would he leave? Or if he did leave, why not come back when the heat wore off?

My heart beats faster as the plan unfolds. I've just got to shake the bushes and let the bugs crawl out.

The prospect of finding that asshole and beating a confession out of him makes me smile. Closing my eyes, I know what I've got to do. I won't let my son down. I will be home soon, and once I'm clear, I'll find my girl.

For a week, I've been coming to the stone cross behind Rainbow Falls. I didn't know much about Golden Gate Park before this, but it's a lot like Central Park in New York City, long and rectangular, with different attractions scattered throughout.

I usually pack a lunch and read a book or listen to music while I sit under the trees and wait. I don't know what I expect to find, but I'm holding onto hope.

Hope.

I miss her. I miss her cute little smile. I miss the way her nose wrinkles when she's teasing or doesn't like something I said or Scout said. I miss the way she used to sneak glances at me when we were driving, when I was so pissed, I could barely unclench my jaw. I miss her soft skin, and the feel of her body beneath mine. I miss her lips, her scent of flowers and coconut, like the beach in summertime.

I'm kicking myself for not getting her phone number. I was so fucking distracted. How the hell am I going to find her?

I've gone to that old beach shack where I picked up the car a few times, but it's completely deserted. I tried calling Car Heaven, but they wouldn't give me any information, citing privacy reasons.

She said her dad was in a nursing home, and her friend with the unusual first name is... somewhere. *Dammit.*

Where are you, Hope?

Frustrated, I lean back against a tree, looking up at the massive falls. Water spills over smooth, gray boulders, and a path with a wooden bridge is about halfway to the top. Hikers and kids walk across it, occasionally stopping to take pictures.

The place smells like damp leaves, metallic water, and skunk weed. Strange, trumpet-shaped flowers hang from the trees like upside-down vases. They're bright yellow with red-orange petals curled back. They look like something from another planet, or maybe I've got a contact high from sitting here so long.

Scrubbing my fingers against my forehead, I do my best to remember Clyde and the two burnouts. When we met, he was dressed like anybody else you'd see in this park, but instead of a laid-back vibe, he was focused, watching. At the time I chalked it up to the supplement he was hawking, but now I realize he was on guard for any sign of a setup.

I was the one being set up.

Another meeting with my asshole parole officer, another week of sitting in the park, and I'm ready to quit.

I have no idea what makes me think I'll find this guy. I watch the water slam against the bottom of the falls, and I feel like one of those rocks. Defeat is heavy on my shoulders and pot is in the air.

I'm ready to walk home when a skinny guy in loose jeans and a poncho strolls up and takes a seat. His dark dreads are tied in a thick bundle at the back of his neck, and a scarf is tied over his mouth and nose. He sits like a Buddha at the base of the cross.

A long strand of jet-black beads is around his neck, and a memory hits me. Clyde wore a similar strand the day we met. I thought they were onyx. He laughed and said no way. They were "magical."

Magically, I did not roll my eyes.

This guy isn't familiar, but he's as close as I'm going to get.

I have to go for it.

Taking a slow breath, I think about Scout. I relax my shoulders and do my best to channel his carefree, laid-back style of talk. "Hey, Namaste, man."

I feel like an idiot.

Bloodshot, eyes blink open to meet mine, and he's clearly high. "Peace and love."

Keeping a safe distance, I do my best to sit in a similar style as him, wondering what these guys say to each other. I don't know a lot about hippie-speak, but I read a book by Stephen Hawking about the history of the universe.

"The world is turning at a thousand miles per hour." I look towards the falls. "We're just along for the ride."

He nods. "Like sands through the hourglass."

"Turtles all the way down."

His eyes widen. "You're into Hinduism?"

"Hawking."

"Good stuff. Happiness is a direction, not a place."

I don't think Stephen Hawking said that, and I don't care. I've got to find Clyde. "I was looking for a friend. Maybe you know him?"

"Maybe." He closes his eyes and starts to *Om*.

I put my hands on my knees and wait. I don't want to rush him.

Ironically, a turtle crawls to the edge of the small lagoon and stretches his head out of the water. I picture a flat earth balanced on the top of his shell and him standing on the back of another turtle and another below that... It's the universe people once believed.

Stoner Dude's lips have stopped moving, and now he's deep breathing, in and out. My stomach is tense, and I'm praying I don't blow my cover.

He exhales loudly and rises to his feet. "Just got my word. I was on another plane, watching the thoughts roll by like pebbles in the stream."

I stand with him. *This is it.* "So Clyde told me to drop by next time I was in town."

A smile breaks across his face. "You know Clyde, man? I just saw him over at Hidden Hemp."

You don't say? "Is he in the same place? Frederick and Clayton?"

"No way, man, he left there two years ago. He's north of Buena Vista now—over the coffee house."

Two years ago, as in right after my shit went down. "Thanks..."

"Arlo." He holds up his hand, palm facing me. "It is not how much we have, but how much we enjoy."

"See you around, Arlo."

"Stay beautiful, Turtle-man."

He wanders off in the direction of the ocean, and as soon as he's out of sight, I take off jogging back towards the bus stop.

Buena Vista is a smallish park east of here. I have no idea which coffee house he's talking about, but I'm pumped. I'm ready to get justice.

CHAPTER
Twenty-One

Hope

"**Y**OU WERE IN HER ROOM, MASK OFF, SAMPLING HER COSMETICS…"
Yarnell stalks around the living room like she's so astounded.

"I wasn't sampling her cosmetics!" I'm on the couch, hiding under a blanket, where I've been since I fled the hotel. "My mask was off because I was scenting her colognes."

"Watching Netflix, going through her stuff, not making the beds…"

"She really overreacted." I recall the scary woman with the Cruella de Vil hair screaming like I had a gun on her. "People are so on edge right now."

"You stole her body spray!"

"I didn't mean to steal it! She kept calling me a thief and yelling for security. I panicked." Pulling the blanket tighter around me, I sink lower on the couch. "She was like a scary witch."

"That scary witch is married to one of the richest real estate developers in California."

"Then I don't know what her problem is. That body spray is only twenty dollars."

I looked it up, thinking I'd mail her the money.

"That's not the point, and you know it." Yars shakes her head. "You're lucky Sonny likes me as much as he does. He's not going to dock your pay. He said you can come back to work after she checks out tomorrow."

"I don't know, Yars." My nose wrinkles. "I don't think I'm cut out for that job."

I think about having to make beds and clean toilets and vacuum.

The vacuuming part I didn't mind, actually. It was sort of gratifying to watch the little bits of dirt or paper or whatever being sucked up by the machine, leaving the dark floors shiny and clean. It took my mind off thinking about JR all the time.

"Not cut out for the job," Yarnell huffs. "The point is it's a *job*. You need a job, remember?"

"I *need* to update my business plan and salvage what I can from the restaurant before my lease expires."

"Then you ran into Mr. Hastings's room." She goes to the kitchen and pours a glass of wine. "You're really lucky he didn't complain. He's the richest venture capitalist in Manhattan."

"That's what he said." Pressing my lips together, I remember how arrogant he was, like whatever he decided was the law. "He was like a king."

"He's about as close as you can get in this country."

"He said he might help me." Pulling the body spray out of my pocket, I give it a pump, watching it rain over my legs. "I think this stuff is my lucky charm. If I hadn't sprayed it at him, he might not have started asking questions."

"You sprayed Brazilian Crush at Stephen Hastings?" She takes another, bigger chug of wine then drops to the couch beside me. "I need to lie down."

"What I really think is it was cosmic karma." I push the blanket back and get on my knees beside her. "All this bad stuff happened right as my dream was coming true. That weights the scale too far to one side. It had to be corrected!"

"You've been listening to your dad too much."

"I need to check on Dad." Walking to where I left my small bag of clothes, I drop the body spray inside. "I'm going to head back tonight. Please tell Sonny I'm so sorry for everything."

"What will you do?"

"The only thing I can do." I shrug. "Chase down my second chance."

DRIVING BACK TO THE BEACH HOUSE, ANXIETY AND OPTIMISM TWIST together in my stomach.

In front of me is the chance to reclaim what I've lost, but it's not guaranteed. I have to decide if I can still see my dream, but see it in a way that has changed, at least locationally. It's only a small change, right?

Sometimes in the waves of change, we find our true direction. I don't know who said it, but could Monterey be my true direction? Dad says, if you really want something, don't hold it too tightly. You have to believe in it, then let the universe take over.

It's a terrifying concept.

The universe has not been very nice to me lately, and I'm not sure I trust it. Oh, God, I'm so afraid. Instead of Hope Eternal, I'm back to the Eternal Hill.

Blinking away the heat in my eyes, I park Metallicar in front of the beach house for the first time in weeks. I sit in the car studying the weathered wood boards, and I realize it's not just my dream changing, I've changed.

The last time I was here, I was sad, discouraged, drunk... Now I'm awake, and I know what I want so clearly. Why does it have to be across this scary chasm?

Taking out my phone, I check the time before dialing his number. *Not too late…*

"Hey, sunshine, what's on your mind?" My dad's warm voice eases the fear in my chest.

"I'm back at the cottage." Dropping the car keys on the island in the kitchen, I head out the back door to where the wooden porch overlooks the ocean far below. The sound of the waves is a soothing hush and the scent of salt water and brine takes me back to being a little girl here, safe with my father.

"I thought you were working with Yarnell?"

"I kind of decided that wasn't for me. I'm a terrible housekeeper."

He chuckles in my ear. "Housekeeping at a big hotel is not easy. People take it for granted."

"I'm so lonely, Dad." I haven't told him about JR.

I should because if anyone would understand a broken heart, it would be my dad. Still, I'd be lonely here even if my heart weren't broken.

"I know, sweetheart. It's going to get better. Remember that saying about that which doesn't kill us?"

"I remember." My voice is quiet as I gaze up at the black-velvet sky.

The cottage is so far from any other homes or businesses, the stars are brilliantly visible at night. A million points of light against an inky black expanse.

"There's no moon tonight."

"How many stars can you see?"

It's a question he used to ask me as a little girl, before I was big enough to understand estimation. "All of them."

He chuckles in my ear, and it helps me smile. "The stars are our loved ones looking down on us when we can't see them."

"I know." It doesn't make me feel better. I want real loved ones, flesh and bone loved ones right here with me tonight.

"What's troubling you, pumpkin?"

Exhaling softly, I sit on the top step. "Dad, how do you know when change is good and when it's bad?"

"Hm…" I appreciate him not rushing to answer. "Change is inevitable…"

"What I mean is, how do you know when it's time to make a change and when you're going in the wrong direction?"

"That's easy." His smile drifts through the line. "You'll know the change is good when you feel calm. You'll know it's right when you have peace in your heart."

"There's no way to know before?"

"Of course, but it's a soft voice. Don't ignore your instinct. Listen to it."

Disconnecting from my dad, I close my eyes and picture JR, his sexy gaze and his full lips parting with a gorgeous smile. I think about him hugging his little boy, and looking at me with so much feeling in his eyes… Were the feelings love?

It warms me to my toes, and I know he's a good change. I imagine him looking at the sky somewhere just like I'm doing right now.

Reaching up, I hold a pinpoint of light, a star between my fingers. I send my warmest wishes across the miles to wherever he is right now.

This one's for you. To protect you…

Maybe I'll find him again now that I'm home.

Maybe we'll have the chance to try again, to see what a life would be like for a sunny girl and an angry boy with a scar.

Maybe we'll fall in love.

Maybe we already have…

CHAPTER
Twenty-Two

JR

I T TOOK THREE DAYS OF SITTING ON THE BENCH OUTSIDE RITUAL COFFEE Roasters for me to find him. He appeared at the counter right at closing time, just as I was leaving to go to the bus stop to head home.

He stood there talking to one of the baristas, and my heart beat so hard in my chest, I had to grip the wood of the bench to keep from charging in there and grabbing him.

Calm.

Self-control.

Do it the right way, not the easy way.

Now I'm at my studio apartment, making my daily Facetime call to my son. Jesse is animated as ever, blue eyes bright as he tells me about his day.

Only today instead of happy, his lips press into a thin line and anger darkens his expression. "Hunter said only pirates could play on his team, and I was not a pirate."

"Do you want to be on his team?" I do my best to be a thoughtful, calm dad and not call the little punk excluding my kid a bad name. "Why don't you make a team with Jimmy?"

"He picked Jimmy first. He said I could be on the team with all the girls."

My hackles are up, and I'm ready to violate parole again. "Where's Uncle Scout?"

"He's here." Jesse hooks a thumb over his shoulder. "He said he's going to call Hunter's dad, but Hunter doesn't have a dad. I told him that."

Lifting my chin, I start to see what's going on. "You know, sometimes missing a dad can make kids act like bullies."

I'm not sure my son is old enough to understand the concept of self-loathing.

His brow furrows just like a little man's as he thinks. It makes me smile. "When you were gone, I didn't act like that."

"That's because you're a smart guy, J. You knew I was coming back. And you had GA and people around who loved you taking care of you."

His face scrunches. He's reluctant, but trying. "Poppy would take me to the park and throw the ball."

My jaw tightens at the mention of my dad, but I don't want my son to see my anger. "Is Uncle Scout doing that with you now?"

"Yeah!" His eyes brighten. "Every day after school. And he taught me to skateboard. I'm the only kid at school who has a longboard."

"That's really cool. Send me a picture."

"We'll send you a video!" He's talking loud again, and I'm glad he seems to have forgotten his anger.

"I can't wait to see it." I'm smiling, and damn, I want to be there with him. "Hey, little man, you know I love you?"

"I love you too, Dad."

"I'm working on getting home, but I need to talk to Uncle Scout now. I need him to help me with something."

"Okay! He's right here." The video zig-zags as he bounces on the bed then runs to find my brother. "Here he is!"

"Hey, J?"

"Yeah?"

"Think about tomorrow, maybe starting your own team first with Jimmy. Then pick Hunter to be on it."

He's quiet a bit, frowning. He's breathing fast from running, but I can see in his blue eyes he's thinking about what I'm saying. "I'll try."

Pride swells in my chest at my boy. "Let me know how it goes."

My brother's smiling face appears on the screen. "What's the latest, bro?"

"Hey, I need your help."

"Shoot."

"I need to record a confession on my phone, but I don't see a voice recorder or anything." I frown, turning the device side to side. "How can I do that?"

"Damn, sometimes I forget you were in the joint the last two years. Technology has come a long way, old one."

"Can you focus? It's important."

He laughs, walking me through how to make a voice memo on my phone.

"What would be even better is if you did video, then there's no question who's talking."

"I don't know how I could hold up a phone and get him to confess…"

"Put it face up on the table." I don't know how that's better, but he walks me through the steps for that as well. "Just be sure you don't accidentally delete it once you're done."

"How the hell would I do that?" Panic tightens my lungs.

"Not save it, hit the delete button, lots of ways."

"Mother…" I don't say the rest, because Jesse could be in the room, but *motherfucker*. My jaw tightens, still I'm not backing down this close to the goal. "I'll have to be careful."

"Call me as soon as you're done."

"Okay. Thanks, bro." I'm ready to say goodnight, but I hesitate. I want to ask him one more thing, even if he'll give me shit for it. He's going to gloat, but I don't care.

"What?"

"Do you know how to get in touch with Hope? Like did she give you her number or anything?"

"About time you got your head out of your ass."

"Just tell it to me."

"I wish I could. She didn't give it to me. She was into you, not me, remember?"

I remember it so well.

Disappointment sinks in my chest. "I just thought you might—"

"Don't worry, bro. You get that video, and we'll find her. It's going to work out. I've got a good feeling about this."

I wish I did. I'm worried and alone out here, and damn this technology. I've got to get that confession.

SUNRISE FINDS ME ON THE BENCH OUTSIDE RITUAL ROASTERS WAITING FOR Clyde Shaw to reappear. Today is the day.

My phone is in my pocket ready to record, and my heart beats hard in my chest. Freedom is within my grasp. I'm going to meet this guy, and he's going to tell me what I need to know. It ends today.

An hour later, my confidence is less strong.

I leave the bench to enter the minimalistic coffee shop. It's a spare, wide-open beige room with a black granite counter in the center. Behind it is a massive, stainless steel mechanism of coffee roasters and brewers.

I order a regular coffee and an egg sandwich. I'll give it to them, it's probably the best damn coffee I've ever tasted. If I cared about that right now.

Two hours later, and the rat still hasn't come out of his hole.

I'm restless, and as I shift on the bench, my phone buzzes in my pocket. Taking it out, I've got a text from my brother. **Did it work?**

Groaning, I swipe open the phone and tap a reply. **He still hasn't appeared.**

Are you texting with your fingers? Text with your thumbs, Grandpa.

Asshole. I don't have time for this.

Stay calm. Inhale for five, exhale for six.

Shaking my head, I tap back, **What kind of bullshit...**

Basic meditation. Let me know when you've got it. Gran's got the prayer chain going.

Sliding my phone into my pocket, I glance towards the horizon. I never felt like the Big Guy was on my side, especially when I got thrown in fucking prison for a crime I didn't commit.

Still...

"I could use a little help if you're up there."

Yeah, I prayed.

People walk past, checking their phones, walking their dogs, ignoring the tense guy sitting on a bench with his whole future hanging in the balance. It feels like an eternity has passed when the wiry asshole finally appears.

He's at the counter again, and I'm on my feet, crossing the street. I don't know if he'll recognize me, and if he does, I don't know what he might do. I'm prepared for anything. If he takes off running, I'll run right after him. Then I'll beat a confession out of him.

But hopefully it won't come to that.

Smoothing my hands down the front of my jeans, I grab a

paper mask and reach for the door of the shop. A little bell dings when I enter, and Clyde turns to look.

He's different than he was two years ago. Back then he had dreads like all his friends, and he dressed in their standard attire. Now he's in jeans and a button-up oxford, and his hair is a short, light-brown afro, kind of like that guy who painted on television when we were kids.

Happy little trees.

He's still wearing those magic beads, and when our eyes meet, my question is answered. He recognizes me.

My jaw sets, and I step to the side just as he tries to dodge. This motherfucker's trying to run. Don't do it, asshole.

"Clyde Shaw?" I plaster a smile on my face, acting like I'm so glad to see him. In a twisted way I am. "I haven't seen you in two years. How've you been?"

"I'm sorry." He looks towards the guy at the counter, who's watching like he doesn't suspect a thing. "I was just leaving."

"Hang on a minute. Surely you have time for an old friend." Reaching out, I grab his bicep in a death grip.

His eyes flinch, but he knows he can't outmatch me. Dumbass better not try. At this point, I would enjoy beating a confession out of him.

The only thing holding me back is I don't want to jeopardize my future. Jesse is waiting for me. I want to believe somewhere Hope is waiting for me. I won't sacrifice them for this piece of shit.

He cocks his head to the side. "Do I know you? I think you might have me mixed up with somebody else."

"Let's have a seat and talk about it."

Still holding his arm, I lead him to the back of the café, to a booth in the corner where we can talk.

We've got the place to ourselves, and he slides across the red velvet cushions. I take the seat across from him, taking out my phone and acting like I'm checking for a text. Instead, I touch the video button like Scout told me to do, say a quick prayer I turned it on, not off, and place it between us on the table.

"I don't have much time."

"You've got time for me." I'm so casual. "Clyde Shaw, right?"

"That's my name."

"The Clyde Shaw who lived at Frederick and Clayton?" I have to establish his identity on the record.

"I lived there. It was a dump, so I moved. What of it?"

"You contacted my father, William Dunne two years ago about buying health supplements, specifically shilajit, to sell in our gym. You offered to be our supplier. Do you remember that?"

"I had several clients back then. You're wasting your time, Mr. Dunne. I stopped selling supplements two years ago."

"How come?"

"No money in it. That particular product was hard to get, and the profits were too small." He's looking around the room like he's planning to bolt. "So I'm sorry you wasted your time—"

"I'm not here about shilajit."

His brow furrows. "Then what is this about?"

"That day, two years ago, your guys loaded my trunk with illegal human growth hormone. I was stopped in a sting operation, and I went to prison."

He's on his feet at once. "I don't know what you're talking about. I only sell legal CBD and cannabinoids now. I don't do illegal shit. You've got the wrong guy."

I block him, smiling with my eyes. "Cool out, Clyde. It's all good. I'm not here to bust you."

"Why are you here?" His eyes move around my face. "You're that kid from South Carolina. Why don't you go home?"

"I was home. I just rolled back into town yesterday specifically to see you." My voice drops, and I lean closer. "Let's make a deal, Clyde Shaw."

He studies me with twitchy hazel eyes, then looking right to left, he slowly lowers to the seat again, and I do the same. "What kind of deal?"

We're across from each other, and every muscle in my body is tense. At the same time, I'm acting so relaxed, I should hire Scout's agent.

"You're the man with the connections, right? You know where to go for everything."

Clyde hasn't relaxed, and I can tell he's not buying my line. "I don't know what you mean by everything."

"I mean just like last time, only I'll be in on the joke."

"Last time wasn't a joke." He stops, like he knows he almost said too much.

"Good thing, because I wasn't laughing when the judge hammered that gavel and sent me to prison. Not a lot of peace and love there."

"That's not what I'm about." He has the nerve to act contrite. "I'm not part of an organization. I had to deliver a package to Charleston. A fellow at your gym said he could collect it and take it the rest of the way."

"Hey, no hard feelings, I get it." I hold up my hands. I'm so close to having him on record. "You didn't think I'd get caught. It was a mistake."

"It wasn't a setup." He looks over his shoulder towards the front of the store, almost like he's expecting the police to enter.

"Don't be nervous, man. It's just me, JR Dunne."

His eyes flicker up and down my face. "I don't understand what you want."

"I want a piece of the action. You say you're not part of an organization, but maybe you are. I've got a kid back home, an ex-wife to support. Times are tough. The gyms are closed... I need money."

"Everybody needs money."

"So last time, you gave me growth hormone when I thought I was getting supplements."

"It wasn't my idea."

"But that's what happened, right?"

He nods, and my jaw grinds. Nods don't pick up on audio, and the camera isn't on him. "What's that? Are you nodding?"

"Yes. Hurry up."

"I want to be in on it for real. Last time I didn't know anything about what was going on…"

He doesn't answer, but I wait. "What?" He's impatient. I want him impatient.

"You knew that, right?"

"What?" He frowns harder.

"I didn't know you gave me HGH last time."

"Why would I tell you we were using you as a mule? You'd have been shitting your pants the whole way home. You'd have been busted at the first mile marker."

"I would've said no." I smile, but my voice is level. "I didn't deal drugs."

"Right, you were Mr. Straight-A, Captain of the football team—"

"I didn't know anything about the drugs you planted in my car."

"You already said that." His voice rises. "Why do you keep repeating it?"

"It's important to me to know you know."

"Of course, I know." He leans across the table. "You say you're not a square anymore, but I'm not buying it. Taking a chance with you is a good way to get killed, and I'm not getting killed for you."

I slide out of my seat, picking up my phone. "You know what, I think you're right, Clyde Shaw. I don't think I'll fit into your drug ring after all."

"That's what I said, asshole. So quit wasting my time."

"You're Clyde Shaw."

He stands and narrows his eyes, mocking me. "Yes, Hero-man. I'm fucking Clyde Shaw, and I run this town. Now beat it. I'd better not see your face again."

I slip my phone into my pocket, praying to God I don't delete this recording. I won't get another chance.

"You won't see me. You'll hear from my lawyer."

Turning, I stride to the front of the shop fast as he yells after me. Once I'm through the double glass doors, I take off jogging, cutting a quick left down an alley in case he's chasing me, and pressing my back to the wall. I whip off my mask, breathing hard, and my fingers tremble as I search for the video recording.

It's in my photos, a long one. I draw it up and hit the red button, and immediately it starts to play back...

I don't have much time.

You've got time for me. Clyde Shaw, right?

Yes, that's my name...

"Ha!" I shout, pumping my fist.

I fucking got it, the evidence I need to get my conviction overturned. I've got to get this to my lawyer. I don't bother trying to text, I hit his number.

"Yo." My brother is too relaxed for how I'm feeling.

"I got it."

"Fuck, yeah, you did!" He shouts. "Send it to me!"

"How the hell do I do that?"

He quickly talks me through the steps of sending a video via text, but it bounces back red. "It says the file's too big."

"Shit." Scout's teeth are gritted. "Shit shit shit."

My stomach is in my throat. "What?"

We're too close for fuckups.

"Do you have access to a computer? You're going to have to hardwire and email it."

"How would I have access to a computer?" A bead of sweat runs down my torso, and my throat constricts. "Scout…"

"It's good. It's all good. The video is fine. It's only your phone until you can send it to me. Maybe you could go to the library?"

"I don't know where there's a library—"

"You know what? Let's don't sweat it." I hear him smiling, and my tension eases a notch. "You got it. That's the most important thing. Now, just don't let anything happen to your phone until you talk to your lawyer."

Rolling my shoulders, I look up at the sky. This fucking tension is too much. "I can do that. I only use this thing to call you and Jesse."

"You're almost free, bro." The ease in his voice helps me breathe. "We've just got to get that confession to your lawyer and clear your name."

Hearing those words is like a rush of warm water on my insides. "I'm going to beat this."

"Yeah, you are. Then we're going to find Hope."

Scrubbing my fingers on my eyelids, I exhale a loose laugh. "One step at a time."

We disconnect, and I'm walking fast in the direction of my apartment. I'm so full of adrenaline and gratitude and anticipation, I'm never going to sleep. The sun is dropping towards the horizon, and I feel so good, so full of hope.

Hope.

Digging in my pocket, I pull out the metro card. The bus doesn't go to her beach house, but it gets close. I've got to try one more time…

CHAPTER
Twenty-Three

Hope

I park Metallicar on the street in Cannery Row.

I've never been to Monterey, but a little quick research last night told me this part of town is a hot spot for young families and tourists. It's where the aquarium is located and some specialty shops.

It's not high tourist time, but a few sets of what look like parents and kids are walking along the sidewalk towards an elevated walkway. It's beige and has *Cannery Row Company* painted in huge white letters on a maroon background.

A little more research before I got on the road this morning told me the area is named after a John Steinbeck novel called *Cannery Row*, and I was immediately plunged into a memory of being on the road, Scout explaining to me the history of their names… John Steinbeck and Phillip Roth… *John Roth*…

God, that feels so long ago. The ache in my chest tells me it's only been a month, but thinking about those few days, the sun on our faces and the wind in our hair. Did it really happen?

Resting my forehead on the steering wheel, I wonder how long it will take before I stop aching for him, before I stop wondering where he is and what he's doing.

It's been four long weeks since I saw him, kissed him, traced my fingers along the lines of his torso. I can still see his dark hair pushing around his temples in the wind. I can still feel the press of his lips against mine. At night, when I'm sleeping, I can still feel the weight of his body holding me down in the most delicious way.

I'll never forget his scent of soap and sweat, the salty taste of his skin on my tongue. He took me like I always wanted to be taken, like a steak dinner after a forty-day fast, water after a three-day walk in the desert. Like he couldn't get enough, and all he wanted was me.

Heat is in my belly, and a tear is on my cheek.

I shove it away. *Snap out of it, Hope.*

Fate has dropped this amazing second chance in my lap, and I can't squander it. Few people get a second chance like this, and I have to explore the area and see if I can find a good location to open a family-friendly restaurant where patrons can let their creativity flow.

I have to get my head back in the game, and my brain back on my dream.

Four hours later, the sun is setting, and I'm walking to Metallicar only partially satisfied with my afternoon exploring.

The buildings are historically beautiful, navy and maroon board with white wooden porches and green awnings. The alleys are wide, and I can imagine tucking Pancake Paradise into one of them with a folding sign out on the main walk sending visitors my way.

Still, I'm not getting that click. Dad said I would know the change was right when I felt the peace in my heart, the feeling of satisfaction.

I felt it in the Embarcadero. San Francisco was my home, so perhaps that's why it seemed so natural to me.

This place is strange. It's beautiful, small with a gorgeous coast and an absolute built-in clientele. It just doesn't feel like home.

A bit discouraged, I park the car outside the beach shack. The night has turned hazy and cold, pretty typical for late summer in San Francisco, and I walk inside the empty place, dropping my keys on the counter and going to the closet.

My teddy bear coat hangs on a peg, and I take it off, walking outside to try and see the stars. I'll be lucky if I see anything tonight.

Tonight I'm on my own, and the loneliness weighs heavy on my shoulders.

I know they're up there. I know if the fog rolls away, I'll see them looking down on me just like Dad said. Holding my phone in my hand, I can't call him again. I'll only make him worry, and I have to be an adult now. I have to stand on my own two feet and face these times of loneliness.

I have to believe this too shall pass…

A drop of rain touches my cheek, and I close my eyes, allowing a tear to join it. It's so poetic for the rain to fall at this point in my story. The darkest night, the fog, the cold rain…

I'm gearing up to feel very sorry for myself when a low creak echoes from the other side of the house. A thump on the boards, and my eyes fly open. My heart skips like a rabbit.

Shit… Someone's here!

The bad thing about being in the beach cottage is the same as the good thing—I'm so far out here on the beach highway alone, anything could happen.

I can't breathe. Fishing out my phone, I unlock the screen quickly and press the two buttons to call 911.

Backing slowly along the rail of the balcony, I make my way

towards the wooden staircase leading down to the beach. It's a long, winding descent, but I know it better than any burglar. I can be away from danger in thirty seconds or less.

"Hello?" A low male voice stops me in my tracks, freezing me to the spot.

"911, what's your emergency?" A higher, female voice cuts through the swish of the waves far below, the push of the wind around my ears, the soft cry of seagulls.

"Hello?" I call back, straining my eyes in the darkness.

The voice sounded familiar, almost like…

Spotlights on the corners of the house point away from where I stand, leaving me dazzled by their light, and concealed in the darkness.

"Hope? Is that you?" The deep, rich voice is like warm caramel in my veins.

"John?" It's a hushed whisper, a prayer. My entire body is tight.

I hear him before I see him. I hear the heavy thump of his feet on the wooden boardwalk, and his silhouette appears, outlined in the beam of the spotlight.

"You're here!" I cry.

"Where have you been?" Relief is in his voice, almost like he can't believe he found me on the back porch of my family's home.

"Monterey?"

Instantly, I'm surrounded by his strong arms, sweeping me up in a hug against his hard body. I never even saw him move. Of course, my eyes are flooded with tears. My hands grasp and cling to his shirt, to his body. My mouth searches for anything, kissing his neck, his jaw, until finally our mouths collide.

He shoves my lips apart, and our tongues entwine as I exhale a noise of gratitude and deep satisfaction. Strong hands grip my ass, and my legs wrap around his waist as he lifts me.

I grasp at his cheeks. I slide my fingers into his soft hair. He's my water in the desert, cool ice cream on a hot summer day…

Our kisses taste like the salt of my tears. I laugh and cry, holding his face as I pull his lips with mine. Our teeth clink together, and I realize we're both smiling. We're desperate and devouring. We're together again at last.

"God, I've missed you so much." His voice breaks in a way that thrills me to my core.

"You missed me?"

He lowers me to my feet, and my eyes have adjusted, I can see him in the hazy darkness. His lowered brow, his chiseled jaw, his perfectly defined lips parted over straight, white teeth. He's such a work of art.

"I've missed you more than I've ever missed anything."

Shaking my head, I blink up at him. "But you said—"

"Hello? Is this an emergency?" My phone is in my hand, and I snap out of the joy of reunion to realize I still have 911 on the line.

"Oh my gosh, I'm so sorry!" I hold my hair back, and JR moves around behind me.

His hands slide around my waist, before he wraps muscled arms like steel bands around my body, pulling me against him.

My breath disappears. "It's not an emergency," I manage.

"Sounds like it's not." The lady on the line has a laugh in her voice, and I close my eyes as warm lips close against the side of my neck. "Have a good night, Miss."

I intend to do just that. Hitting the end button, I turn in his arms to find his mouth. I'm off my feet again, only this time he's walking, carrying me inside the house.

Once we're through the door, he lowers me to my feet, and I take his hand, leading him down the short hall to my bedroom. I'm not wasting any time.

The room is open, with a balcony that overlooks the beach.

It's too cold to open the doors, but it creates a shushing ambiance in the air around us.

Lust and need drive us. JR's strong hands are on my hips, moving under my thin sweater and lifting it over my head, leaving me in a white lace bra that just covers the bottom half of my breasts.

He exhales a groan. "You're so beautiful."

A flash of need shoots to my heated core, and my fingers circle the buttons of his shirt, quickly unfastening them, doing my best not to rip his clothes off. The fabric falls open, and I slide my palms along the planes and ridges of his lined torso.

"I was afraid I'd never see you again." Leaning forward, I trace my lips along his skin.

He's here.

He came to me.

My eyes close as heat rushes through my chest.

Large hands cup my cheeks, lifting my face and tilting it so he can devour my mouth. My lips part willingly, hungry for his kisses, his possessive touch.

His hands leave my cheeks and circle my back, unfastening my bra. As it falls away, a whisper of cool air hardens my nipples. His hands cover them, tweaking the tips, sending sparkling waves of energy between my thighs.

"John." My head falls back with a moan.

He lifts me off my feet, carrying me to the bed. With a toss, I fall back, laughing at his Tarzan style. He shoves his jeans down, and I do the same, tossing them across the room as I lick my lips.

I gaze at his thick, hardened cock, and his voice is rough. "The way you look at me... It makes me want to do very bad things to you."

Dragging my eyes up his Adonis body, I meet his smoldering eyes. "Please do very bad things to me."

The smolder turns to blue fire, and he catches my ankle,

dragging me towards him on the bed and flipping me onto my stomach.

My stomach jumps, and he slides his fingers along the line of my thong, hooking one inside the fabric and ripping it away.

"Oh!" It's a startled cry, but I love it.

Catching me by the hips, he lifts me to my knees and leans forward, tracing his tongue up and down my pussy, melting my insides. "Oh, John... Oh, God..."

My elbows give out, and I can't take it. The pleasure shooting through my body trembles in my thighs. I've missed him so much. I'm going to come so fast for him.

"You taste so good." He kisses my bare ass cheek before standing. I hear the rip of foil and a shush of rolling, and he slides his cock along my slippery folds. "Ready?"

"Yes..." I gasp, and he fills me, driving all the way to the hilt.

Eyes squeezing shut, my hands reach forward on the bed, clawing at the fabric as I let out a low moan. He places a knee between my thighs and thrusts deeper, spreading my legs wider. He's moving fast, pushing me higher in the bed, erasing my mind.

Hot breath is behind my ear, and I turn my face, searching for his lips. Our mouths unite, and he holds my waist, pumping and groaning, kissing and pulling, sliding his tongue against mine.

It's hot and hungry and wild. Prickles of orgasm radiate through my pelvis, and I arch my back, meeting his movements as best I can with my own.

We're devouring, fucking like we can't get enough. Our sounds are groans and whimpers, broken yeses and desperate oh Gods. I arch my back, rising higher, and his hand moves from my hip to my clit. One thick digit slides up and down that hypersensitive bud, and my orgasm erupts suddenly, like I've touched a live wire.

"John!" I cry out.

His fingers curl on my stomach, and one, two more thrusts

and he holds, groaning low as he pulses inside me, filling the condom.

We're panting as we collapse together. Reaching out, he draws me close to his chest and buries his face in my hair, inhaling deeply. I love when he does that.

"Hope." Satisfaction permeates his tone, warming me to my toes.

Turning to face him, my arms snake around his waist, and I scoot myself closer to him, loving the feel of our skin against skin, from our shoulders to our stomachs to our thighs. It's incredible. I wasn't sure I'd have it again. *I have a dream…* Is it coming true?

"Why did you come here?" My chin is at his chest, and I look up at his cool blue eyes.

Again, they're so full of that emotion. I don't know what to call it. "I've been looking for you since I got back."

I'm afraid to ask why. I don't want to give him any ideas. Still… "I thought we had to wait."

"I missed you." His full lips tighten, and he dips his head, taking a deep breath of my hair and kissing my head.

My stomach squeezes so tight. Inside I'm jumping up and down and doing a cheer. *He missed me!*

Clearing my throat, I'm very cool. "I missed you."

"You changed your scent?" He sniffs again, and all my cool is gone.

"You don't like it?"

"It's not that…" He gives me another sniff. "It's just different."

"It's my lucky charm."

"What does that mean?" He shifts to the side, and I prop on my elbow beside him.

Being so close to his face, chatting, it's something we've never had time to do, and it makes my stomach tingly. He's so intense and focused.

"You asked where I've been. I was with Yarnell, working at the Lodge in Half Moon Bay."

"Yarnell... I couldn't remember her name."

"Her parents were big Shields & Yarnell fans."

"The mimes?" He frowns. "They were creepy as fuck."

"They were the original pop and lockers!" I push his shoulder. "They started a whole dance craze. Anyway, we weren't allowed to watch a lot of mainstream stuff growing up. I'm surprised you know who they are."

A smile curls his lips, and it makes me so tingly. "Tell me about this lucky charm."

"So I was working at Half Moon Bay Lodge in housekeeping, and I really sucked at it." He slides a finger along my forehead, moving my hair behind my ear. I lose my train of thought for a second, then I remember. "Oh, and I stole this lady's body spray."

His full lips part, and I put my finger on them. "Before you judge. I was cleaning her room, and I got distracted by all her cosmetics. I just picked up the body spray to smell it, she came in and started screaming I was a thief, so I ran."

His pretty, pretty eyes twinkle, and he exhales a short laugh. "I'm sorry." He clears his throat when he sees my eyes narrow. "That doesn't explain why it's good luck."

"Oh!" I shift in the bed. "I ran into this guy's room to hide, and we got to talking, and I told him about Pancake Paradise, and he offered to give me money so I could reopen. Only he wants me to move to Monterey..." JR's brow lowers, and his eyes go from glowing and loving to super pissed. I exhale a little laugh. "What's wrong?"

"Some guy you don't know offered you money?"

Biting my bottom lip, more warmth flares in my chest. *Is he jealous?* "No, no. It's not like that. He's an investor. He said to update my business plan and send it to his secretary."

"How do you know?"

"I Googled him." It's my turn to slide the hair off his forehead. Such pretty hair. "Yars already knew who he was. She says he's the richest man in Manhattan."

I realize that sort of rhymes, but JR is not buying it. "I don't like it. He wants in your pants."

"John Roth Dunne, he does not." I shake my head and laugh. "Stephen Hastings is a happily married man with two children—"

"And you're a beautiful young girl who turns into this beam of sunlight whenever you talk about your restaurant. You're fucking irresistible."

This time I can't resist. My eyes warm, and I press my lips together before pushing my arms around his neck and kissing him firmly on the mouth. Our lips part, and our tongues slide together as he rolls me onto my back, deepening the kiss, taking my breath away.

He lifts his head, and when our eyes meet, it's hot and demanding. "I don't want some strange guy giving you money."

My insides are sparkling, and I'm sure it's showing in the grin I can't hide. "That's kind of how investors work."

"Then I want to meet him."

"What are you going to do?"

"Make sure he knows this is strictly a business transaction."

I kind of super-love this possessive side of him. "I'm pretty sure he already knows that."

"I want to know that he knows that."

"Tell you what." Lifting my head, I kiss him again briefly. "If I even see him again in person, I'll be sure you're there with me."

"Good." He leans down and kisses me again, slower, heating my core. "Although I still don't like it."

My forehead crinkles. "Why not?"

"I want to give you everything you need."

"Oh." I shake my head, hugging myself closer to him, pressing my bare chest to his and loving the feel of our bodies together. "You already do."

CHAPTER
Twenty-Four

JR

HOPE IN MY ARMS IS LIKE COMING HOME.

Her body molds to mine like we were made to be together, perfect and beautiful. I bury my nose in her hair and breathe deeply... Vanilla and something different. Caramel?

Her talking about some guy making her dream come true has me angry and hot. I want to fuck her again. I want to wrap her body around mine and make love. I want to be the man who gives her everything she wants. I want to make her life mine. We've never had a chance to say the words, but I think she feels the same.

When I realized I had Clyde's confession, my first thought was *I'm free*. My second thought was *Find Hope*. Nothing stands in our way now. I can come to her with clean hands.

I can ask her if she wants to try.

I can make a promise...

I can tell her the truth. She fills a part of me I didn't know was lacking. The sunshine in her hair, the sparkle in her eyes, all of it turns the anger in my chest to peace. She changed me. Hell, she kept me from punching my dad in the face. She made me have faith again. She's my hope.

Her soft cheek is against my chest. Her finger traces the lines along my stomach, and it feels so good. She's in my arms, and I'm on the right path again. It's all coming back to me now, and I'll do whatever it takes to hold onto her.

"That 911 operator sure got an earful." She lifts her head. Our eyes meet, and she's so adorable.

Threading my fingers in her hair, I chuckle. "You called the cops on me."

"I thought you were a burglar." Slim fingers lightly trace the lines of ink above my pec. *"This much is true..."* What does it mean?"

I take her fingers in my hand and kiss the tips. "People lied to me, and because of their lies, I lost everything, my son, my freedom, my reputation... I decided the only thing I can believe, the only truth is me."

Her pretty brows furrow, and her eyes are sad. "Sounds lonely."

"I was in a pretty dark place." Remembering it makes my chest cold. "The system took everything I had and left me with nothing."

"It's like what you told me that night?" Her voice is quiet. "Like when you were a football star?"

I forgot I'd told her that. "Yeah."

Her fingers move from my hand to trace the line of my jaw. Her blue eyes are focused on them, so careful. "Do you ever think you can trust someone again?"

She has no idea...

In that moment I make a decision.

"I don't like you being here alone. I should stay with you, or you can come back to my place."

Her brow arches. "You have a place?"

"It's just a studio on Divisidaro, but it's better than you being out here alone and vulnerable."

"I thought you said we couldn't be together." She's teasing, and I roll her onto her back.

"Something changed my mind."

"Something... like?"

Leaning on my elbow, I gaze down at her angel face. "Like I think I got a miracle."

Her pretty blue eyes widen. "How?"

"GA has a prayer chain, and she insists they make shit happen—"

"Shit like what?"

"I found the guy who set me up." Shaking my head, I still kind of can't believe it. "Not only that, I got him to confess."

"John!" She pushes up to sitting, and I shift onto my hip beside her. "Oh my God! That's incredible... That's..." She hesitates, shaking her head as if she can't find the words.

I get it. This changes everything.

Dropping my chin, I kiss the top of her shoulder. "I know."

It's a big moment, the break we need, and I want to hold her, linger here.

Her breath swirls in and out, and I feel the excitement tight in her body. I remember what we said, if there's any chance...

It's our chance.

Our heartbeats slow, and I can't resist. "You know, it's pretty cool, but it's nothing like pulling a copperhead out of a wooden box."

"Brother Bob." Her head drops back with a groan. "Talk about a liar. He was not incredible. He was insane."

"He sent his goons after us."

"And you kicked their asses." She grins, sliding a finger along my brow. "It was hot."

"It was a close call." Shifting, I lean back against the headboard.

"So what now?" She bounces beside me, and I can't help noticing her small tits bobbing.

My fingers trace from her waist to her breast, and I think how amazing it would be to have her any time I want. She covers my hand with hers, threading our fingers, and my train of thought disappears at the sight of her body.

"Hellooo..." I look up, and her head is tilted to the side, a sexy smile curving her lips.

"Sorry, what?" My thumb slides around the stiff peak of her nipple, and she leans forward, threading her fingers in the side of my hair and tracing her lips along my brow.

My dick perks up... almost like it's been four weeks since I've seen her.

"What happens now?" Her voice is low, and her lips feather against my cheek.

Gripping her waist, I pull her across me in a straddle. "Now I take it to my lawyer and clear my name."

Her tits are right at my chin, and I lift them in my hands. Soft and tight, just like the rest of her. Leaning forward, I pull a taut nipple between my lips and give it a gentle bite.

I'm rewarded with a sharp gasp, and her slim hand fumbles between us, guiding my cock to her hot little pussy. I don't have a condom, and I'm about to stop us when she lowers her body, moving onto her knees and riding me.

"Shit..." My eyes squeeze shut, and my hands grip her soft ass.

I need to stop her. I need to be responsible and put on a condom.

"Hang on, beautiful." It's almost more willpower than I have. "I can't get you pregnant yet."

"John..." Her lips seal against mine, and she hugs me.

She's so hot and tight and slippery and tempting. She's killing me.

"Hold that thought." Shifting our positions, I lay her on her back. I'm still inside her as I thrust, sliding in and out as our bodies heat and tense. My jeans are just within reach, and I pull out a condom.

Leaning down, I pull her warm lips with mine, sliding my tongue along hers as I lift my hips, coming out with a long pull. I'm on my knees above her, and she rakes her fingernails up my thighs, tracing them around to the center. It's insanely hot, and my fingers tremble as I roll on protection.

Her knees rise, and hot blue eyes meet mine. "Fuck me, John."

She doesn't have to ask twice. I catch a knee with my forearm, lifting it higher as I bury deep, thrusting hard and fast. Her back arches, and she moans. Rotating her hips like a dancer, she blows my mind.

We move in a primitive dance, like the waves on the ocean. Leaning down, our mouths collide, and it's all instinct and desire. The air is filled with soft moans and low grunts, It doesn't take long before we're coming again. Her insides clench, and I kiss her small breasts. I drag my mouth higher, kissing her shoulder, behind her ear. I taste the sweet salt of her skin.

She's velvet and sugar and spice. She's hot liquid and warm depths. She's my best fantasy come to life. She's the promise of a better life ahead, something richer and fuller.

Something true.

We're coming down, and I quickly dispose of the condom before gathering her in my arms again. This time her back is to my chest, and my arms wrap over hers. My face is at her ear, and I kiss her neck.

She exhales a laugh, and I do it again. It makes me smile to feel her happy in my arms.

It makes me do something I haven't done in years.

It makes me believe in a bright future waiting at the end of this long, dark road.

"I'LL DRIVE YOU TO YOUR APARTMENT." HOPE IS SITTING ON A BARSTOOL across from me, holding a piece of jelly toast in one hand and a mug of coffee in the other.

She's the cutest ray of sunshine in faded jeans and a long-sleeved green sweater.

"Thanks." Taking out my black iPhone, I study the face. "The confession is stuck on this phone. I'm guarding it with my life."

"Why don't you back it up on a computer?"

"Don't have one."

Her brow furrows, and she looks around the cottage then back at me. "Isn't that weird? Not so long ago everybody had a computer. Or at least a laptop."

"Either way, I can't lose this recording. Nothing can happen to this phone."

"Why does that make me feel terrified?" Her voice is a whisper, and she stands, carrying her plate to the sink.

"Let's get going. I'll call my lawyer first thing and play it for her." I tuck my shirt into my jeans. "Maybe she can record it through the phone."

"Good idea." Hope nods, snatching up the keys. "Did you get enough breakfast?"

"I'm good." Polishing off my cup of coffee, I place it in the sink before catching her waist and pulling her to me. "You're going to your restaurant?"

"My retail space," she corrects me, and I can't tell if saying it makes her sad. It seems not. "I've got to get what's left out of there before the lease expires."

"Let's plan to meet up at noon." Leaning down, I kiss her.

She melts into me, kissing me back.

I love how she does that.

"Your place or mine?" Her voice is sultry, but I don't have time to carry her to the bedroom. It'll have to wait.

"Here. We'll come here."

"I wish it were now."

We're out the door, and at this hour, it doesn't take long to get from her beach house to my apartment in town.

As we drive, I take her phone and study the face. It's a picture of her smiling on the beach, her blonde hair falling over one eye. "How would you feel about going back to Fireside with me? Once all of this is done."

Her eyes are on the road, but a smile lifts the corner of her mouth. "I'd love to see everyone again, Scout and Jesse and your grandmother."

"I don't have your number."

She parallel parks at the sidewalk in front of my apartment and takes her phone from me, unlocking it and handing it back. "Type in your number." I do as she says, then she nods. "Now type in Scout's."

My brow furrows, but I do it. As soon as I'm done, she takes the phone again and quickly thumbs out a text. So that's what Scout's always bitching about.

Seconds later, my phone buzzes, and I lift it, reading her text on the face. *Who's up for another road trip?*

It doesn't take long for my brother to answer. *Is this Hope? You found her?*

I chuckle as my chest expands. Unlocking my phone, I slowly tap out. *I found her.*

She smiles, and when our eyes meet, hers are warm and glistening.

Leaning across the seat, I kiss her long and slow before I get out. Hell yeah, I found her, and I'm never letting her go again.

Before I get out, I think about what I'm about to do. "Everything's going to change."

"It's going to be amazing." Her voice is quiet, eyes bright.

Leaning in one last time, I kiss her soft lips, then I'm out the door, heading inside to call my lawyer and start our new life.

ONLY LIFE NEVER GOES THE WAY YOU CHOOSE.

Pacing my apartment, I listen to the phone ring. Checking the time, it's after eight. I guess my lawyer doesn't get into her office until nine, but she's got to have an answering service or a machine or something.

A loud banging on my front door makes me disconnect. I'm holding the phone, looking down as I go to it, thinking about that text Hope sent, thinking about another road trip.

"Can I help you?" My voice has an edge. I'm not expecting a delivery.

I don't think Clyde would come here, but I'm not certain. I am certain I could kick his ass, but would he bring a gun?

"Open the door, Dunne. It's Deputy Blank."

My chin draws back. What the hell is my parole officer doing here? I turn the locks and remove the chain. I'm just turning the doorknob when it flies inward on me, causing me to take a few steps back.

"What the hell?" The words barely leave my lips, before I'm surrounded by masked cops, jerking my hands behind my back. "Hold up!"

My phone slips from my grip and falls, hitting the wood floor with a crash. My stomach crashes with it, and I try to dive for it.

My struggle gets me a knee to the ribs, knocking the wind out of me. Still, desperation twists in my chest. That phone is everything.

"Stop resisting, asshole." The men gripping my arms aren't asking questions or reading my rights. Handcuffs are slapped over my wrists, and they jerk me upright, pushing me towards the door.

No… My throat is tight. My heart thuds fast in my chest. My entire future is slipping away with that shattered phone lying on the floor.

Hope…

"Why are you doing this?" My voice cracks.

I'm still struggling, needing to get my phone, but the more I twist, the tighter they grip my arms, pulling them behind me so hard, I think my joints will pop.

"Please…" I gasp, blinking the heat in my eyes.

"Don't make me tase you." The biggest guy growls at my ear.

He's holding my arms behind my back, and he drags me up so straight, my feet nearly lift off the floor. It hurts like hell, then his black boot heel lands directly on my phone's face.

"God… NO!" I shout. "I'll go with you. Just stop… My phone."

The first guy, the smaller of the two, looks down to where his partner's foot is on the device holding my key to freedom. "Is this your personal device?"

His sarcasm makes me sick. I've only wanted to kill a person one other time in my life.

"I need that to call my son." For some reason, I don't trust them with the truth.

I don't know why they're doing this, and all I can think of is Deputy Blank's disgust at me walking around on parole. She hates me.

"I told you," she steps between the officers and me. "You should've thought of your son before you started dealing drugs." Deputy Blank circles around to the door, her hands on her hips. "We got a tip this morning you've violated your parole. You went to South Carolina without prior authorization. Authorization I already denied."

Fucking Becky. It's interesting how easily murder takes up residence in your mind. I now want to kill two people.

"I wasn't running. I'm not a flight risk." Struggling strains my voice, but I do my best to hide my rage.

"Tell it to the judge." She nods to the door. "Take him to the car. You're going back to prison. This time for good."

The men lift and shove me into the hall, not even caring that my phone is on the floor broken and stomped on. I look over my shoulder at my whole world lying there in pieces.

If Hope comes back, I'll be gone, and she won't be able to reach me. If the landlord comes, he'll think I've skipped town and have the apartment cleaned.

They'll throw my broken phone in the trash. My last chance at freedom will be swept away with the garbage. Anger like an iron fist surges in my chest as the door slams. It can't happen…

I'm still struggling as they muscle me to the car. It can't end this way.

CHAPTER
Twenty-Five

Hope

AS I WALK THROUGH THE OPEN SPACE OF THE ORIGINAL PANCAKE Paradise, I can tell I've changed.

When everything shut down, when it was clear I would lose the business, I couldn't come here anymore.

The thought of entering this big, empty space after our gigantic grand opening celebration, after a weekend of smiles on people's faces, happiness and laughter, photographs on Instagram, group photos on Facebook, sharing and eating and so many pancake creations…

I walked away and never came back.

My manager handled the online auction, where we sold all the kitchen equipment, tables, chairs, flatware, napkins… anything anybody wanted to buy.

I used the money to pay my employees one week's salary, which left almost nothing for me—and is why I was selling Dad's precious Impala.

If I had opened the restaurant and absolutely sucked at it; if I'd been irresponsible or made bad business decisions, and it had simply flopped, that would've been difficult.

Correction, that would have been devastating, but I could have lifted my chin, and said I tried. It wasn't meant to be, but you never know until you try. Right?

This was something entirely different.

This felt like some cruel, invisible hand, smacking me from behind. I'd worked hard. I'd planned and consulted advisers. I'd done everything right. It wasn't my fault…

Which is why it's coming back now with benefits. JR and I are both getting a second chance, and we've found each other. I'm so sure, all the way to my bones, it's meant to be and it's going to be better than what we'd originally planned.

I spent the morning loading the industrial-sized bags of flour, sugar, and cinnamon no one wanted into the back of the car. Dry ingredients keep for a while if they're kept cool. I also discovered a mop and a step ladder stuck in a back closet. I guess they're mine like all the rest of it.

So I have four bags of dry ingredients, a mop, and a step ladder. They'll go with me to the new Pancake Paradise, and like the Brazilian Crush, they'll be my omens of something better to come… Now I just have to figure out where.

I stroll out onto the Embarcadero, down to Pier 39 where the sea lions live. Tourists love to come here and gaze at the giant mammals lying in the sun, but it smells like raw fish and the air is stuffy. Wrinkling my nose, I continue up Fisherman's Wharf.

The sky is blue, and it's slightly warmer, but the crowds are thin. I wander past the carousel, towards the giant metal crab, wondering if it's too soon to call him.

Last night was so amazing. The last thing I expected was for him to appear at my house in the foggy darkness. Then he kissed me.

My stomach tingles as the memories rush into my mind. All of it was so amazing and hot and thrilling. He's so possessive. He's so perfect.

I'm craving his touch when my phone goes off in my bag. I dig it out quickly, hoping it's him. I want to spend the rest of this beautiful day together. Maybe we can hold hands and walk along the beach.

I don't recognize the number. It's a strange area code, and I'm about to dismiss it, when I get a feeling, almost like something's wrong.

"Hope, thank God." It's a voice I haven't heard in weeks—and it's different, no longer laid-back and teasing.

"Scout?" My heart beats faster. "Why are you calling me? What's wrong?"

"JR's been arrested. Somehow they found out he violated his parole."

"But…" I'm walking fast, heading to where I parked my car. "I don't understand. If he's cleared of the charges, won't that mean he didn't violate parole?"

"He never talked to his lawyer. He said he was trying to call when the cops showed up." Scout's speaking fast, and I grab my keys.

"He called you?" I hate feeling jealous, but I can't help it. I want to be the one he calls when he needs help.

"He called Jesse. He wanted to tell him he wouldn't be home as soon as he said."

"Oh…" Tears fill my eyes. "He must be devastated."

"It's going to be okay." Scout's voice is determined. "I told Jesse we were going to get his dad home. I'm flying to San Francisco tonight."

Swallowing the knot in my throat, I nod quickly. "How can I help?"

"I need you to go to JR's apartment and get inside. Find that phone." He's moving quickly in the background. "We've got to get it to a lawyer. This time we'll be there for him."

Scout texts me the number of the apartment, but when I arrive, the door is locked.

Standing in the hall, I look all around trying to figure out how I'm going to get into a second-floor apartment with no key.

"He's not here." A raspy voice comes through the door across the hall, and I clutch my neck to stop a squeal.

My heart beats faster as I face the closed door. "Hello? Are you talking to me?"

"If you're looking for the guy in 213, they took him away this morning." I can't tell if the person is really old or really sick.

Hesitating, I decide to take a chance. "I'm a friend of his. He asked me to come here…"

The door flies open, and I jump back with a little yip. A very small, very old woman with frizzy gray hair and a mask with a smiling sloth on it appears.

She can't be taller than four-foot-eleven, and she squints one eye at me. "Are you selling encyclopedias?"

"Um… no…" I hold up both hands. "I just need to get into this apartment."

"Why?" She squints even harder. "Is there a cat in there?"

I'm not sure how to answer this question, so I'm careful. "If I say yes, will you let me in?"

"No." She shakes her frizzy gray head. "I don't have a key."

My shoulders drop, and I collapse against the door. "What am I going to do?" It's a whispered sigh to myself, but the old lady holds up a finger.

"The fire escape is in the alley. If he leaves his windows unlocked." Her small arms cross. "Would he be that irresponsible?"

"Only one way to find out!" I push off the door, running down the hall.

"Remember to feed the cat!" She calls after me, and I don't bother to argue.

Slamming into the stairwell, I fly down the stairs. Outside, I skip quickly along the sidewalk, looking for any break in the buildings to access the alley.

Finally, half a block down, I spot a narrow passage almost obscured by ivy. Pushing through it, I jump back and yelp when a dog barks loudly right at my head.

"Holy shit!" A window is between us, but he paws at the glass. "Good doggy!"

I dash farther down the passage, tracing the buildings with my eyes, trying to count the windows so I can figure out which is his.

At last I locate a metal stairwell covered in flaking white paint I'm sure leads to JR's building, but I'm stumped. The ladder is pulled all the way up, and it's too high for me to reach.

"Shit." I look all around the tiny, square area.

Boxes and crates are tossed around. A dumpster is against one wall, and it's clear nobody comes back here except for garbage. Shoving both my hands into the sides of my hair, I try to think. If only I had something to stand on... Or something to reach up and catch the bottom rung so I can pull down the ladder.

If only I had a mop and a step ladder! I jump up and down then take off running back to Metallicar. Jamming the key into the trunk, I open it quickly and pull out the supplies.

"Is this some kind of miracle or what?" I'm breathless as I run back to the fire escape.

I'm sure I look like a deranged maid in a paper mask running down the sidewalk with a mop and a step ladder. If I weren't so desperate, I'd probably stop and take a picture to send to Yarnell. As it is, I'm in the alley, looking up to where the metal fire escape ladder is all the way up.

"You're coming down!" I'm not sure why I've decided that ladder is my enemy, but here we go.

Carefully, I climb to the top of the step ladder and reach with the mop as far overhead as I can. It's super awkward, and I nearly lose my balance twice. Still, I manage to catch the bottom rung with the hair of the dry mop and pull it down to the ground. It's spring-loaded, so as soon as I step onto it, the ladder starts to rise.

Not losing time, I climb with it, reaching the second floor quickly. Sure enough, JR's window is unlocked. I want to yell to Crazy Lady across the hall he *is* that irresponsible, but there's no time.

I dive into the one-room apartment, and quickly begin my search. Spare and very clean, JR's bed is neatly made in one corner of the room. A brown wood dresser is beside it with a framed picture of him and Jesse sitting on it.

Picking it up, I smile at the two of them. Jesse looks about three. He's on his dad's hip with an arm around his neck, and they smile with matching cheek dimples. Jesse does resemble his uncle, but he's clearly JR's son. I think about having them both in my life, and my chest shimmers. Jesse wasn't a fan of my football skills, but maybe I could win him over with some pancakes. It's such a happy dream. I want it so much.

Returning the picture to the dresser, I continue searching for the phone. Scout didn't tell me where it would be. I go to the kitchen, which is clean with only a few circulars on the bar.

A bottle of whiskey is on the counter, but it's barely been touched. My mind flickers to the night Scout bought whiskey for us. JR and I danced in the headlights, he kissed me for the first time...

I could get lost in that delicious memory, but I don't have time for distractions.

I go quickly into the small living area, and when I step around a chair, my eyes land on the black device lying on the floor.

"Oh, God, no." I fall to my knees beside it, desperation tightening my throat.

It's not just shattered. It's demolished. The face is splintered into a million pieces, and it looks like something heavy was dropped on it for good measure. Picking it up carefully, I grab a bit of paper towel off the end table and wrap it around the device, doing my best to preserve every bit.

I'm scared now. JR said this was his only chance at a reversal. Slipping it into my pocket, I go to the door and open it.

Crazy Old Lady is still there waiting. "Did you feed the cat?"

"Oh!" I jump back with a squeal. "Yes… It's all good. Thank you, Miss…"

"Ronnie. Short for Veronica." She turns and goes back inside her apartment, slamming the door.

Shaking my head, I run to Metallicar. I'll have to come back for my supplies. I've got to get to the nearest phone repair shop and pray they can work a miracle.

"Try ten, four, twenty fifteen." I quickly repeat the numbers to the guy behind the counter.

When I pulled out JR's demolished phone, the repairman's face drained of color, but I wouldn't let him discourage me. We've come too far.

He attached a bunch of wires to the dead device. Then he needed the passcode to unlock it. Thankfully, Scout was on a layover.

"That did it." The tech winces at me. I think he meant to smile, but he's been pretty bleak since I pulled out the phone.

"You're a genius." I tell Scout.

"When my brother gets out, I want you to be sure and tell him that."

I have to hand it to him, even in the face of this dire situation, Scout still manages to try and keep things light. Of course, he hasn't seen this phone.

"What were the numbers?"

"Jesse's birthday."

"Got it." I make a mental note, October fourth. "How much longer until you get here?"

"I'm supposed to be there at seven."

Glancing at the clock, I see it's two more hours. "I'll be glad to see you."

"Same here, girl. You know, we were only together a few days, but it felt like the three of us could face anything after that road trip. Didn't it?"

A surge of warmth fills my stomach. "It did."

It really did.

"Here's your receipt." The guy hands me a long piece of paper, and he shakes his head. "Nothing is guaranteed, and we're not promising we can fix it."

Taking the sheet, I give him a pleading look. "Please, please do everything you can. You have no idea how important the information on that phone is."

"You just need something off it?" His brow furrows.

"A video. It was made two days ago, and it's vitally important."

He nods. "Usually it only takes a day, but it might take a little longer in this case."

"As soon as you can." I think about what Stephen Hastings said about having faith in each other.

I do have faith, and I have to believe this guy can help us.

"Here's another number just in case you can't get me." I quickly write Scout's number on the receipt. "Call either of us as soon as you know something."

TWO HOURS LATER, I'M PICKING UP SCOUT AT THE AIRPORT.

"What's the latest?" He hops into the passenger's side dressed in faded jeans and a long-sleeved tee.

His light hair is messy, and instead of the carefree expression he usually wears, he's focused.

"The guy at the repair shop wasn't very encouraging." I glance over with a worried face.

He gives my shoulder a squeeze and shifts in the seat, taking out his phone. "I've got a backup plan. We're going to see JR at the prison."

My heart beats faster. I want to see him so badly. "You think we can?"

"We have to try. I need him to help me find this Clyde guy."

"You think he's still there?"

"Only one way to find out." Scout's jaw tightens. "JR didn't beat a confession out of him, but I will. Then I'm going to find a good lawyer and get my brother free."

CHAPTER
Twenty-Six

JR

FOR TWENTY-EIGHT HOURS, I'VE BEEN ALONE IN THIS CELL.

The warden said we're isolated for our safety, but it only intensifies the thoughts pressing hard against my brain.

My one call was to my son. I wanted to call Hope. I ache every time I think about her, but I had to call Jesse.

At the sound of that boot crunching my phone, he was the first thing on my mind. He's waiting for me. He believes me when I say I'll be back soon. He's also five—too little to understand why. He'll only know I never came back.

Again.

Exhaling a low growl, my fist tightens as all the rage roars to life in my chest. I'd released my dad. I'd kept myself from beating the shit out of that asshole Clyde, but injustice still won. I'm back to where I was when I left this place a month ago. I want to hurt somebody. Not somebody, three people in particular.

The bitterness in my chest is a physical pain. My one chance at overturning this wrongful conviction is gone… There's no way it survived, and powerlessness is a cruel driver.

Scout said he was getting on the next plane here, but it's hard to believe it'll make any kind of a difference.

"Just hang on, bro. I'm going to get you out of there." My brother's voice was level.

Then he put Jesse on the line.

"It's taking a little longer than I expected, buddy." Despite the flames in my throat, I managed to quiet them for him.

"How much longer?" Jesse's wobbly whisper clawed at my heart.

"I'm not sure. I'm not sure…" My voice cracked as I said the words, and I blinked up at the overhead lights, doing my best not to lose it.

"I did what you said." His small voice turns positive, hopeful. "I invited Hunter to be on my team."

"You did?" Leaning my head back, I fight to match his optimism. I imagine being there with him. "How'd it go?"

"Just like you said. We're all friends now."

"That's good. I'm really proud of you." *God, this is so hard.*

"Uncle Scout said he's going to get you and bring you home. Will you come home with Uncle Scout?"

"If there's any way…" I swallow the knot in my throat. A beeping on the line tells me my time is up. "I have to go now, buddy. I love you, little man."

"I love you too, Dad."

Ever since that call, I've sat waiting. I should have a meeting with a lawyer, but according to the guards, everything takes longer these days. All I can do is wait and hope.

Hope…

Dropping my head into my hands, I can't stop thinking about her, her soft skin and bright blue eyes, her sweet laugh and sexy little body. After weeks of searching for her, there she was, back at that old beach house. We shared the most amazing night. When

I left her, we were making plans. I'd asked her to go with me to Fireside, and she said okay.

Now it's all shot to hell.

My fingers curl against my forehead. I believed. I actually *prayed*. Snapping my gaze up to the ceiling, my jaw tightens along with my fist. Why would I find something I've never had only to have it taken away?

The thought of never touching her again, holding her, burying my face in her hair… It's the definition of hell.

I push off the floor, pacing the small square room and breathing hard. I'm about to start throwing things when a buzz at the door, cuts me off. Turning to face the sound, I see a masked guard approaching.

"You've got a visitor." He stands outside the door waiting, and I check the clock.

Is it possible Scout got here that fast? Is it Hope? Looking down at the heavy, light blue shirt I'm wearing, I wince.

It's the same thing I was wearing the first day we met. The same shirt she slipped over her naked body in the motel room that night. I'll never forget her standing in the shaft of light from the bathroom like an old-school centerfold.

Even if she knows it's wrong and I shouldn't be here, I hate for her to see me this way.

The guard motions for me to go into a glass-windowed room, again, saying it's for safety.

"My brother, the jailbird." Scout's voice greets me from the other side of the glass. He's grinning, but I don't smile.

"You made good time." My voice is flat. "Did you find the phone?"

"Hope did." His smile fades, and he shakes his head. "She said the guy at the repair shop was pretty grim."

My chin drops as the wave of anger surges through me. "So that's it."

"Nope." His voice is sharp, determined. "New plan. You're going to tell me where I can find Clyde Shaw, and I'm going to get his confession myself."

Our eyes meet, and I'm conflicted. "I can't let you do that. If you got in trouble—"

"The way I see it, you don't have much choice. I came here to help you. You've got a little boy praying his daddy will come home every night."

My throat aches, and I can't escape how much that hurts. "I don't want to let him down."

Scout steps closer to the glass. "So tell me where that asshole is hiding."

That makes me laugh. "He's not hiding. At least he wasn't. He's right out in plain sight living over the Ritual Roasters at Buena Vista Park."

"That's all I needed."

Looking up at him, I'm not sure what to say. "How did it come to this? I tried to look out for us. I wanted to be a good dad—"

"You're the best dad. You got hit hard, but you've thrown me the ball, and I always catch it. I always run it in for the win." He puts the side of his fist on the glass. "I won't let you down this time."

"You've never let me down." I put my fist up across from his.

"Not even when I was Rammin' Rod?" His eyes twinkle, and I just shake my head.

"Don't get arrested. Can't have you in prison with that reputation. I'll never get any sleep."

"I won't." He shoves his hands in his pockets and looks down. "Hope's here. She wants to see you."

Shame flashes in my chest. "I don't want her to see me like this."

"Like what? You look like you did all the way to Charleston. Except for when you shaved your beard."

Reaching up, I scrub my fingers through my stubble. "I guess you're right."

"She's the one. I'm telling you. Marry her."

"I'm not tying her down to a jailbird. Fuck that."

"When I spring your ass out of here, the first thing you're going to do to repay me is propose to her."

"I can't propose to a girl I've only known five weeks."

"You proposed to a girl you knew five years. How did that work out?"

My jaw tightens, and I turn away from the glass. "I still can't believe Becky did this."

Scout's quiet a minute, and when I look back, he's mad. "You think Becky turned you in?"

"When I told her I wanted Jesse full-time, she threatened to call the parole board."

His blue eyes flash, and he steps back from the window. "I've got a call to make. I'm sending Hope in now." He pauses at the door. "You look at her and tell me if you don't see your future there."

"I can't see a future there until I don't see a future here."

"Your days in this shit hole are numbered. Next time I see you, I'm coming with a lawyer."

He strides out of the anteroom, and I hesitate. I'm not sure if she'll enter immediately, or…

"JR?" Her soft voice hits me right in the chest.

"Hope?" I step forward, putting both hands on the glass.

She's rushes to it, putting her palms flat against mine. Still, this fucking barrier is between us. Tears are in her eyes, and it causes my chest to ache.

"I'm sorry, Hope."

"No!" She shakes her head. "It's not your fault. We're going to fix this. Scout's here, and he's determined—"

"Listen to me." I pause, letting my eyes drink in her face, her bright blue eyes. The waves of pale blonde hair that fall around her temples. She looks just like her name. I can't get over it. "I know my brother is determined. I don't know what he's going to find or how it'll go—"

"We're going to find that guy, and we're going to get you out of here."

"Maybe. I hope so." *God, can I say these words?* "Just in case that doesn't happen, I want you to keep going with your pancake dream. Go to Monterey, take that guy's money, and start your restaurant. Don't wait for me."

"I have to wait for you. I'm not giving up on any part of my dream."

Our hands are on the glass, and her eyes are so warm. *This girl.*

"I want to kiss you."

She smiles, and her cheeks flush a pretty shade of pink. It matches her fuzzy pink sweater. My arms ache to hold her.

"When we come back." She moves her forehead close to the glass. I do the same. "I'll be waiting for my kiss."

"I won't make you wait."

Her blue eyes meet mine, and that fist releases in my chest. It happens every time. Maybe my idiot little brother is right. This girl is my future.

CHAPTER
Twenty-Seven

Hope

"**S**HE SAID SHE DIDN'T DO IT." SCOUT IS IN THE PASSENGER'S SEAT looking at his phone.

"Who?" My brow furrows.

We crashed last night at the beach shack after he arrived then went straight to the prison this morning to visit JR and get the location of Clyde Shaw. We're in a good position to find him and get this done today. I'm just waiting to hear from the phone repair guy as a backup.

And praying.

"JR thinks Becky called the parole board and turned him in."

My jaw drops. "That bitch!"

"Yeah, she's a bitch all right, but when I called Dad, she swore to him she didn't do it."

I'm fuming driving the car. I want to fly all the way to Charleston and slap that woman right across her stuck up, bitch-assed face. "Do you believe her?"

"I don't know. I mean, Becky's a gold-digging whore, who it seems was always in love with our dad, which is weird and gross, but I mean, I guess he's a good-looking man...?"

As much as I hate to admit it, their dad is a very good-looking man—for someone as old as my father. His sons look just like him.

"It just doesn't make sense." He continues. "Dad doesn't want to have Jesse full time. Gran's got him at her house. Why would Becky do it?"

Guilt weighs in my chest. "Do you think it was because of me?"

Scout glances over at me and squints. "You're pretty damn cute, but eh." He shakes his head. "It doesn't feel right."

It doesn't matter, because we're at the park. Steering Metallicar to a spot behind a bush, I parallel park, and we mask up and get out.

"How do you want to do this?" I look down at my fuzzy pink sweater and white leggings. "I didn't really dress for beating a confession out of anyone."

"Just leave it to me." Scout strides across the four-lane highway like he owns the place.

I think he might be reenacting a part in a movie, but I take off after him. All I care about is getting JR out of prison and figuring out what comes next.

The coffee shop smells delicious as we walk through the door. It smells so good, I almost need to take a seat.

"I'm not sure I could live over a coffee shop," I whisper. "I'd stay broke."

Scout holds up a hand and looks around the space. It's all pale wood and very open and empty. In the center is a stark, black granite station where it looks like they take orders and roast and prepare the coffee.

He turns to speak right in my ear. "You must not be able to access the apartments from here."

"What are we going to do?" I look over his shoulder at the barista watching us. "We've been spotted."

Stepping back, he grins, and I swear a twinkle flashes in his eye. "Hey, there... Betsy." He reads her name tag. "I was looking for a guy... Clyde Shaw. I think he lives around here?"

Betsy blinks several times, and I think she might have forgotten how to talk. Scout does have the power to strike women dumb.

Stepping up beside him, I smile. "Betsy?"

She finally tears her eyes away from my handsome friend to look at me. "Sorry!" She shakes her head like she just woke up from a daze. "Welcome to Royal Roasters. Would you like to try the Buena Vista special?"

"Actually, we're looking for a guy... Clyde Shaw? I think he lives around here."

"Oh! Clyde's right upstairs..." She inhales sharply, almost like she just remembered something.

Twenty dollars and I'll tell you what.

"Thanks." I grab Scout's arm, and we head out of the shop, running first left then right along the sidewalk until we see the entrance to an apartment overhead.

"Hurry," I hiss, as we press all four of the buzzer buttons until one of them goes off, releasing the front door.

Falling inside, we catch our breaths. Scout grips my upper arms. "You stay here. I don't know what might happen when we go in there."

"No way." My eyes flash. "I'm not letting you do this alone."

I know what Scout plans to do, and I want to be able to bash Clyde Shaw over the head should things go wrong.

"If anything happened to you, JR would kill me."

"Nothing's going to happen to me. Or you."

We find the apartment number and charge up the stairs. I'm right behind him when we get to the landing, and he bangs on the door.

We back up to wait, and my heart is beating so fast, I'm not sure I can breathe. I want to hold out my hand and say wait a minute, but it's too late.

The door jerks open, and everything stops. A guy dressed in jeans and a beige oxford shirt stands in the doorway. He has a light brown afro and short beard, and he looks like Bob Ross. I half expect him to smile and say it was all a happy accident.

Instead he blinks several times then does break into a smile. I'm completely confused until he speaks.

"Oh my God." He takes a step back, putting his hand on his chest, seeming star struck. "Are you... Are you... *Rod?*"

My hand flies to my mask to cover my laugh. I pass it off as a sneeze.

Scout's entire demeanor changes as he stands beside me. The fight disappears, and he grins. "Sorry, I'll just put this on..."

He lowers his chin and shakes his hair as he loops the mask over his ears, giving Clyde a little wink. "I see you've heard of me."

"Yes." Clyde looks like he might faint. "I mean, I've *seen* of you."

He starts to laugh like a hyena, and my nose wrinkles. *Ew.*

Scout doesn't react. He waits, putting a hand on his hip. A few seconds tick past, and suddenly Clyde seems to snap out of it.

"Would you like to come in? I don't know to what I owe the pleasure..."

"Well, I'll tell you, Mr. Shaw." Scout casually swaggers into the apartment. "Or can I call you Clyde?"

"By all means, call me Clyde."

I close the door and stand back, unsure what's about to happen.

"My assistant and I are here because I'm in need of supplements... if you know what I mean."

"Of course. I can get you anything you need—Acapulco

Gold, Blue Dream…" He goes to the kitchen, opening and closing cabinets. "Do you need to be calm or energized?"

Scout gives me a glance, slipping his hand into his pocket. I know he's turning on his voice recorder, and I dig around in my bag for my phone. Clyde is completely ignoring me, and I plan to make the most of it.

"No, Clyde. I need something for my physique."

Clyde turns to him and pops an eyebrow. "Last I checked, your physique's doing just fine, Rod." He chuckles, and I force my face to remain neutral.

Scout walks to the guy, getting just close enough to make me squirmy. "I want to bulk up. I heard you're the guy to help me."

"I'm glad to help you… Did you have something particular in mind?"

"HGH. Growth hormone."

Scout's gaze levels, but Clyde's chin pulls back.

He seems to lose all his swoon, and instantly he's on alert. "Who told you that?"

My heart beats faster, and I'm not sure what to do.

Scout grins, holding out a hand. "Hey, now. Take it easy. *Who told me* isn't as important as *can you get it?*"

He's quiet, looking from me to Scout. I'm convinced it's over. We're going to have to return to Plan A, beating it out of him, and I have no idea if that means we'll end up in jail or on the news… More like TMZ, *Rammin' Rod Attacks Bob Ross.*

"I just like to be careful." Clyde's shoulders relax. "I don't have that on hand."

"My bad. I was told you could get it for me… You know a guy named Ritchie? Ritchie Deemers out of Charleston?"

Again, Clyde tenses up, and I might have to step into the hall so I don't blow our cover. My heart is in my throat.

"Deemers?" Clyde's brow lowers. "It's been a while. Funny you're the second guy this week to mention him."

"What are the chances of that?" Scout laughs, shaking his head. "There's just no accounting for this year, is there?"

"No, there isn't." Clyde isn't smiling, he's studying us, and I could never be an actress. I'm totally panicking.

"Just between us..." Scout walks to the bar so casually, like it's all business as usual and our cover isn't teetering on the brink of being blown. "I'm working on a screenplay, sort of a second career type of thing, and I wanted to do something similar to *The Mule*—you know, that Clint Eastwood film? I thought maybe you could be my consultant. Have you ever been to LA?"

That changes Clyde's tone. "A Hollywood movie?"

"Yeah, Bigelow has indicated interest. Shia LaBeouf is attached. Maybe he'd play you..."

"I thought he was out of the game."

"Nobody's ever out of the game, my friend. Deemers said you'd used a mule before. How does that work?"

Clyde only hesitates a moment. "One of two ways. Either we can add additional packets to a regular order or in the case of Deemer's, his entire order was HGH."

"That so?" Scout makes a face like he's taking mental notes. "And it worked?"

"It would've. The asshole got caught."

I'm definitely going to have to step into the hall. I'm ready to beat him for saying that, and I don't even care if we get a confession.

Scout watches me, and fury must be shooting from my eyeballs like lightning bolts. He comes to me and puts a hand on my forearm. I glance up at him, and his expression says *calm down*.

He waits a beat, then asks, "What was the mule's name?"

"What difference does it make? He's in jail." Clyde laughs. "Actually, he got out and came here threatening me. One call, and I had him back behind bars."

I'm about to scream at him, but Scout's grip on my arm

tightens. I try to jerk it away. I'm ready to jump on Clyde's back and start hitting him over the head with my shoe. Then maybe I'll cram it in his smug, smiling mouth.

"I'm just curious." Scout's voice is as tight as his grip. "Maybe I could interview him. Get his side of the story, add a little heartbreak."

"I don't know. I don't feel comfortable—"

"You said he's behind bars." Scout is facing me, and his eyes close. "If you're going to be my consultant, you have to trust me."

I'm holding my breath. Could Clyde be that stupid? Could his lust for fame cause him to confess? I start to pray, *Be that stupid… Be that stupid…*

The apartment is quiet, and I think I'm going to be sick.

Clyde walks to the bar and picks up his phone. "Let me see. It was initials… JT or JD…" My lips part, and my eyes lock with Scout's. *This is it…* "Here it is. William Dunne."

My shoulders drop, and I silently swear.

Scout exhales a chuckle, releasing my arm and turning back to Clyde. "Is it JT or William?"

Clyde looks at him, and his eyes dazzle. I can only thank our lucky stars Scout is such a hot gay porn star. "William was the contact. It was his son, who made the pickup."

"Poor guy." Scout leans on the bar. "I've got to go, but maybe I'll drop by again."

"If I'm not here, leave your number with one of the baristas." Clyde's rat face looks suspicious, and I'm afraid he's onto us.

"I'll do it." Scout's hand is on my arm, and he leads me to the door. He does a finger-gun. "Thanks for being a fan."

"Thank you for sharing your… endowments."

Turning to the door, I roll my eyes so hard, I'm surprised they don't get stuck. We're out in the hall, and I'm stomping all around pissed. Scout taps his phone, turning off the recording, and grabs my wrist, dragging me down the stairs behind him and out onto the sidewalk.

"Holy shit!" He puts both hands on his forehead and exhales deeply.

"Motherfucker!" I shout, pacing a small circle. "Did we get it? Is that enough to nail his ass? I want his ass nailed!"

He throws an arm around my shoulders and pulls him to me, laughing. "You are something else, you know it? For a minute, I thought I'd have to pull you off that guy."

"I'm surprised I didn't have to pull you off him." I'm still raging.

"Getting that confession was the most important thing. He didn't exactly say JR's name or initials, but he said Dad's name. He said William's son. We need to talk to a lawyer."

"Let's go." He releases me, and we head to the car.

CHAPTER
Twenty-Eight

Hope

"IT'S WEAK." WE'RE SITTING IN FRONT OF THE COMPUTER SCREEN, talking to the Zoom lawyer, and I'm getting more and more frustrated.

"He clearly stated they planted the drugs on JR without his knowledge." Scout pushes, but the lady shakes her head.

"He doesn't clearly state it. Also, it could be argued he was bragging to impress you. He can come back and say he made it all up. It's too vague."

I'm out of my chair, walking around the living room and shaking my arms. It's so frustrating to be this close, to know the guy is a guilty, lying piece of shit, and not to be able to use it.

"So what do we do?" Scout won't give up.

"He needs to clearly say he planted the drugs in your brother's car without his knowledge. That's the most important piece. Without that, it won't hold up."

"I don't know if he'll say more a second time." Scout looks at me, worried.

"What if Ritchie Deemers confessed?" I lean into the camera.

"How would you convince him to talk?" Zoom lawyer studies her notebook. "The pickup never occurred, so as it stands, he's not implicated in any of this. If he comes forward, he'll basically be confessing he's part of an international drug ring."

"Can you offer him protection? Make a deal with him or something like a plea bargain?"

The lawyer only laughs. "It's not that big of a case."

"I'll wait a little bit and try going after Clyde again. Thank you. We'll be back." Scout hits the end button, and we both sit, staring at the blank screen.

For a minute, neither of us speaks. I look out the glass doors towards the ocean, while Scout stands and walks into the kitchen.

"Well, I didn't want to have to do this…" He exhales dramatically. "But it's been a while since I've had my dick sucked."

My eyebrows shoot up. "You're going to—"

"Maybe I'll just masturbate in front of him. I do have an appealing cock."

I cover my eyes with my fingers. "You'd do that?"

He stares at me a beat, his eyes dead serious.

I'm starting to think he might…

Until he starts to laugh. "You are so gullible."

"Scout!" I scramble to my feet so I can cross the room and hit him on the arm.

"I got you."

"That… I…" Shaking my head, I can't deny it. "It seemed a little extreme."

"A little!" He cries, laughing more. "We're pretty desperate, but I think we have a few more options before I start prostituting myself."

Walking to the doors, I look out at the ocean, wondering if we do. From where I'm sitting, it looks like we're back to beating it out of him.

"That Rammin' Rod thing really put you on the map."

"Or took me off it. I couldn't get an acting job for years. Casting directors wouldn't even speak to me."

"Seems so unfair. You couldn't help it." He makes a noise, and I pick up the keys off the table. "I'm going to see him. I can't stand thinking of him sitting alone in that cell all day."

Scout's eyebrow arches, and he gives me a little grin. "Okay."

"You want to come?"

"I'll see what I can come up with around here. Tell him I said hey."

TWISTING MY FINGERS, I WAIT FOR JR TO APPEAR THROUGH THE DOOR. I didn't really think it through coming here without better news. Still, when he enters the small room, I dismiss all my doubts.

His blue eyes light when they meet mine, and I rush to the glass. His beard is fuller, and his arms extending from his short sleeves seem more defined, like he's been working out again.

I put my palms against the barrier between us, aching to touch him.

"Hey." My voice is soft.

He places his palms opposite mine. "Hey." His voice is low, and when he smiles, I almost cry. "What are you doing here?"

Blinking up at him, I trace my finger along the glass like I would along his skin if I could. "I missed you. I hate thinking of you here all day alone."

He shrugs. "I'm used to it. How'd it go with Scout and Clyde?" The hint of optimism in his tone aches in my chest. I hate to disappoint him.

"Scout got him on record admitting they put the drugs in your trunk, and you got caught, and they were using you as a mule… It was him who reported you for violating parole."

His glittering eyes harden. "And?"

I inhale slowly before answering. "The lawyer said it

wouldn't hold up. Clyde said your dad's name as the initial contact, but he never directly named you as the mule... She said because Scout's a celebrity, his lawyer could argue he was bragging, making it up to impress us." I exhale sadly. "She said it's not enough."

He looks away, over his shoulder, and I can feel his body tense through the barrier. He turns away, and before my eyes, it's like a wall goes up between us, more impenetrable than the one currently standing.

My heart beats faster, and I want to break through this plexiglass and hold him, beg him to keep believing. I'm afraid it's too late.

"So that's it." The resignation in his voice makes me panicky.

"We're not stopping. Scout and I are both thinking of new ways—"

"It's over, Hope." His voice is flat. "I knew it when I lost my phone. It's time to stop fighting and do this time."

"No!"

His eyes flicker to mine, and his expression turns dark. A cold stream of dread filters through my veins.

"I've been thinking about it, and I made a decision…" His brow is lowered. "You need to get back to your business. You've wasted enough time on me. You need to follow up with that guy and get his help while he's offering it."

"But you said—"

"I said a lot when I thought things were different. You've got to live your life."

The pain in my chest radiates up to my temples. "Are you taking back what you said to me?"

"Things change. You have to walk through the doors when they open. Next time I hear about you, I want it to be for the grand opening of your new Pancake Paradise."

My heart is in my throat, and I'm doing my best to keep the

tears from falling. "Would you even hear about something like that in here?"

"I'll hear about it."

I can't bear it. I can't let him push me away without telling him, if only this once. "I love you, John."

His eyes close, and his chin drops. The sexy muscle in his perfect jaw moves, and he shakes his head. I watch him inhale slowly, then exhale before he breaks my heart. "Don't."

"Don't?" My voice goes high. "Don't love you?"

"Don't say that." He lifts his face, and our eyes meet. His are stormy and sad. "Don't come here anymore. I don't want to see you. I want you to get on with your life and leave us where we belong, in the past."

A hot tear hits my cheek. His eyes flicker to it, and his throat moves. He puts his mask on and goes to the door, waving to the guard and leaving me alone in the visiting space, staring at an empty room, an empty chair.

My chest is a bleeding hole. More tears start to fall, and I hiccup a breath. Oh, God, I'm going to break down. Cupping a hand over my mouth, I quickly go to the exit. I run to Metallicar before the uncontrollable sobs begin. I hold my hand against my face and close my eyes, fighting for control. I have to hold on. I have to.

It takes a few minutes before I'm able to complete the blurry drive back to the beach house. When I get there, Scout has left a note saying he's running an errand. I can't talk to him right now. I can only talk to one person.

Going to my closet, I take out my weekend bag and pack fast. Anger and sadness and misery make me slam the clothes harder than I normally would.

JR Dunne has pushed me away twice now, and I can't keep holding on, waiting for him to see how right we are together. If he wants me to do it, I will. I'll seize my opportunity.

Before I go, I pull the long receipt from my purse and place it on the bar with a note to Scout.

They have your number. You have mine.

If anything changes, let me know.

Lots of love,

Hope

CHAPTER
Twenty-Nine

JR

TELLING HOPE TO LEAVE WAS THE HARDEST THING I'VE DONE... SINCE the last time I did it.

Fuck. I tighten my fist, slamming it against the top bunk in my empty cell again and again. I don't want to treat her like a yo-yo, but my whole damn life has turned into one, and I'm not holding the strings. She doesn't deserve that.

She deserves to be out there making her dreams come true. Some asshole wants to help her... He probably wants to sleep with her, too. My throat tightens and I lift the metal bed, shoving it hard against the wall with a growl. Sending her to him makes me crazy with rage, but it's her second chance. She's got to take it.

As an added layer of insurance, I ask the guard, I think his name is Mel, to remove her name from my visitors list. Scout must have added it, because I never did. It's like pouring acid on a wound, but it's the only way I can be sure she doesn't come back and try to see me again. I'm not strong enough to send her away a third time.

It would be the most selfish thing I ever did.

Walking away from her was like giving up on my life. It was letting go of my hope.

It's resigning myself to being stuck in this place as long as the judge says, and then when I finally get out, I'll have a whole host of new hassles to deal with.

Still, it's the right thing to do. I knew it when those cops slapped the cuffs on my wrists. I knew it when that bootheel ground my phone into the floor. No more wishing on stars. I have to put my head down and do the time. Fair or not, this is where I am.

My next call will be to my brother. Somebody has to take care of Jesse.

WHEN I CALLED SCOUT, HE FILLED ME IN ON THE DETAILS OF WHAT happened. It was basically what Hope said. He told me she left, and he tried to get me to tell him why. I told him to go home to Jesse, tell my son I love him and it's breaking my heart not to be there.

Another week passes. Another week of my life I'll never get back.

I watch the news until I can't listen to it any more. I don't need assholes telling me cops can be assholes. No shit, Sherlock.

I lift weights. I read, and every day I walk around the yard for the two hours they give us as recreation. Only a handful of inmates are allowed out at a time, and we're all sectioned off.

I never made friends or had a group on the inside, so I'm fine keeping my distance. Walking to the chain-link fence, I look out towards the water. When I was in here before, somehow it was easier. I was fueled by rage and so focused on getting answers and making people pay. My entire mindset was on my dad and his part in putting me here.

Now I know the truth, and it's harder than it was before. It's like a fucking soap opera, where I got caught on the wrong side of the aisle. If it weren't so fucking stupid, I'd laugh. Or maybe I'd cry.

"I've known a lot of guys in here say they were innocent."

I'm lying on the bottom bunk of the metal beds in my room, and I look up to see Mel the Guard speaking to me. It's quiet and boring in here, so I answer.

"That so?"

"Yeah. This one guy Levi said he fell asleep in the backseat of his cousin's coupe. Woke up and the cousin was armed robbing a 7-Eleven."

"Let me guess." I shift to my side, not sure I want this kind of camaraderie.

"He got sentenced to life. Accessory to first-degree murder. The cousin shot the clerk in the face."

"Jesus." I shake my head, realizing it could be worse. I'm only on the hook for two to four more years, which is a lot, but shit.

We're quiet a little while. I look at the book I've been reading, something about the Vietnam war protests in the 1960s.

"Of the guys who claim they're innocent, the ones who do best, are the ones who don't give up and don't get hard."

I exhale a laugh. "Easy for you to say."

"I know." Mel nods, going down the short passage. "But I see you. I know you." His hand slides over the light switch. "I'm on your side."

It's lights out, and I lie in bed thinking about what he said. I want to be encouraged, but guards get transferred. Nothing's permanent here. The last thing I should do is trust somebody on the inside is on my side.

MORE DAYS PASS. I'VE LOST COUNT.

I'm lying on my back, looking at the iPhone Mel smuggled to me, wondering in the course of my life, where does this fall? Am

I living in the space between… Beauty came before, with football and Jesse. Now I'm in the pain. Is more beauty waiting on the other side of this, or will it be more pain… or a void?

The irritating thought is in my head, when I get a message from my brother. *Are you sitting down?*

It makes me frown, and I peck out a reply, doing my best to use my thumbs more than my fingers. *What else would I be doing?*

Don't want to give false hope, but something big just happened.

What?

Can't tell you yet.

I'll kick your ass.

Focus on that. I'll be back soon with instructions.

Swinging my feet to the floor, I look at the wall, my constant companion since I returned to this fucking hole.

My chest is tight, and of course, my first thought is seeing Hope again.

It doesn't matter if I sent her away. It doesn't make a damn bit of difference I listened to her say she loved me and didn't answer back. I love her.

I love her face, her pretty hair, her bright blue eyes and sweet smile… She haunts me every night.

In the daylight hours, I can keep her memory at bay. I can exercise, lift weights, walk around the yard, watch television, talk to Mel, play games on my phone, meditate…

Yeah, I meditate a little.

But at night, there's no escaping her.

I close my eyes, and I see her beautiful body. My fingers curl against the mattress, and I feel her round ass beneath them. I crave her taste, her soft lips, her small tits, her flat stomach.

She's the goddess of my dreams, and now I'm standing here, pacing this room, furious at the torture my little brother has conjured. Hoping against hope, the girl of my dreams might be on the other end of it.

I collapse onto the bed, dropping my face to my hands. The last time I prayed, I got kicked in the nuts so hard, I didn't think I'd recover. What's wrong with me?

Still, I can't help myself.

God, please…

CHAPTER
Thirty

Hope

"I T'S LIKE I'M DAWN." I'M LYING ON THE LOUNGE CHAIR ACROSS from my dad.

I had to wait two weeks to be this close to him. Until then, I stayed at a Holiday Inn nearby and talked to him through a plastic screen like he was the Bubble Boy.

It didn't matter. I just wanted to be near him. I needed my dad.

"Who's Dawn?" He frowns at me, shoving his longish brown hair behind his ears.

I was right, although he's more *Road House* than *Deadwood*, and he isn't wearing a mustache.

"Are you kidding me?" I slap the side of the lounger and sit up. "Frankie Valli and the Four Seasons?"

"Oh." He leans his head back and laughs, brown eyes brimming with love. "You can't just pull something like that out of left field."

"I'm so glad to see you, Dad." Even though it's safe, I lower my cheek to his chest and hug him that way.

"I'm glad to see you too. I missed your sunshine." His kind hand smooths my hair back. "Now tell me more about this Dawn situation."

"Oh, Dad." I sigh, sitting up and falling against the cushions. "He's been wrongfully convicted of dealing drugs... And stop!" I hold up my hand. "Before you ask me how I know, trust me. I know. I was there when the guy who set him up confessed. Only the lawyer said it wasn't a strong enough confession because the liar fingered his dad as the target rather than him..."

My dad's thick brow furrows. "That isn't right." His low voice rumbles slowly, and I couldn't agree more.

"That's where we are. I told him I loved him, and he sent me away. He said I couldn't wait for him. I had to get on with my life."

"He sounds like a good man." Dad leans back on the lounge chair beside me.

We're lying next to a sparkling blue pool at the Shady Rest nursing home, although nobody's swimming. Still, it's a nice ambiance. A small waterfall is trickling at the far end, and palm trees are strategically planted at the corners.

It has more the feel of a luxury resort than an assisted living facility.

"He's the best kind of man." Tilting my head to the side, I remember how he was with his brother, his son, me. "He's an amazing dad. His little boy is so adorable, and he's a loving grandson. His brother adores him..."

"Says a lot about a man when other people care about him that much."

"I really do love him. I think he loves me, too."

Dad's lips twitch, and he slants an eye at me, giving me a little grin. "If that's the case, then it's going to happen. The universe doesn't let true love go unanswered. It wouldn't be right."

"I hope so."

"Hope eternal."

We spend the rest of the day walking along the shore. I meet his new girlfriend Karla, and she's really beautiful. Slim with brown skin and thick, spiral-curled brown hair. She's smart and wise, and she clearly loves my father.

We have dinner and she tells me about her yoga practice. She specializes in middle-aged patients, and as much as she never gets involved, she couldn't resist my fit, handsome father.

I'm not harshing on her. Dad's a silver fox all right. And she's really calm and steady. I think she'll be good for him.

When he walks me to the Impala that night, I'm not sure I'm ready to say goodbye, but I know it's time to get back to San Francisco. Two weeks is a long time to be away from home, and I have to make a decision one way or the other.

"If you really love him, hold onto him." Dad smooths a lock of hair behind my ear. "You're not an easy girl to let go."

"Sure you're not just saying that because I'm your daughter?"

"No." He shakes his head, and it makes me laugh. I put my face against his chest and hug him again, longer, not wanting to let him go.

"I'm so glad I got to see you. Karla is amazing."

"You're amazing. I love you, Sunshine." He steps back, inspecting Metallicar. "I knew you'd take care of my baby. I have to say, you look like a badass driving it."

"You're the badass." One last dad hug, and I think I'm ready to face the real world again.

Still, there are times when I wish I was a little girl, laughing and screaming from the treehouse out back, not a care in the world.

I'm pulling up to the beach shack when my phone goes off with a text from a number I haven't heard from in weeks. *Are you back in town?*

Are you back in town? I reply. Last I heard, Scout was returning to Charleston to be with Jesse.

Would you do something for me if I promise it'll make you happy?

I can't imagine what he's talking about, still, I'm curious. *Only if it's quick and easy.*

When did quick and easy ever equal happy?

Touché. Still make it quick.

An hour later, I'm walking on the pedestrian path along the Golden Gate Bridge. I haven't done this since I was a girl with my dad. We used to try and see if we could run the whole way across. I always ended up not even halfway across with a cramp, holding my side and laughing.

Traffic is still pretty sparse at my back, and I stop in the center, looking out over the waves far below. It's dark, and I close my eyes, remembering a time when I believed I could hear the angels singing over the waters.

It's been a long time since I believed that.

I don't even get sad anymore.

"Hope?" The deep voice pulls me up short, and my eyes flash open.

My breath disappears, and my body trembles all over. What's happening right now?

He comes closer, breaking into a jog until he's right in front of me.

I still can't find my voice, and now I'm having a hard time seeing his face. Tears blur my eyes.

"Did he…" He looks over his shoulder in the direction he came, and I take the chance to reach up and lightly touch my fingers to the ends of his dark hair.

At last I find my voice. "What are you doing here?"

Ice-blue eyes blink back at me under a dark, furrowed brow. He's so brutally handsome, for a moment I'm lost in the sight of him.

"My phone." He stops short, shaking his head like he's in disbelief. "The guy you gave my phone called Scout and said he couldn't fix it… But he was able to retrieve the file you needed. The last video."

An ache fills my throat, and I almost can't speak. "He got it?" Blinking, a crystal tear hits my cheek.

JR reaches up to wipe it away with his thumb. "You saved me."

His body is so close to mine, I can smell his luscious scent of soap and sweat and spicy-man. "You made the recording. I only took it to the repair guy."

His fingers slide along the side of my hair, and I close my eyes, leaning my cheek into his palm. He lifts his other hand, tracing the side of his thumb along my bottom lip. He touches me like he's remembering something…

"The judge dismissed the case. She threw out my conviction. They cleared my name."

My chest tightens with every word, and I huff an excited laugh. "She did?" My hands rise to my lips.

"Not only that, GA did some digging. Found out my mom left us a trust fund when she died. A pretty big one."

"You didn't know?"

"Our dad used some of it to start his gym. Which means we own all of it. The house, the gym, his wellness line of products."

Blinking, I try to understand what he's saying. "It's what you said you'd do…"

"It's what I figured I'd do. Now I fucking own it all."

"Is that good?"

His eyebrows rise, and he nods slowly. "Yeah. It's really good. Trust me. It's better than good."

Rising on my toes, I clasp my hands together under my chin. I want to hug him. I want to kiss him and tell him he's amazing and he deserves every good thing that's coming to him. I want to tell him I still love him…

Instead, I stick to the basics. "How's Jesse?"

"Great." Warmth permeates his tone. "He's here. We've been spending every minute together since I got out. I've taken him everywhere… but he keeps asking about you."

"Me?"

"Yes."

A bloom of warmth floods my chest. "But why are you here?"

"My brother said a dream I had would come true if I showed up here tonight."

"A dream?"

"Something I didn't know I wanted until it dropped in my lap on the road between San Francisco and Los Angeles."

I can't hold back a laugh. "What is it?"

Strong arms wrap around me, lifting me off my feet. My legs wrap around his waist, and I rest my hands on his cheeks. Looking into his blue eyes, I see heat and desire and longing and… something more?

"I'm glad to see you smiling." My voice is soft. "What will you do now?"

"I was thinking I'd settle down, maybe get married, give Jesse the home he deserves."

"You're a handsome man, JR Dunne. Any woman would be lucky to have you."

"Is that so?" He lowers me to my feet, and I look up at him, nodding. Warm hands cup my cheeks, and he leans closer. "Only one man could be lucky enough to have you."

My nose wrinkles, and I lift my chin. "Who might that be?"

"This man." His voice is rough, sending heat sizzling all the way to my toes. "Can I kiss you?"

"I wish you would."

Warm lips cover mine, pushing them apart and sweeping his tongue inside. A high whimper escapes on an exhale, and I'm off my feet again. My legs are around his waist, and I hold him, chasing his lips, doing my best to keep up with his kisses. It's divine and delicious, and bubbles of happiness rise in my chest.

I lift my chin, and his lips trace a hot line down my neck. Lowering me to my feet, he cups my face and holds my head as he takes a long inhale of my hair. Shimmers move from my head to my toes.

"Hope?" He steps back, putting both hands on my shoulders. I blink my eyes open in dreamy satisfaction, meeting his gaze. "I love you."

My throat tightens at the words. Heat fills my eyes, and I have to blink quickly to clear it. "You…"

"I love you so much. I want you to marry me. I want you to come home with me to Fireside, and I want us to find a place for your restaurant. I want your life to be with me. I want to make your dreams come true. I want your dreams to be my dreams. I want you to be my hope eternal."

"You…" I can't speak. It's too much for my blissed-out brain to handle.

"You don't have to answer me now. I only want you to know that's what I want." He leans forward, kissing the tip of my nose, the top of my lips. "The rest is up to you."

Mist is so heavy in my eyes, I can only grin and kiss him back. "I can answer you now. My answer is yes."

Warm hands slide along my waist, slipping beneath the hem of my white sweater, rising higher to cup my back. My entire body is humming with delight.

We're here together. We're making promises. It's the culmination of my dream, and it's with the man of my dreams.

Closing my eyes, our lips reunite, and electricity races from the tips of my hair to the tips of my toes. JR's lips capture mine, and our tongues slide and curl together. It's incredible. It's everything, and when my eyes flutter open to gaze at the brilliant stars above us, it's there.

To the average pedestrian, it might sound like the hum of tires on the metal bridge, but it's not. Far away, over the ocean, it's them. Angels are singing. It's the first time I've heard them in a year.

Lifting his head, he looks into my eyes. "Do you hear that?"

My eyebrows quirk, and my stomach flutters. "Hear what?"

He looks to the side and waits, but after a moment, he shakes his head, a sexy smile curling his perfectly full lips. "I thought I heard singing."

Bouncing on my toes, I squeeze my arms tighter around his neck, speaking in his ear. "It's the sound of our future. It's going to be brighter and more beautiful than we ever knew."

He smooths both hands along the sides of my face, cupping my cheeks. "You're my hope, and I'm holding onto you as long as I live. I'll never let you go."

Placing my hand on his chest, over the spot where his ink lies, I look into his eyes and make a vow. "This much is true... You can count on me. I'll never let you down. I'll always stand by your side."

Another kiss, and while our lips part in a swirl of desire and passion and longing, our mouths seal in a promise we'll keep. It's a promise of hope and of a future. It's a promise born of hardship and refusing to let go.

It's a promise that says this much is true... I'll never let you go.

Epilogue

JR

'M BALLS DEEP IN THE WOMAN OF MY DREAMS, AND SHE'S TAKING ME TO paradise.

Hope's back is to me, and she rocks her hips, moving faster as I thrust my cock deeper into her hot little pussy.

"John…" She gasps, arching her back.

I sit up behind her, sliding my hands along her flat stomach up to her soft breasts, cupping them, tweaking her nipples. Her insides clench, and my mind blanks. I'm so close to coming.

"So good…" I groan, biting the top of her shoulder lightly.

Her body shudders, and I wrap my arm around her waist, sliding a hand between her legs and circling firmly over her clit. It's just enough to take us both over the top.

She breaks with a loud moan, clenching and falling into me. Her fingers curl in the side of my hair, and I close my eyes as the orgasm races through my legs, centering in my pelvis and pulsing into her.

It's so fucking good.

We're breathing fast, and both my arms are around her now. I turn my face to kiss her behind the ear, inhaling soft flowers and caramel. She reaches both hands over her head, caressing my neck, pulling my hair.

"Mmm..." The smile on her lips makes me smile. "My sexy husband."

Yeah, we did it. We decided not to waste any time getting married. As soon as we got back to Fireside, we had a small ceremony down by the shore in Oceanside, just the two of us, GA, Scout, and Jesse. When we're able to get everyone together, we'll fly out her dad, Karla, and Yarnell and have a big celebration.

On the way back, we took a detour through Oceanside Village, and stopped in a pretty little cake place. The owner was a friendly girl who said they did a steady business with tourists coming up from the strip.

Hope and I exchanged a look, and as soon as we got home, she got to work on her business plan, altering the location to a boutique community near a thriving beachfront tourist destination.

As luck would have it, Stephen Hasting's investment partner Remington Key is located not too far away, and he made a day trip to check it out. They agreed to give her half the startup money she'd need. As her husband, I'm investing the other half. Pancake Paradise is on track for a grand re-opening in the summer of next year, just in time for high season at the beach.

"My beautiful wife." Sliding my hands over her flat stomach, I kiss the side of her jaw, speaking in her ear. "I'm ready to put a baby in you. A little girl that looks just like her pretty mamma."

Hope slides her hands along my arms, threading our fingers. "Not until after the grand opening. It's going to be crazy until then."

"You'll be adorable barefoot and pregnant."

"Just because I was barefoot when you met me doesn't mean I won't wear shoes." She's teasing, and I kiss her neck.

Her shoulder rises with a squeal. I love that little sensitive spot. "To think, I almost left you on the side of the road."

"You wouldn't have done it." She climbs out of my arms, and I miss her already. "I'd better get moving. Alice is bringing Jesse for breakfast, and he wants peanut butter pancakes."

Jesse lives with us full-time now in our big house in the older part of town, but he spends every weekend with GA. He says he doesn't like her being alone. I tried to get her to move in here. We've got plenty of room, but she's stubborn and said she likes having her own place.

"Is Scout coming over?" I toss back the blankets as she emerges from the bathroom.

"I don't know. He's been spending a lot of time in Oceanside since the wedding. I think he's got a girlfriend there. You know, he never found that girl he told me about."

Her slim brow furrows over her bright blue eyes, and her hair is up in a high ponytail. She's dressed in jeans and a short black tank that shows off her cute little navel, and I can't resist. I catch her around the waist, kissing the back of her neck.

"John!" I love it when she fusses, especially when she's laughing like right now.

I only ever want to see her happy after all the shit we went through to get here.

An hour after my brother texted me in that prison cell, Mel the Guard came to the door and told me it was time to go. At first, I was confused, but a big grin split his fat cheeks. He told me the judge had reviewed new evidence on my case and threw out the charges.

I was a free man.

My brother's instructions were to get in the brand-new Tahoe he'd left for me and drive to Hope's beach house, which I was eager to do.

I walked through the door, and the first thing I heard was my little boy's voice. It hit me right in the chest, and I dropped to my knees to catch him in my arms for the longest hug we'd shared since the last time we were together at the airport.

It's possible tears were in my eyes. I'm not made of stone.

The whole place was decorated with balloons and streamers and a sign reading Welcome Home. Scout had flown back to get Jesse as soon as the lawyer said my phone recording would do it. Hope was with her dad, and I wanted to drive out to be with her.

Only, my brother had a different plan.

"I thought you might want to know what happened to that rat in Buena Vista," he'd said.

Fucking Clyde Shaw.

My joy at being released, being reunited with my son, reclaiming my life was shadowed by the fact that asshole was walking around free.

"Not for long."

We piled into my new ride, which is a whole other story, and Scout drove us into the city.

He parallel parked in a space behind a bush and killed the engine. "I've been working with the cops ever since Hope and I came back here. The detective called and said if we wanted to watch, now was the time."

My brother was still speaking as a swarm of cars surrounded the building.

A black Camaro pulled into the alley and a white police cruiser blocked the front entrance. Two uniformed officers burst through the apartment entrance with Clyde Shaw in handcuffs.

"Cool!" Jesse cried from the backseat watching. "They got the bad man!"

I looked at Scout. "How?"

"The evidence on your phone was the break they needed. Clyde was just a middle man, but he was connected to an international drug ring that extended from Mexico all the way to Toronto. Cops had been trying to break it up for two years."

As much as I'd wanted to kick his ass from here to Ocean Beach, seeing him dragged away in handcuffs had been pretty satisfying.

"Remember that con artist Brother Bob?" Scout sits at the kitchen table holding a coffee mug while Hope and Jesse are at the counter behind him in front of a large mixing bowl.

"Add a third of a cup of peanut butter." Hope holds a silver measuring cup over the bowl while my son scrapes the contents with a wooden spoon. "The snake handler who recognized you?"

She gives my brother a wink, and my son's head jerks around. "Who got a snake?"

My brother stands and goes to where my son is on a stool beside my beautiful wife. "A bad man who took a bunch of people's money." He leans closer. "That smells good. How much longer?"

"Finish telling us what happened!" Hope gives him a bump with her hip.

"He got caught with a fan of Rod's in his hotel room playing hide the sausage."

"What's hide the sausage?" Jesse's little nose curls, and I cut my brother a look.

"It's something you shouldn't play until you're a grownup." Hope kisses the top of his head.

"Because sausage is messy?"

"Yes." She grins, looking at me, and I shake my head. "Sausage can make a big mess if it's not handled properly."

"Some people like their sausage messy." Scout waggles his eyebrows, and I punch him on the arm hard.

"You don't say?"

"Ow, shiiooot." He rubs the spot. "That's going to leave a bruise."

"What kind of snake was it?" Jesse's stirring the pancake mix, and Hope puts her hand over his to help him.

The way they get along so well warms my heart.

"Copperhead." Scout grabs a handful of chocolate chips. "He was a bad man, and he got what was coming to him."

"Scout!" Hope fusses. "Don't eat all our decorations."

"What was coming to him?" Jesse watches his uncle while Hope pours the pancake batter into a squeeze bottle.

"Nobody listens to him anymore."

Jesse is confused, but Hope pulls him back to their preparations. "Good. Now, Jesse, you're going to use this to make your pancakes. I'll show you."

"Where's GA?" I step up beside my brother, grabbing a few chocolate chips.

"John!" Hope bumps me with her hip while she holds the squeeze bottle over the frying pan. I give her cute little butt a pinch and she squeals. "You messed it up..."

"She had to go to the church for some reason. Probably more prayer chain."

"I think it looks like a turtle." Jesse watches his pretty stepmom drizzling batter on the hot pan.

"It was supposed to be a heart." She narrows her eyes at me.

I wink. "There's more where that came from."

Hope snorts a laugh, shaking her head as she passes the bottle of batter to my son. The two of them spend the next few minutes spelling out their names, my name, Scout, Gran, then they make shapes. After they've finished playing and flipping the pancakes, we're all around the table spraying whipped cream and adding chocolate chips or banana slices or walnuts or all three.

"This is the best pancake ever!" Jesse is shouting again, which means he's happy. Or hopped up on sugar. Or both.

I expect to see my grandmother when I hear voices at the back door. I do not expect to see my ex-wife and father standing in the small mud room at the side of the kitchen.

"Sorry to interrupt." Dad seems uncomfortable. He and I still haven't come all the way around.

"Oh!" Hope jumps up from the table. "Jesse's soccer game."

Becky strides into the kitchen, looking around and crossing her arms. "What's all this?"

"Hope makes special pancakes, and we wrote our names and made shapes. I even made one that looked like Dad!" Jesse is turned up to eleven.

"Inside voice, Jess," his mother scolds. I wish she'd give him a hug and smile at him like Hope does. "Chocolate and whipped cream? Not a very healthy breakfast."

Hope returns to the room carrying Jesse's cleats and shin guards. Her eyes are worried as she scans the empty plates. "I did use whole wheat flour, and the peanut butter is organic…"

"That's a lot of sugar." Becky's eyes move up and down my wife in her typical judgey way. She's not smiling.

I step up beside Hope, putting my arm around her waist. "He'll burn that up in five minutes playing soccer." Giving Hope a squeeze, I kiss the side of her head. "The most important thing was spending time together."

Hope gives me a grateful glance. Becky's still watching us with her arms crossed and her upper lip curled. She'd better think twice before she tries to make trouble with Hope.

"Let's go." She pats our son on the head and turns for the door. "We'll have him back in time for dinner."

"Have fun!" Hope calls, and Jesse makes a U-turn running back to where she's standing. Hope instantly drops to her knees, and he throws his arms around her neck, giving her the biggest hug.

"Thank you for the pancakes." He kisses her cheek, and I'm ready to high five him. "Bye, Dad!"

He takes off running out the door, and Hope stands, clasping her fingers in front of her mouth. "He's so adorable."

"I remember when I used to get the hug bye."

I watch my father leave and think about how I started this journey, burning with rage and hell-bent on revenge. Karma has settled the scores far better than I could've.

He has nothing, he's married to that shrew, and he works for me. I actually feel sorry for the guy—when I think about him.

I have my son, and I have Hope. Her eyes meet mine, and it's sunshine breaking through the clouds, warming my heart and calming my anger.

GA plops down at the table. "That Rebecca St. John is so horny, I swear."

Hope and I jump back, but Scout slides in beside our grandmother unaffected. "*Ornery*, Gran. The word's *ornery*."

"That's what I said!" GA snaps. "She's so damn horny. I wish she'd try a little kindness sometime."

Hope's hands move from in front of her mouth to covering her face, and we both start to laugh. I'm collecting plates, and Scout joins me at the sink to wash them. I'm not sure how we got stuck with dish duty, but it started that day at GA's house when we first rolled into town.

"You've been spending a lot of time in Oceanside." I glance at my brother, taking the clean dish from him and drying it.

For the first time all day, he grows serious. "You remember Daisy Sales?"

Leaning against the counter, I try to remember. "Was that the little girl you were so into junior year?"

"We dated senior year."

"I was gone your senior year."

"I remember." He drains the sink, seeming pissed at me for graduating. "They tried to make me quarterback that year."

"Mistake." I fold the towel, thinking. "Her dad owned a furniture store?"

"Antiques."

"Teachers would pay her to do interior design for them."

"How the fuck do you remember all this?" He shakes his head.

"She set me up with Becky."

"Yeah, well, don't hold that against her. Becky had us all fooled." He puts his hands on the sink and looks out the window at the elaborate yard around my equally elaborate house.

This big ole place is a century old, with five bedrooms and five baths. It's on the historic register, and recently renovated. GA picked it out because she said I had to have a bigger house than my dad's. She's still pissed he hid our mother's trust fund from Scout and me.

I only agreed to buy it because I wanted her to move in with us. Then she insisted on staying in her tiny little house.

"She lives in Oceanside… with her little girl, Melody. She's three now." The way he says it piques my interest.

"Is she the one you were telling Hope about? The one you hoped was still waiting for you?"

He steps away from the counter and seems to shake it off. "Yeah, I gotta go."

"That's it?" I holler after him, but he's telling GA and Hope bye, heading for the door quick. "Scout?" I step after him, catching his shoulder. "What's going on?"

He shakes his head. "I'll tell you more when I know more."

He seems frustrated, embarrassed, maybe a little angry—all strange emotions from my little brother. I want him to talk to me, but I'll let him have his space.

For now, I lean against the doorjamb, watching my pretty wife chatting with my crazy grandmother, thinking a twisted path led me to here.

LATER THAT NIGHT, HOPE IS SNUGGLED AGAINST MY CHEST. WE'RE sweaty and satisfied, and she's tracing her finger along the lines of the new tattoo on my chest. *Hold onto hope…*

It's right under *This Much is True...*, inked at a time when I only believed in myself. Now I realize how wrong I was, this beautiful girl in my arms changed my hatred to love.

"They say it's bad luck to get a tattoo of your significant other's name." She props her cute little chin on her hand, blinking up at me.

Tracing my finger along the line of her hair, I push a silky lock behind her ear. "You're my wife, and it's not your name, it's a reminder. You're my hope eternal."

Her eyes mist, and I cup her cheeks, kissing her gently. "Don't cry. I want you to be happy."

"I'm crying because I am happy." She blinks smiling, and a crystal tear falls to her cheek. "Hope Eternal Dunne. No more hills."

I gather her close, rotating her naked body so her back is to my chest. Holding her in my arms, pressing my lips to her shoulder, inhaling her beautiful scent... It makes all the shit I went through worth it.

I'll never get back the time I lost with my son, but Hope is so loving to him, I think it evens the scale. They're my new family, my new life, and it's so much better than the old.

Hope's dad says a lot of things, but when I asked for Hope's hand, he told me *Love lights more fires than hate extinguishes*. He said it was a quote by a female writer from a long time ago, but it feels right now. It feels right always.

The love we share is powerful enough to burn away the bad. It's bright enough to guide us home through the darkest times, and it's warmth melted the ice that had formed around my heart.

I found my hope eternal, and this much is true, I'll never let her go.

Thank you so much for reading JR and Hope's story! I hope you fell in love with this quirky, beautiful couple as much as I did!

TWIST OF FATE is **Scout's** story…
It's a sports romance; it's sexy and fun and a little angsty.
Scout goes away to pursue his dream of Hollywood stardom, and when
he comes back home, Daisy is holding a baby girl who looks just like
him.

Get into TWIST OF FATE **Spring 2021!**
What to read NOW?
Meet Daisy and the whole Oceanside gang in **WHEN WE KISS,** a
super fun and sexy, "enemies to lovers" romantic comedy—**FREE** in
Kindle Unlimited!

Keep turning for an Exclusive Sneak Peek…

Already read it?

Stephen Hastings is the hero of **STAY,** an enemies-to-lovers romance
about a single mom living in Manhattan who marries her billionaire
ex-crush to save her son…

It's sexy and fun and **FREE** in Kindle Unlimited!
Also available **as an Audiobook!**

Keep turning for a short sneak peek…

Never Miss a Sale or New Release!

Sign up for my newsletter (http://smarturl.it/TLMnews) so you don't
miss it—and get a **FREE 3-story book bundle…**
and/or
Get a New Release Alert by messaging TIALOUISE to 64600 now!*
*Text service is U.S. only.

Stay

Special Sneak Peek

Stephen Hastings is a control freak.

He's arrogant. He's smart as a whip and *sexy AF.*

He has too much money. He's bossy, and he's usually right.

All I saw were his clear blue eyes, tight ass, and ripped torso.

I gladly handed him my V-card that night, ten years ago.

I was so stupid. I swore I'd never be that stupid again…

Emmy Barton works for a dry cleaner?

Yes, that Emmy Barton—long, blonde hair, bright blue eyes, pretty smile…

Sexy little ass. Smart mouth.

She was the only girl who interested me, but I was leaving to be an officer in the Navy.

Now I'm home, running my business. My life is perfectly ordered until I bump into her, divorced and struggling to make ends meet.

I hate seeing her like this. I hate that she married Burt "The Dick" Dickerson. *What an asshole.*

She says she hates me, but when we fight, it's all heat and lust.

I won't leave her this way.

She *will* let me help her and her son. She will *stay*…

It's a thin line between love and hate, and this line is on fire.

(STAY is a STAND-ALONE enemies-to-lovers, second-chance, marriage of convenience romance. No cheating. No cliffhangers.)

PROLOGUE

Stephen
Ten years ago…

S TOP CRYING, KID. LIFE ISN'T FAIR.

Humans invented fair as a pacifier, because they needed justice. Animals don't know fair. In nature only the strong survive. You're kind, loving, honest? Nice try.

If you're weak, you die.

Or poor.

"What are you thinking, *Esteban*?" Ximena lowers herself carefully into a dingy-brown, worn-out armchair, and I blink these thoughts away. "You were always the smartest boy in the room."

The gray strands outnumber the black in my old housekeeper's hair. It's thinner than it was when I was a boy, and she keeps it twisted in a low bun.

"Now I'm a man." I kiss the top of her head. "And I'd wager the whole city."

Her muscles tremble from exertion, but her eyes are bright. She still greets me with a smile, just like always when I visit. "Smartest man in the city. What is that like?"

"It sucks." I look around her crumbling one-bedroom apartment.

It's a second-floor walkup, outdated but clean. She works hard to keep it clean, even with the cancer eating her insides. Even with the years passing, drawing her closer to death.

The thought of her dying fans the darkness inside me. "Where's Ramon?"

"He moved downtown. He got a good job, working at the shipyards." Her accent is thick despite all the years she's lived in Manhattan, her English sprinkled with Spanish.

"That's a long way from here."

He won't visit. He might want to, but he won't have the time or the energy to check on his dying mother.

Her neighborhood is shady as fuck, and she's too weak to climb stairs. And I'm leaving for a long time. I'll have to count on her neighbors to do what I can't.

Slipping a fat business envelope from the breast pocket of my coat, I place it under a mug on her coffee table. "This should last a while. I'll send more, but I won't be able to check on you. I'll be gone eighteen months, probably longer."

"I'm so proud of you. So proud." Her cheeks rise, and she slowly shakes her head. "A Navy officer."

Every line in her face wrinkles with her grin. Her faded purple housedress is as thin and old as she is. I remember her fat and jolly, shining cheeks and hair, every word out of my mouth would make her laugh, even if it wasn't funny. I didn't understand her, how she gave love so generously to a boy who wasn't hers. To the son of a man who didn't even consider her worth his time, who thought he was doing her a favor hiring her to keep his oversized brownstone.

She takes my hand from where she sits, and I take a knee beside her. Every time I visit she's smaller, slipping away. Her grip tightens, and the scent of her drugstore perfume drifts faintly around us, dried flowers and talcum powder. It draws a memory of me as a little boy sitting on her lap, crying against her neck after the death of my mother. She would hug me against her soft body, rocking and humming a sad song I didn't recognize.

"Your father will cut you off if he finds out you're giving me money, *Esteban*."

I exhale a disgusted laugh. "Thomas is too proud to cut me

off. It would make him look bad at the club. Unruly boys are to be tolerated, bragged about even."

Her eyes close, and her head leans back as she exhales a weak chuckle. "Men are the same everywhere. *Machismo.*"

Pissing wars. I rise to standing in one fluid movement. "I'll never forgive him for doing this to you."

I blame him for her illness. I blame him for her deteriorating health. I blame him for her inability to find work after he ruined her reputation. No one would hire her after he branded her a thief in his home. All the Upper East Siders shut their doors in her face, and she was left to scrounge a living wherever she could.

I've brought her money from my allowance for five years, and I'd love him to come at me for it. Pompous bastard. So worried about his appearance. So offended by a missing watch.

"He did what he had to do." Ximena still defends my father's actions. "My son stole from him. Your father could not keep me in the house after he stole."

"Ramon stole to buy you medicine. He didn't steal to party or do drugs."

He might've gotten away with it, too. If only he hadn't stolen my father's favorite Rolex—not one of the other seven he never wears.

"He did not put my son in jail." She nods her head, as if my father, Thomas Hastings has the ability to throw anyone in jail.

He's just a grown-up trust-fund brat who knows how to invest the massive wealth he inherited from our bootlegger ancestors. At least he's good for something.

Pride beams in her eyes when she looks up at me. "Now you will go and be a hero. So handsome, serving your country."

I smooth my hand down the front of my jacket, contemplating hypocrisy. "It's what my mother always wanted. Her father was in the military."

"Yes, and she can see you from above. She is so proud of you. Just like I am proud."

I study the woman who filled my mother's role for a little while. I can't heal her. I can't change her situation, and I want to leave her with happiness, not bitterness.

"Thank you, *mamá*. I love you."

"I love you, *Esteban*." She takes a slow inhale and forces a chuckle. "Now why are you here with an old woman? Why are you not out celebrating with friends? You have too much spirit. You should be with a girl tonight, release some energy."

Energy. She's encouraging me to go out and get laid. "I'm not looking for a girl."

"A boy then!" My eyes snap to hers, and I see a joking sparkle.

After all the medicine, the chemotherapy, the drugs, she refuses to be beaten. She still manages to tease me. She's the only person who can get away with it.

"I'm not gay. I'm leaving in the morning."

"Which means you have all night." She carefully rises out of her chair and takes my arm, pulling me to the door. "No more hanging around here. Go out and live your life."

I wrap my arms around her in a long hug. The feel of her bones beneath thin cotton is physically painful to me. "I'll find someone to check on you while I'm gone."

"I have my friends. I have my neighbors. Stop worrying about me." She shoos me away. "When it's my time, I'll be ready." Touching my cheek, she says her final words to me. "Be brave, *Esteban*. Laugh often. Take care of yourself."

"Take care of you." I kiss the top of her head and hesitate one last time before I go.

It's the last time I'll ever see her…

* * *

Emmy

"HARLEY QUINN IS WAY SEXIER THAN BLACK WIDOW ANY DAY OF THE week." Burt Dickerson's voice is too loud.

He's on one of his DC versus Marvel fan-boy rants, and I'm staring into the bottom of my empty red solo cup. I need refill number four.

"Fuck that. Black Widow. Hands down." My older brother Ethan yells at him, but he's only yanking Burt's chain. Ethan doesn't give a shit about comic universes. "Give me a redhead any day. Fire crotch."

My nose wrinkles, and I want to punch my brother in the junk. "She was a blonde in the last movie. You just like Scarlett Johansson." *Why am I still standing here listening to them?*

"What's wrong with that?" He pokes me in the ribs, and I'm ready to call it a night.

It's almost midnight, and I've been watching the door so hard, my eyeballs hurt. Ethan threw this big college-graduation-slash-summer kick-off party for all his old school friends, and I made sure Stephen Hastings got an invitation.

Stephen Hastings... the love of my life.

Ethan said he wouldn't come. He laughed at me and said Stephen hates most of these guys. It looks like he was right.

God, I'm such a fucking moron. How long can I save myself for a guy who doesn't even know I exist? I'm a college woman now. Time to ditch the crush and start living my life.

I just...

I hoped.

With a sad exhale, my mind flies through all my cherished spank-bank memories of Stephen growing up... Tall, lean, dark, wavy hair that looks like he never touches it, but it's always just perfect. He was on the rowing team with Ethan, and when he'd take off his shirt... holy shit, my core clenches at the memory of his broad shoulders, his perfectly sculpted arms… So muscular and tanned. The lines in his stomach would flex, and my mouth would water like Pavlov's dog.

I'm ready to trade this beer for a pint of Ben & Jerry's, curl up in my bed, and cry.

He's not coming.

Walking down the steps, away from the landing at the door, I've reached the edge of the crowd when my brother's voice freezes my insides.

"Stephen! Hell, I don't believe it." Ethan laughs, and a few of the guys join in greeting him. "Didn't think you'd come."

"I didn't either." Stephen's low baritone tickles my lady bits, and I turn slowly to look up at him.

He's wearing a brown tweed jacket over a white button-down shirt and dark jeans. He hardly ever wears jeans, but shit, his ass is so fine in them. He always seems just a bit impatient, and when he scans the crowd, his blue eyes seem to glow from under his dark brow.

He's so fucking hot.

My heart beats faster as I contemplate my next move. He *will* see me tonight, dammit. I'm giving myself one last chance.

He turns again to Ethan, and the muscle in his square jaw moves. "I'm pulling out in the morning."

"Last day as a free man. Sucks to be you." Ethan shoves a whiskey in his hand.

He inspects the glass. "I thought it demonstrated my good character."

"Good character." Burt's loud voice interrupts them, and Stephen visibly cringes. "Still think you're better than us, Hastings?"

"Only you, Dick." Stephen takes a long drink. "Only you."

Girls actually swoon over Burt all the time, but he's nothing compared to Stephen.

"Let's join the party." Ethan puts his hand on Stephen's shoulder, and they start down the stairs in my direction. "Find a chick and get your dick wet."

"Right. That sounds like me." Stephen shrugs off my brother, and Ethan staggers away.

He pauses at the bottom, scanning the crowd with a frown. I follow his gaze over the mob of former classmates. Most are buzzed. Most are familiar. We passed each other daily at Pike Academy four years ago—until he left for Yale. Tonight we're reunited.

Girls sway in colorful silk dresses with thin, spaghetti straps, practically lingerie. Their hair hangs in waves over their shoulders and their eyes sparkle as they listen to guys tell exaggerated stories of their prowess, either in the stock market or on the playing field. The guys evaluate their breasts, their hips, their lips. I'm sure they'll be fucking like good little rabbits before the night ends. Our classmates can be so predictable.

All I know is Stephen is wide open. It's now or never.

"That's a fierce scowl." I'm amazed at how confident my voice sounds, loud and commanding. *Thanks, beer.* "Don't like what you see?"

I hop up on the bottom step beside him. It puts my head at the top of his shoulder, and I lift my chin, looking over the crowd with a scowl, imitating him. "You're right." My nose wrinkles, and I meet his gaze. "They're a bunch of horny assholes."

I manage to come off casual, teasing, and his frown morphs into a narrow-eyed grin. "Emmy Barton. Ethan didn't say kids would be here."

His voice is like warm butter, and I'm thrilled he remembers me. "I'm not a kid anymore, Stephen Hastings. I started at Sarah Lawrence last year."

"Bully for you." He takes a drink of whiskey, but I'm stronger than his sarcasm.

"I wanted to stay close to home."

"Why the hell would you want that?"

Blinking up at him, I smile, going for honesty. "I miss my dad. I miss Ethan. I guess family feels more important when you lose someone."

"Oh, right. Sorry." He looks down at his tumbler, and his expression darkens.

My mom lost her long battle against lung cancer a few years ago. It was devastating watching her suffer, and her death was a mixture of heartbreak and relief she was out of pain. It still hurts if I think about it too much…

Stephen's mother died of cancer when we were kids, but I remember how it changed him. How he smiled less, played less.

"We have that in common, don't we?" My voice is gentle.

"It's not so fresh for me." His softens, and I'm encouraged. I'm not inside the wall, but I'm closer.

"Here you are." Burt appears at my side, putting his hand on my lower back. *What the hell?*

Stephen's eyes go to where he's touching me, and all I can think is *fuck no*.

"You're drunk." I shove Burt's hands off my short denim skirt.

He immediately puts both hands on my waist and turns me to him, leaning closer. "You're not blowing me off for this asshole are you?" His breath smells like vodka, and his flat brown eyes are intoxicated.

He makes a move like he's going to kiss me, but I duck and twirl away, moving to stand beside Stephen, holding his arm. "Stephen and I are having a nice chat. You need to call it a night."

Burt's attention turns to Stephen, and his brow lowers. Stephen is ready when Burt lunges at him. His strong arm shoots out, gripping Burt by the shoulder and holding him back.

"Walk it off, Dickerson." It's a low growl, and I know Stephen could wipe the floor with Burt's drunk ass.

"Don't tell me what to do, Hastings." Burt grips his wrist.

Stephen's fist rises, and I hold my breath. I've never seen Stephen fight, and my heart is flying. I'm sure it's about to go down when Ethan and a big guy appear. They corral Burt, dragging him to the right, and I take my chance, catching Stephen's arm and pulling him into the crowd.

He stops and straightens his jacket, jaw clenched. "That asshole. I'm taking off."

"Wait!" I gently pull his arm again. "I know where we can get a refill... away from all this."

He hesitates a beat, then our eyes meet and his shoulders relax. I quickly lead him past everybody, waving at old friends as we weave through the crowd.

Ethan put a keg out on the terrace near the wet bar, and Stephen goes to refresh his whiskey while I step over to the corner balcony overlooking Central Park. It's a beautiful night, and I can see the moon and a few stars. I make a quick wish.

Warmth at my side causes me to turn. He's standing beside me in the moonlight, dark hair, blue eyes, that dimple in the side of his cheek. "So, what's your major?"

The way he says it makes me laugh. I push a strand of long, wavy blond hair behind my ear. "Art history."

The scene flips. He actually groans, rolling his eyes and turning his back to the railing. "Not planning to work after college?"

His disgust offends me. "I most certainly am. I want to get a job at Sotheby's or at one of the museums downtown. Maybe something in SoHo. Or maybe I'll move to London!"

A moment's pause, and he slants an eye at me. "Is that so?"

"It is." My feathers are still ruffled, and I straighten my button-up cropped top. "What will you do now that you're out? Take a job with your dad? Have a wife in New Haven and a mistress in the city?"

Two can play the stereotypes game.

He drifts a little closer, and my pulse ticks faster. "Is that what we do?" His voice is low, and his eyes drop to my lips.

My voice is softer, higher compared to his. "Isn't it?"

A slight grin from him, and that humming is back in my veins. "You're smarter than I gave you credit for."

"Is that a compliment?"

"It's actually an apology. I underestimated you."

Now it's my turn to hesitate. Still, it's not like I didn't know Stephen was arrogant. It's one of the things I love about him.

"Apology accepted." Reaching out, I trace my finger down the front of his blazer. "Now. Wasn't that easy? You don't have to fight with everybody."

Taking a chance, I put my hand on his chest. It's firm and warm, and he covers my hand with his. It's a gentle touch, but it radiates heat to my chest, fanning out into my belly, warming the space between my thighs. I want this so much... I've dreamed of it. I know if he'll let me in, everything will change. He'll change.

My voice is just above a whisper. "When you look at me like that, I wonder what you're thinking."

Our eyes hold, and I know he feels it, this pull between us. My breath stills, and I'm humming with desire.

But he throws on the brakes. "I'm thinking I've had enough whiskey." His tone is level, and he releases my hand, moving away.

I have to stop him.

I can't lose this moment.

"What do you want?" I'm sassy, flirting. "Do you even know?"

He stops, giving me the full force of his scowl. "I don't want a wife in Connecticut, and I definitely don't need a mistress in the city."

Closing the distance, I put my hand on his waist this time,

sliding it back and forth, working my way lower. "Maybe you need me."

He stops my downward progress with a strong grip. "You're playing with fire, Emmy Barton."

"I'd rather be hot than cold."

His grip on me tightens, and he pulls me against his chest. I can barely breathe, but I blink up to his lips, slipping my tongue out to touch mine. His erection is against my stomach, and I'm so wet.

"Are you drunk?" His voice is a rough whisper.

"No. Are you?" Stretching higher, I touch my lips to the scratchy stubble of his jaw.

Leaning down, he kisses me fast. His lips shove mine apart, and his tongue invades, finding mine. My knees start to give out, but his arm is around my waist, scooping me up against his chest.

It's a rough kiss, not kind or gentle, and my fingernails scratch up to his shoulders. A little noise escapes my throat, and he rumbles in response. Heat floods my panties.

Our mouths break apart with a gasp, and his blue eyes are blazing. "Do you want this?"

Nodding, I step back, holding out my hand. "Come with me."

He hesitates as I go to the glass doors leading to Ethan's dark bedroom. When I pause and look back, he's watching me like a predator. His hair is messy from my fingers, and his lips are parted with his breath. He looks like pure sex.

"This way." I'm holding still, hoping, until…

He follows me inside.

MY SHIRT IS RIPPED OPEN. STEPHEN DOESN'T BOTHER REMOVING MY BRA. He shoves the cups down under my small breasts, and devours me, pulling a taut nipple into his mouth and giving it a bite, sending electricity straight to my core.

"Stephen…" I whimper as his large hands cup and kiss me.

I'm on fire, threading my fingers into his hair. His mouth feels so good against my skin, and he lifts me like I weigh nothing, perching my ass on the edge of the sink.

We're locked in my brother's small half bathroom, and he's making my dreams come true.

"You still want this?" His voice is hot at my ear as he shoves my skirt up to my waist.

"Yes." I gasp, gripping his neck. *God, yes...*

His belt clinks, and I wait as he rolls on the condom. Our eyes meet once more, and his burn with desire. Everything's going to change after this. He's going to fall in love with me. I just know it.

Large palms go under my thighs, lifting them, and I feel the tip of his cock touching me, probing... It's about to happen... Then all at once...

Oh, holy shit! My eyes squeeze shut, and I bite my lower lip hard, letting out a little moan of pain.

"Fuck, Emmy," he groans in my ear. "You're so fucking tight."

I make a little noise of assent, gripping his shoulders. His massive cock rips through my virginity, and it hurts so much more than I expected. He has no idea, of course, and I have no intention of telling him. I know for certain Stephen Hastings would not deflower me so roughly.

Rotating my hips, I do my best to accommodate this distinct sense of fullness. My eyes are squeezed shut, and I focus on his scent, spicy sweat and fresh soap. It's warm and good. He groans again, thrusting faster at my movements.

"Yes..." His lips find mine, kissing me quickly, a touch of his tongue leaves me wanting more. "Like that."

His face is in my hair, and as he moves faster, somehow the pain begins to subside. It transforms into numbness, until gradually, gradually, the smallest flicker of warmth blooms in my lower belly.

"Come for me." Hot breath is at my ear, and my forehead tightens. *Can I?*

Warm hands cup my ass, lifting me off the sink and turning us to the wall. The pain is gone, and my body slides up and down against his hard pelvis. His cock glides in and out, the ridge of its head working my insides. My clit is against his shaft, and something begins to happen. Prickling warmth starts to grow. It gets stronger, and I forget everything but chasing it down.

My thighs tighten around him, and I'm pumping my body up and down, riding him, wanting that tingling heat to keep getting hotter. I'm desperate, gripping his skin and moaning as the orgasm creeps higher up my thighs.

"Fuck, Emmy." He groans, fucking me harder.

"Yes..." It's almost there. "Yes!" It's right there... the tightness in my lower stomach.

It bursts through me, and I moan so loud. It's like a million fireworks shooting through my veins. My vision goes white. I'm flying, and I feel it when his orgasm breaks, pulsing deep inside me as he comes with a loud noise.

I'm shaking. My thighs shudder and grip him, and he holds me. He holds still as we both fly through space together, soaring past galaxies, touching the stars. It's amazing.

Gradually, I blink open my eyes, and through the haze, I see us in the mirror, our bodies molded perfectly together. It's just like I dreamed it would be. My arms are around his neck, our bodies flush. It only lasts a moment.

The noise of the party outside creeps into our little cocoon. He reaches between us, lowering me to my feet as he grips the condom and quickly disposes of it. I feel like a newborn colt, my legs are so shaky.

His back is to me, and his shoulders broaden as he takes a deep breath. Then he moves to the sink to wash his hands. "It's been a while since I've done that." He sounds apologetic.

Shoving my skirt down, I straighten my bra, struggling to get a grip. "What? Bathroom fucked at a party?" I'm shook.

He cuts off the water and dries his hands on the towel as I button my shirt. I've managed to get myself together when he steps to me, putting one hand above my head on the wall and leaning close. "Had sex, period." Leaning down he kisses my cheek. "You were great."

He steps back, and just like that, he's ready to go.

"That's it?" I'm confused. The devastation hasn't hit me yet.

"I think I'll head on home." He reaches out and pats my upper arm. "Good luck at school."

I recoil from his touch. *Are you kidding me? Good luck at school?*

Loud banging startles me. A female voice shouts through the door, "Hurry up in there!"

The banging grows louder, and I go toward it, looking over my shoulder but not meeting his eyes. "Seems I overestimated you."

Pushing through the door, I run into the crowd. The party surrounds me like a wave, and I let it pull me under, drowning my tears in noise and sweeping us apart.

Read STAY today!
It's available in print, free in Kindle Unlimited, and also on Audio.

When We Kiss

Exclusive Sneak Peek
"Kiss me...
You're too law-abiding for me.
What makes you say that?
That uniform. Those handcuffs.
Maybe I should put you in handcuffs.
Maybe I'd like to see you try..."

Tabby Green:
Preacher's niece.
Website designer.
Bad Girl.

Chad Tucker:
Retired military.
Deputy sheriff.
Hero.

He's a hot cop with a square jaw, a sexy grin, and a tight end. I'm a bad girl, a "Jezebel"—just ask all the old biddies in town. We're oil and vinegar. We don't mix. *But when we kiss...*

She's got flashing green eyes, red-velvet lips, and luscious curves in all the right places. She's a bad girl all right, and after what I've lost, I'm not looking for trouble. *But when we kiss...* Oil and vinegar DO mix, And when they do, *it's electric.*

A full-length, STAND-ALONE, opposites-attract romance about heroes, bad girls, and what happens when you stop fighting and surrender to love.

CHAPTER 1

Tabby
August, last year…

THE AIR IS ELECTRIC WHEN YOU'RE BEING BAD.

Little currents zip through your veins like lightning bugs grazing the tips of tall grass, and your stomach is tight. You're right on the edge, holding your breath…

Or maybe it's just me.

"Climb through." Blade squints up at me, the devil in his blue eyes.

He's holding the corner of a chain-length fence, and it makes a metallic screech as he lifts it higher.

Eleven thirty, and the night air is hot and humid—a warm washcloth on my bare skin. I duck through the opening, putting my hands up to protect my hair, my ears.

The space is just big enough for me to fit, hidden behind the tool shed. A rustling and a *BANG!* lets me know we're both through the breach. My naughty escort stands grinning in the moonlight. His hair is dark, his skin pale, and shadows deepen his eyes, nose, and mouth. He's like one of those scary-sexy vampires.

Or maybe I'm a little high.

"Let's do this!" He lets out a whoop and jerks off his black leather jacket.

His white tee is next, revealing a coiled serpent tattooed on his upper back. Jeans off, I catch a glimpse of his tight ass as he runs straight to the pool and breaks the glassy surface with a loud splash.

I shimmy out of my calf-length jeans and unbutton my short-sleeved shirt. I'm buzzing from the pot we just smoked at my small house, the old parsonage in town near the church, before we got the idea to break into the Plucky Duck Motel pool.

The Plucky Duck is off the Interstate, too far from the beach to be a tourist attraction. It's a million years old and completely deserted.

"Nobody ever stays here." I walk slowly down the steps into the shallow end.

The water is warm as it rises up my calves, to my knees, to my panties, to my waist. Blade is under the diving board watching me, his mouth submerged like a shark or a crocodile. His eyebrows rise as the water reaches my waist.

Through a blue haze of pot smoke, he demanded we do something I've never done before. I said there isn't much in Oceanside I haven't done. Until I thought of this old place.

Skinny dipping with Mayor Rhodes's tattooed bad-boy nephew is the perfectly spontaneous, irresponsible way to kick the last memories of Travis Walker from my heart.

Acid burns in my stomach. Tattooed Travis blew into town three months ago on a Harley, kissed me, and said I was the prettiest girl he'd ever seen. We screwed around for six weeks, until I caught him sneaking out of Daisy Sales's bedroom window.

He didn't even deny sleeping with her. He said Oceanside was getting "too restrictive," then he hopped on that Harley, lit up a cigarette, and drove away.

Asshole.

Serves me right for letting my guard down.

Pushing off the bottom, I keep my head above water as I glide to where Blade waits at the deep end. It's darker under the diving board.

"How long you planning to stay in Oceanside?" I don't really care. Blade's a fling I'm going into with my eyes wide open.

"Not sure." He reaches for my waist, his palms hot against my bare skin. "Ma said Uncle John needs to straighten me out."

He grins, and a dimple pierces his cheek. That bit of information makes me laugh, and I rest my elbows on his shoulders.

"I've been told something like that before." I give the field where we came in a longing glance. I wish we had more pot or at least a six-pack.

"Who's trying to straighten you out?" he asks, running his fingers up and down my sides.

My eyes return to his, and I do a little shrug. "My uncle's Pastor Green."

"No shit!"

The way he says it with a laugh makes him seem young, like a kid. I don't like the way it makes me feel, especially with the iron rod of his erection pressing against my stomach.

Twisting my lips, I reach up to hold the sides of the diving board, moving out of his arms. "I lived under his roof, his rules, until I was old enough to get out."

"I hear that." Blade reaches up to hold the diving board, mirroring my behavior.

We're facing each other, and I admire the lines of his lean muscles. Another snake is tattooed around his upper arm, but it looks amateurish, almost like he did it himself.

"So you're staying?" My red velvet lips purse, and he winks.

"That's what they tell me."

His muscles flex as he walks his hands forward, bringing our bodies closer together.

"Future's a lot brighter now that you're here."

I don't know if I'm sobering up or if his enthusiasm is killing the mood.

Blade had waltzed into the bakery where I work earlier this afternoon looking for trouble. The memory of Cheater Travis was looming large, and I decided I needed to do something reckless to blow off steam.

"You're new in town," I had said, cocking my hip to the side.

"My uncle's the mayor," he'd replied with a swaggering shrug.

"Good enough for me." I'd trotted out the door behind him, down the steps, and into the beat-up old Buick he'd parked out front.

We started on the strip at Oceanside Beach, where the high-rise condos line the shore like a wall and the tourists block up the sand. Then we had a few beers at the Tuna Tiki, the local beach bar-hangout, before he pulled out a dime bag of weed and we went back to my place to smoke it.

All in all, it was a fun, reckless day, but my buzz is definitely wearing off.

He gives me a boyish grin, and I decide I'm not looking for some *Grease*-inspired Danny and Sandy summer romance.

He walks his hands closer until my boobs smash against his chest. His legs pull my lower half flush against his, and I feel him hard against my panties. It's been a while since I've had a non-solo orgasm, and I'm not opposed to a fling with the town's newest bad boy.

He flashes a cocky grin before tilting his head to the side and kissing my cheek. His lips are soft, and I turn my face, ready to kiss him.

Still, before I do, I issue a warning. "Don't get attached."

His laugh reminds me of a young James Dean, and I'm ready. Our mouths inch closer. Another second, and they'll meet, tongues entwining. The space between my legs grows hotter, and I briefly consider I don't have a condom.

There's no way in hell I'm doing this without protection, when...

FLICK! It's a loud switch, like the throwing of a main breaker.

The entire pool floods with light, and I let go of the diving board, lowering my body into the water.

"What the fuck?" Blade does the same, joining me at the side of the pool.

The water offers little protection, as the lights fully illuminate our half-naked bodies under water. Looking up, I see we're surrounded.

"There she is! I knew I heard her voice." Betty Pepper is on the side of the pool, leaning down. Her lavender bouffant glows around her aged head, and she's wrapped in a peach terry-cloth robe pointing a bony finger in my direction.

"What are you doing in my pool, Tabitha Green?" Her voice is stern as always, the quintessential school marm.

"What does it look like I'm doing?" I snark. "Having a prayer meeting?"

"The pool closes at dark, *Tabitha*. And it's for registered guests only." She says it like I don't know very well we're out here breaking the law. "Who is that with you? Is that Jimmy Rhodes? Jimmy, is that you?"

My eyes flick to Blade. His face is downcast, and if it weren't so dark, I'd be sure his cheeks were red.

"It's me, Mrs. Pepper."

"I told your mamma I'd be looking out for you today. Did you check in with Wyatt at the hardware store? What are you doing running around with Tabitha Green?"

She says my name like it's a bad word.

Like I'm the bad influence.

I hiss at him. "You know Betty Pepper?"

He shrugs, and a male voice cuts through my irritation. "Tabby, did you take Jimmy to the bar at the Tuna Tiki?"

My brows tighten, and I squint up at Sheriff Cole. He towers over us from where he stands at the side of the pool, and his cowboy hat blocks the security light from blinding me. Otherwise, it's pretty much a police interrogation.

I answer truthfully. "I rode down to the strip in his car."

"We need you to get on out of the pool now," Sheriff Cole says, tipping his hat.

I look down at my transparent bra and panties, and there's no way in hell I'm climbing out in front of Sheriff Robbie Cole, Betty Pepper, and what I now see is a tall, quiet guy who's also wearing a khaki uniform.

He's quite a bit younger than Robbie, although he's older than me, and he stretches that polyester in a way I've never seen before.

Muscled arms hang from broad shoulders, leading down to narrow hips. His dark hair is short, and from under his lowered brow, I can see he's observing everything.

"Who's that?" I jerk my chin in his direction. "A storm trooper?"

The big guy's square jaw tightens as a muscle moves in his cheek. He gritted his teeth at me, and the heat in my panties reignites.

"Now's as good a time as any." Sheriff Cole, steps back gesturing to Mr. Tall, Dark, and Sexy. "Chad Tucker's my new deputy sheriff. He'll be working with me until I retire next year."

My lips press together. *No, thank you.* No Sheriffs. I don't care how square his jaw is or how well he fills out that uniform.

"Chad," Robbie continues. "This here is Tabitha Green, Reverend Green's niece, and this young man is Jimmy Rhodes, Mayor Rhodes's seventeen-year-old nephew."

"Seventeen!" The words are like a splash of water in my face, and I jerk off the wall, dog-paddling as fast as I can away from Jail Bait to the shallow end, humiliation burning in my chest.

"You hear that, Tabitha?" Betty shrills after me. "Not only are you breaking and entering, you're contributing to the delinquency of a minor."

Robbie continues introducing the baby wanna-be bad boy. "Jimmy is staying with his uncle until he finishes high school next year."

Every word is a cringing flash of shame, and I stomp up the pool steps, scooping my shirt off the tattered lounge chair and over my shoulders. My tight jeans are next, but it's a challenge getting them up my damp legs.

"What would your uncle say if he saw you?" Betty continues regaling me.

I stomp back to where Sheriff Cole and his new storm trooper stand, not even casting a glance at the kid in the pool. "Are you planning to arrest me?"

Lines form around the sheriff's eyes as he suppresses a grin. "Well, Mrs. Pepper here has listed your potential crimes."

"You're turning into a Jezebel," BP continues nagging. "If you're not careful, you're going to end up just like—"

My eyes flash at her, and her voice dies. She'd better not say my mother. If she knows what's good for her, she'd better not say it.

Instead she tightens her robe. "It's a slippery slope."

"What do you think, Chad?" Robbie exhales, straightening his posture and tugging on his waistband.

Mr. Silent But Deadly's eyes skim the front of my transparent bra before meeting mine. When they do, I realize they're light brown. I also realize they're hot, and chills break out over my skin in the warm night air. It strikes me this sexy future sheriff might be the real bad boy in the group.

His voice is a nice, low vibration. "I think you're playing a dangerous game... Miss?"

"She's single," Betty interrupts, as if not being married is another of my offenses.

Chad's eyebrows twitch ever so slightly. I'm pretty sure he doesn't think my being single is a crime.

My stomach is tight, and I swallow the knot in my throat. *Get a clue, Tabby.* The last thing on God's green earth I have any intention of doing is getting mixed up with a lawman.

"I don't play games, Mr. Tucker." My voice is higher than his, but just as determined. "And I don't check IDs on people I've just met."

"Maybe you should start." I can't tell if Chad Tucker is being a smartass or if he's just naturally cocky.

Seeing as he's a deputy, I'm willing to bet it's the latter.

Robbie's chuckle breaks the tension. "I think we can let you off with a warning this time. Do you need a ride home?"

I've managed to get my feet into my slides, and I see Jimmy standing on the side of the pool, pulling on his jeans and tee. He looks so skinny and young now. I wonder why I ever fell for his counterfeit tattooed bad-boy routine.

My phone is in my hand, and I tap the icons quickly. "No thanks. I just ordered an Uber. Looks like it'll be here in two minutes."

Gripping my shirt closed, I stomp up the sidewalk that leads to the front of the hotel.

Betty Pepper calls after me, getting her final jab in. "Consider your ways, Tabitha!"

I grind my teeth and fight the urge to flip her off as I round the corner. I'm saved by the headlights of a Dodge Dart with a white U in the windshield. It's too late to call my best friend Emberly, but when I get to the bakery tomorrow...

A billboard on the Interstate catches my eye, and I get an idea. Not Robbie Cole, Betty Pepper, or even Mr. Tall, Dark, and Sexy will see this one coming.

Get WHEN WE KISS and fall in love today! Free in Kindle Unlimited.

Books by
TIA LOUISE

Descriptions, teasers, excerpts and more are on my website
TiaLouise.com!

Never miss a new release!

Sign up for my New Release newsletter and get a **FREE Tia Louise Story Bundle!**
smarturl.it/TLMnews

Acknowledgments

There's a little bit of me in all my books, but there's a whole lot in this one. I can't begin to thank all the wonderful family, friends, and readers who worked with me on TMIT.

Mr. TL and my girls, having you with me this year has been such a blessing. Your encouragement, love, and support makes me so grateful for my blessings.

My readers, who send me excited messages, who love TMIT, who make those gorgeous graphics, send cards and gifts, and tell their friends to read my stories... You make this job so worthwhile.

Huge thanks to **Ilona Townsel** and **Renee McCleary** for reading as I wrote, giving notes, and just keeping me encouraged... **You are EPIC**.

So MUCH LOVE to all my author-buds, in particular **Kate Farlow** and **Harloe Rae**. You two are just the best.

To **Kylie, Jo** and all the gals at **Give Me Books**—thank you for unparalleled promo support. You are a Class Act.

To my incredible betas... **Jennifer Christy, Sarah Green**, **KC Caron**, and **Maria Black**—you ladies give amazing notes. Love you!

Thank you so much to editor **Jenny Sims** and eagle-eye proofreader **Jaime Ryter** for cleaning me up!

To my Mermaid VEEPs, **Ana Perez, Clare Fuentes, Sheryl Parent, Cindy Camp, Carla Van Zandt, Jaime Long, Tammi Hart, Tina Morgan**, and **Jacquie Martin**. You ladies have no idea how much you mean to me!

Every author who helped me... I love this community more than I can ever say. I have the BEST author friends. **I love you.**

Special thanks to **Lori Jackson** for the masterful cover design, and to **Wander** for another gorgeous, *inspirational* photo. And HUGE THANKS to Stacey Blake with Champagne Formats for making my paperbacks so gorgeous. Love you three!

To my **Mermaids** and to my **Starfish**, *Thank You* for giving me a place to relax and be silly, and for showing me all the love…

THANKS to all the **bloggers and bookstagrammers** who have made an art of book loving. I appreciate your help so much.

To everyone who picks up this book, reads it, loves it, and tells one person about it, you've made my day. Without readers, there would be no writers.

Thank you,
Stay sexy,
<3 *Tia*

About the Author

Tia Louise is the *USA TODAY* bestselling, award-winning author of super hot and sexy romance.

Whether billionaires, Marines, fighters, cowboys, single dads, or CEOs, all her heroes are alphas with hearts of gold, and all her heroines are strong, sassy ladies who love them.

A former teacher, journalist, and book editor, Louise lives in the Midwest USA with her trophy husband and two teenage geniuses.

Signed Copies of all books online at:
http://smarturl.it/SignedPBs

Connect with Tia:

Website: www.authortialouise.com

Pinterest: pinterest.com/AuthorTiaLouise

Instagram (@AuthorTLouise)

Bookbub Author Page: www.bookbub.com/authors/tia-louise

Amazon Author Page: amzn.to/1jm2F2b

Goodreads: www.goodreads.com/author/show/7213961.Tia_
Louise

Snapchat: bit.ly/24kDboV

** On Facebook? **

Be a Mermaid! Join Tia's **Reader Group** at
"Tia's Books, Babes & Mermaids"!
www.facebook.com/groups/TiasBooksandBabes

www.AuthorTiaLouise.com
allnightreads@gmail.com

Printed in Great Britain
by Amazon